Robert White

Robert White is an Amazon best selling crime fiction author. His novels regularly appear in the top ten downloads in the Crime and Action and Adventure genres. Robert is an ex cop, who captures the brutality of northern British streets in his work. He combines believable characters, slick plots and vivid dialogue to immerse the reader in his fast paced story-lines. He was born in Leeds, England, the illegitimate son of a jazz musician and a factory girl. He hated school, leaving at age sixteen. After joining Lancashire Constabulary in 1980, he served for fifteen years, his specialism being Tactical Firearms. Robert then spent four years in the Middle East before returning to the UK in 2000. He now lives in Lancashire with his wife Nicola, and his two terrible terriers Flash and Tia.

Novels

Rick Fuller Thrillers:

THE FIX
THE FIRE
THE FALL
THE FOLLOWER
THE FELLOWSHIP
THE FIGHTER

Det Sgt Striker Thrillers:

UNREST
SIX

Stand alone novels:

DIRTY
BREAKING BONES

THE FIGHTER

A Rick Fuller Thriller
Book SIX
(The CIA Diaries Pt3)

By

Robert White

www.robertwhiteauthor.co.uk

ISBN: 978-1702508391

For my wife, Nicola

Acknowledgements

I spent fifteen years of my life as a police officer, five as a member of a tactical firearms team. After leaving the Service I spent four years working in the Middle East and during that time I had the pleasure of meeting and working with several retired members of Her Majesty's Special Forces.

One evening, sitting in an Abu Dhabi bar, I was having a quiet beer with two such ex-servicemen I had grown to know quite well.

Casually, one broached the subject of a job offer. They needed a third man to complete a team who were to collect a guy from Afghanistan and deliver him across the border to Pakistan. The job was worth several thousand pounds each and would last three days.

I was extremely flattered to be asked.

I knew my two friends would be soldiers until they took their last breath. Even then, in their mid-forties, they missed the adrenalin rush only that level of danger could bring.

Personally, I didn't feel qualified enough to join them and turned down the offer, something incidentally, I have regretted ever since.

I would like to say a big thank-you to those two men, who, with their many late night tales of war and adventure, inspired me to write this work.

"Success is not final; failure is not fatal. It is the courage to continue that counts."

WINSTON S. CHURCHILL

Des Cogan's Story:

Throughout my life, I've heard a lot of talk about hard men. In some quarters they hold a status close to royalty. Most of you will have met one or two. The guy down the local bar with the bad reputation. The one best avoided when he's had one over the eight. These men, these subjects of local folklore are revered and feared in equal amounts. I've often noticed that women fawn over them, the age old instinct of protection mixed with sexual attraction making them irresistible. And it doesn't stop at the girls either. Oh no, there's many a boy eager to be associated with a roughneck. How many times have you heard that no one messes with wee Charlie, cos he's big Norman's bestie?

Protection comes in many guises.

I grew up in a city where being tough was preferred to being rich. If you'd asked many of my pals raised in the slums of Glasgow which they favoured, many would have chosen the ability to punch their way through life, rather than the silver spoon.

Now, being tough and being brave don't always go together. Just because a man wields a fearsome right hook, doesn't mean he has heroism in his veins. Indeed, I've discovered that many a formidable scrapper could be found lacking when the real shite hit the fan. That is where the lines get blurred, and the hard man becomes little more than the school bully.

Well, as the old saying goes, ye cannea choose yer folks, but ye can pick yer pals, so do it wisely. The thing is, no one is perfect. Therefore ye must forgive some idiosyncrasies in people, or ye'd find yersel on yer Bill more often than not. The flaws we have, are sometimes what makes us most interesting.

I suppose this tale, or at least some of it, is about such things. About honour, friendship, loyalty and love.

I was just shy of my eighteenth birthday, had just completed 'P Company' at Catterick in North Yorkshire and had been handed my maroon beret. 'P Coy,' is basically one long beasting, a series of eight horrendous tests undertaken over a 5-day period, designed to break you mentally as well as physically. My next move was the basic parachute course, but before then, I had five days leave to enjoy back in my hometown.

Anne and I were already talking marriage, something that is unheard of today, but quite normal back then. Many of my peers were married before they got the key to the door. And quite a few found themselves teenage parents, too. We were hopelessly in love and wanted to spend every available moment together. However, a mixture of peer pressure and stubbornness ensured that one night of the five had been reserved for my mates, and an evening on the tiles to the 'Barras.'

The Barras, or the Barrowland Ballroom to give it its full title, was a two thousand seater venue situated in the heart of town. Me and my two old school pals, Jimmy McCreery and Big Gerry Galloway were off to see one of the great bands of the day, The Cure.

Suffice to say, the Barras was not to be our first port of call. Oh no, we'd started at Granny Black's in Candleriggs. A popular pub located beside the city's Merchant Square. The place was busy from early morning, as tired traders downed dawn pints and tucked into full, fried breakfasts. It was a grand wee place that I visited for many years. Now, I'm not one for dwelling on the past, but long before Glasgow disappeared up its own arse and pandered to bearded hipsters, sipping craft beers and eating pulled pork in brioche buns, Granny Blacks was a top night out. Our merry band of brothers left there four pints deep, with smiles on our faces. Sadly, the place is gone today.

Next was The Ben Nevis on Argyle Street. A corner boozer, famous for its selection of whiskeys and traditional Scottish folk music. At first the landlord had refused to serve the baby-faced Cogan, but when Big Gerry slapped his full week's wage on the bar top, the guy gave us a beaming smile and the drink flowed.

Three single malts were added to the four pints of Guinness and our small but intrepid band, ever so slightly staggered to our next venue, The Toll Booth.

Situated close to The Barras, on Saltmarket, and a regular haunt of the Celtic fan, The Toll Booth was just about as Irish as you could get in Scotland. My old man used to sneak me in alongside my older brothers on match days and I loved the place. Big Gerry pushed his way to the bar, ordered our Guinness and the three of us began the age old game that young men played when allowed out drinking without their girls to keep an eye on them.

Talent spotting.

The Toll Booth was a drinkers pub and men outnumbered the women by quite some percentage. However, the fact that the place was considered a 'real' Irish bar, ensured that it attracted tourists from all over the world, particularly Americans, determined to find their long lost Gaelic ancestry.

These holidaying Yanks were not difficult to spot, with their perfect teeth and All American good looks. They also appeared to have money to burn and quite often, even in the brash and noisy atmosphere of the Toll Booth, you heard them before you saw them.

My eyes were drawn to a group of six such valiant travellers, three boys and three extremely attractive girls.

Now, as I've already alluded to, I was very much in love with my school sweetheart, and therefore, this game was just that, a game, where Gerry, Jimmy and my good self would eye up the girls and give each a score out of ten. Never played?

Of course you have.

The girls were all of similar age to us, late teens, early twenties. Two brunettes, one blonde. All had slim trim figures and wore skin-tight jeans to show this off.

"The arse on the blonde is a ten," said Big Gerry. "No danger."

"That's as maybe," offered Jimmy, stroking the bum fluff on his chin that he insisted was a goatee. "But the wee brunette has a fine pair of tits."

"I like the tall dark one," I said, throwing my own opinion into the mix. "She has lovely teeth."

"Teeth!" laughed Gerry almost spitting out his Guinness. "What are you scoring here Cogan, fucking Red Rum?"

"Aww the boy's in love, eh?" offered Jimmy. "He's too scared to score any good bits in case Anne hears about it."

"That's not so," I said, doing my best to stay with the program.

Gerry downed his pint and gestured towards the coltish beauty. "Go on then, Cogan," he said mid burp. "What score for that tight little bod?"

I gave the girl another once over. Long slim legs, pert bottom, close to perfect proportions. She reminded me of a darker haired Dee Hepburn, the star of the movie Gregory's Girl that Anne and I had watched the night before.

"Nine point five," I offered. "Tits could be a bit bigger."

I turned triumphantly to the lads to judge their reaction of my assessment. Unfortunately, rather than a raft of jovial banter, I was met with total silence and a pair of wide eyed statues.

"There's someone behind me isn't there?" I asked.

Big Gerry nodded slowly. He spoke to the mystery person over my shoulder. "We was just having the craic mate," he said. "No harm done, eh? Just a Scottish thing, really."

"Really?" said the deep American voice from off to my right. "Well I think, in fact we think, that you have insulted our girlfriends."

I turned to face the voice. He was a tall broad shouldered guy; the typical Jock type we'd all seen in the American teen films flooding the cinemas. All suntanned gym bunny, floppy blond fringe and pearly white teeth. Standing behind him, were his two pals, both similar height and build and both looking particularly pissed off.

Now, I must mention at this point, that Big Gerry, was only called 'Big' because he was clinically obese. His fighting prowess was about as good as his ability to sprint the hundred metres. In fact he resembled the Milkybar Kid, except he looked as if he'd eaten all Nestle's stock in the process. That said, Jimmy McCreery was a different kettle of fish. Of similar physique to myself, built like a racing snake, he was a wiry little fucker who didn't know when he was beat. I'd known him all my life, but always kept one eye on him, as you never knew which way he'd go if someone upset him.

As we were outgunned and outnumbered, I'd hoped that he'd have his diplomatic head on, but it wasn't to be.

"Well yer out o'luck, pal," shouted Jimmy over the jigs and reels blasting out overhead. "Cause we dinnea give a shite what ye think. So I reckon ye should just haud yer wheesht, and do one, eh?"

Now, I'd just completed twenty one weeks of gruelling training. That is twenty one weeks of having someone screaming in your face, demanding you attack and kill another human being. I'd been taught to live alongside aggression, to learn to love the pain of battle. This is all very well in the controlled environment of the barracks as all that violence could be channelled positively, but take it out into the real world, add alcohol, and you had a very volatile mixture indeed.

I'd always been a fiery fucker as a teen. I lacked the self-control that I developed in later life. At that age, I could no more have played the grey man as plait fog. There was viciousness in the air, and I'll be honest, I relished it. The Yank had no idea what Jimmy meant by 'hauding his wheesht,' so I helped him out.

"He means, keep that stupid mouth of yours shut and fuck off," I shouted, feeling the skin on my back twitch as the adrenalin coursed through my body.

The American set himself, bounced on the balls of his feet and raised his arms. He then did something that I'd only ever seen in the movies. He hit himself in the face with each of his balled fists then shook his head as if telling me he could take the blows.

He looked a proper twat.

His two mates shouted encouragement from a safe distance.

"Go get him, Brad," shouted one.

"Knock him the fuck out," yelled the other.

What the Americans hadn't counted on, was their surroundings. The Toll Booth was a Celtic pub. In essence, a Roman Catholic fortress where folks bled green and white hoops. What the boy should have done, was offer us outside into the street. More room to move, and more importantly, less likelihood of involving any of the Parkhead faithful.

Brad may well have been a college student. He may well have come from a very well to do family who were paying for his European adventure, but he wasn't too bright. He swung an almighty haymaker in my direction and missed by a good foot. His momentum spun him around and he clattered into one of the more robust locals who was enjoying his ninth pint of Beamish.

This resulted in total chaos. I'm sure that Brad had seen many bar room brawls as he watched his favourite John Wayne movies back home. However, he wasn't prepared for his first 'Glasgow kiss.'

ROBERT WHITE

The guy took one look at his half empty pint pot, scrutinised Brad for a second and then stuck the head on him. Brad's nose exploded and he fell backwards onto a table of four. These Bhoys, unsure of who to blame for their upturned drinks, set about the nearest customers to them. Within ten seconds, the place was in uproar. Less than a minute later, our little group were running up Saltmarket towards the Barras, laughing our bollocks off, unscathed, bobbing and weaving and singing the Rocky theme as we went.

The Cure weren't too bad that night and I liked some of their songs. But I didnea care for all that eyeliner.

As I knew it would be a late night, I'd planned to stay over at Jimmy McCreery's flat so as not to disturb the Cogan clan. As it had been all my life, my own gaff was still full to bursting, my mother unable to say no to any of my brothers when it came to food or a bed for the night. Therefore, after close to six months of my own bed, hot water and three squares, I had little appetite to go back to sharing with my remaining siblings and their offspring.

Jimmy was a year older than me and had moved out from his family home at the tender age of sixteen. For the first two years, he'd shared, but now, working three shifts at Allied Vehicles as a fitter, he had his own small flat in Possilpark.

As you know, I was dragged up in the Gorbals and you didn't get much rougher than that, but Possil was a whole new ball game to me. The housing had been built for the employees of the Saracen Foundry, but when they closed their doors in the mid-sixties the place fell on hard times. By the time Jimmy rented his wee one bed, the place had become the hub of Glasgow's heroin trade. Gangs roamed the streets and it was not a place for a stroll after dark.

Luckily, our taxi had dropped us right to Jimmy's door and I sat in a worn but comfortable armchair, sipping a cold can of Tennents and looking out of his window at the mean streets below.

At the corner, under the lamp, was a dealer. He had two other guys looking out for him, one, across the road, the other a few yards behind him. The second boy ominously carried what appeared to be a baseball bat.

I watched as a steady stream of people, both in cars and on foot, came and bought his wares.

"It like this all the time?" I asked.

"Every fuckin' night, pal," said Jimmy flopping down in an identical chair to my own. "First time in ages there ain't been used needles in the lift."

"That's fucked up," I offered, lighting an Embassy.

"Too right, pal," said Jimmy, popping his can. "Wouldn't catch me taking drugs, eh?"

"Me either," I said taking a long drag.

Jimmy put on some tunes and turned up the gas fire. We sat in silence for a while, but I could tell that something was eating at him.

"You all right there, pal?" I asked.

He looked at the ceiling for a moment, then into my face.

"D'ya like the army then, Des?"

I nodded, took a drink. "Aye, I do. What makes ye ask, Jim?"

He shrugged and looked ever so slightly sheepish. "I was just thinking, y'know? Interested like."

At my tender age, I wasn't the reader of folks I am today. I should have known what his issue was, but I hadn't seen it coming.

"Thinking about what, pal?"

Jimmy put down his can. "I've known ye since you was wee, eh? Your family and mine, living in the same street, going to the same chapel."

I nodded. "Aye."

"What drew ye to the military like?"

I took a deep breath. "Remember James McFee?"

"The big tall fella fe Drumchapel?"

"That's him. Well he came to ours for tea once, mate of my eldest brother he was. My Dad made a right fuss over him. That kinda planted the seed. Got me interested."

"Is that right?"

"Aye."

"But what about…?"

"About what, Jimmy. Something's bothering you, eh?"

He took a long swig of his can. The beer was doing most of the talking, but I could see he had to get whatever it was off his chest.

"You're one of them Paras, eh? The same as the ones who shot all them Catholics in the back over in Ireland. How does yer old Dad feel about that, Des?"

I was a young lad, and yes, maybe a little naïve, but I'd sat down with my father, long before choosing the Parachute Regiment. To me, they were the guys who made it to the sharp end before anyone else. The first to be deployed. They were where the action was, and that was exactly where I wanted to be.

I looked at Jimmy, a skinny angry young man, scraping a wage, living around junkies, waiting for Friday so he could blow half his pay-packet in the pubs and clubs in town. He was me, without the Army, and I wanted to tell him that, show him that, but I didn't have the words back then.

"He's proud of me, Jimmy," I said. "You know my old man. He's of Irish blood and he's more Catholic than the Pope himself, but he's still proud. All he wants is for us boys to have a better life than he had. He's never been one for the politics of it all. Neither should you be."

"So yer happy to do the Englishman's bidding? Is that it?" said Jimmy, face screwed up, anger seeping into his tone.

I lay down my drink and found my coat. "Like you said, Jimmy, we've been pals a long time, and I reckon I'd like it to stay that way. We've both had a good night and a good drink. Let's leave it at that."

Jimmy stood. "Aww, don't be daft now Des, eh? I'm sorry, I didnea mean to piss yer off. Sit back down. I've made a spare bed up fer ye."

I grabbed the door handle and turned it. "Another time, pal," I said.

* * *

Over two years later, I attended the funeral of James McFee, killed in action during the Falklands conflict, a war I missed due to applying for selection for 22 SAS. By that time, our family home was almost empty, Ann and I were married and living in quarters and all but one of my brothers had found love and moved on. My father wasn't in the best of health, but still wanted to hear all about my escapades, even those across the water, which got me to thinking about my old pal, Jimmy.

The day after James was laid to rest, against my better judgement, I decided to try and look up John James McCreery.

I drove my beloved Cortina back to Possilpark and pulled up outside Jimmy's building. It seemed that the area had fallen even further from its fine pedestal and now reminded me of some of the areas I'd patrolled in

Belfast. It certainly felt as dangerous.

On this occasion, not only did the lift contain all the evidence of heroin use, it also held an emaciated young woman, who smelled worse than she looked.

"Blow ye fer a ten bag," she slurred, as the doors mercifully opened.

Jimmy's flat door was ajar, and I tentatively pushed it wide open and called his name. There didn't appear to be any furniture in the living room. Gone were the two comfy chairs, the big old TV and VCR. All that I could see, was a filthy mattress pushed into one corner of the room, a few takeaway boxes and what was definitely drug paraphernalia.

"Jimmy?" I called again, wary that I may be classed as an unwelcome visitor.

There was the sound of movement, slow and stuttering; finally, a wee girl staggered from the bedroom.

She was no more than seventeen, a kid. There was no mistaking that had she been in better condition, she would have been a bonny wee thing. Unfortunately she was equally as skinny as the girl in the lift, with long straight dirty blonde hair that fell to her elbows. Dark rings sat beneath her ice blue eyes. Her full lips were cracked dry and bleeding. There were large black bruises around her thighs, and she had track marks on her pitifully thin arms. All she wore was a once pink t shirt and a pair of tiny white panties.

"What de ye want, pal?" she said, her eyes screwed up against the daylight.

"I'm looking for Jimmy McCreery, hen. Is he here?"

The girl blew out her cheeks, staggered and sat on the floor with a thump. Once down there, she immediately began to rummage through bits of tinfoil. "Ye ain't got any brown on ye, have ye?" she said picking at the stinking carpet with a bitten fingernail.

"It's Jimmy I'm after hen, I told ye."

She looked up at me all doe eyed. "Well, no offence, but Jimmy's always got gear sweetheart, so I figured..."

"That I would too?"

"Yeah, suppose. But he don't stay here anymore. He's big time now. Got one o' them new apartments in town."

I nodded and turned to leave.

"Ye couldnea sort us out, eh?" asked the girl.

I threw her a packet of fags. "Best I can do," I said.

She blew air down her nose. "Thanks fer nothin."

Once back in the sunshine, I noticed that my shiny Ford had company, in the form of two young lads. One leaning against the driver's door, the second sitting on the edge of the bonnet.

"Away ye go, boys," I said, pleasantly enough. "Dinnea be scratching my paint now."

Neither moved.

"What's yer business with Jimmy McCreery?" said the lad at the driver's side.

Obviously the Possilpark jungle drums had been beating whilst I had my chat with the wee girl upstairs.

"Whatever it is," I snapped. "It's none of yours. Now fuck off away from my car son."

The pair remained stubbornly still.

I reckoned that both lads were in their late teens, just a couple or three years younger than me. They sported straggly long hair and wore denim jackets with the sleeves rolled up, as was the fashion of the day. As I reached the boy with the mouth, I grabbed at his hair with my left hand and gave him an almighty slap across his cheek with my right. Now, quite often, a slap is far more effective than a punch. It gets your point across, no danger, yet leaves you room for manoeuvre should you need to increase the pressure.

Holding the boy by his neck, I pushed him against my motor and squeezed. Then I quickly patted him down, after all, no one wants sticking with a blade on your weekend off. His mate must have thought I looked preoccupied and started towards us. I gave him a look, shook my head and he thought better of it.

The boy I held made a few choking noises and began to turn the colour of a ripened plum. My point made, I released him, and he fell to his knees coughing and snotting between expletives.

"I want to speak to Jimmy," I said, finding my spare pack of Embassy and lighting one. "We're old pals. He used to live in these flats here, and he wouldn't take too kindly to you two eejits, messing with his best mate's motor."

"What's ye name?" croaked the kid, lifting himself upright.

"Cogan," I said. "Des Cogan. Me and Jimmy go way back."

The boy that had stayed out of arm's reach stepped forward nervously. "We can take you to him, if ye want, pal… fer a tenner like."

Jimmy had definitely gone up in the world. Gone was the poky Possilpark three roomed number. Oh yeah, bye bye shitsville, and say hello to millionaires row. Well, maybe not quite that, but moving in the right direction. My pair of now very helpful entrepreneurs took me to a very nice three bed penthouse flat on Great Western Road, Kelvinside.

With a fiver and my second pack of Embassy in their pockets the lads wandered off, no doubt looking for the best way to spend their ill-gotten gains.

I stood at Jimmy's door and knocked. It took a while, but finally he answered. He looked flustered, was red faced and sweating. "Fuck's sake," he spat. "Can't a man have a wee bit of peace, I told yees…"

Then he recognised me.

"Well, fuck me, if it isn't my old pal, Cogan." His face lit up with a beaming smile and he grabbed me in a hug. Once released, I took a better look at him. "You look well, pal," I said.

"I am son, very well indeed… hey come on in."

Jimmy turned and walked down his hallway. He spoke with his back to me as I followed. "How the fuck did ye find us?"

"Oh, I asked around. You seem to have celebrity status back in Possilpark."

He turned and beamed again. "You know what they say, pal, if ye cannea beat 'em…"

A door opened to my left and a very attractive blonde appeared wearing very expensive underwear, killer heels, and nothing else. I instantly realised why Jimmy was red faced and not happy to be answering his door.

Before the woman could speak, Jimmy snarled at her. "Put some fucking clothes on. Have you no respect. Can't you see we have a guest?"

Jimmy's mood swung from angry young man to perfect host with each sentence. No sooner was the girl out of sight that his beaming smile returned, as if nothing had ever bothered him. This had always been the case when dealing with my old mate. Sublime one minute, ridiculous the next.

"Sit down, Des, come on. Take the weight off. My God, how long has it been, eh? Must be over a year?"

"Over two, pal."

"And what brings ye home. Some leave I take it."

"A funeral, actually. Remember that last night we spoke, and I told you about James McFee, my brother Tom's pal?"

Jimmy looked a little blank but nodded anyway.

"Well it was his funeral, I came for. He was killed in the Falklands, at Tumbledown."

Jimmy shook his head. "And fer what, eh? So that Maggie can stay in power, that's why. Take everyone's mind off how shite things really are."

I managed a smile. "Like I said to ye the last time we met, Jim. I don't go in for the politics of it. I just do my job." I looked around the luxurious room. "And you seem to be doing just fine, I reckon."

He shrugged as if his newfound wealth was of no importance.

"And what exactly is it that ye do now, Des? You still jumping out of planes?"

I couldn't exactly say too much about selection, so I kept my counsel. "I get to travel about a bit. Should be off to the Far East after Christmas, Jungle training, nine weeks."

"Fuck that, pal. Oh no, all them creepy crawlies in yer boots, no way, not fer me. I'm best where I am." Jimmy frowned and turned his attention to the still missing blonde.

"Chantelle! When ye finally find the right fucking dress, can ye bring me and my pal here a couple of beers, eh?"

I shook my head and lowered my voice. "Look, Jimmy, I didnea mean to drop in on ye so unexpected like. Maybe I should just get on my toes and we can reconvene when it suits ye better?"

"It suits me just fine, the now, pal. Dinnea be worrying about the girl. She gets paid by the hour."

I raised my brows at that one. "Ye mean she's a prossie?"

Jimmy shrugged. "She's a dancer at my club in town. She's just earning a little bit of spending money on the side, eh?"

As if on cue, Chantelle teetered in on those same impossibly high heels carrying a tray that contained two glasses of what appeared to be lager. I took one, sipped at it and eyed the woman appreciatively. She was indeed a fine looking girl. "Thanks," I said.

"My pleasure," purred Chantelle. She turned to Jimmy. "You still want me to hang around Jim? Or should I go home, and ye can see to yer company?"

Jimmy turned down the corners of his mouth, checked what appeared to be a Rolex watch, and then looked at me.

"You like Indian food, pal?" he asked.

"Aye, I certainly do," I offered.

He stood, rummaged in his jeans pocket and pulled out a wad of notes bigger than I'd ever seen in my life. "There y'go hen," he said, handing the girl what looked to be several hundred pounds. "You go buy yourself something nice, eh? I'll see ye at the club later."

Chantelle squealed like a spoilt child and gave Jimmy a big hug. Moments later, she was gone. Jimmy gave me another satisfied look. "Worth every penny, mate."

"I'll bet," I said. "Nice you can afford it."

"Aye, well I can, so it's ne bother, eh? Give me a minute to get a shower and we'll have a run into the city. I know a great place. Best curry in town, pal."

I sat on Jimmy's oxblood leather Chesterfield sofa and took in a bit more of the opulent lounge. It all looked pretty tasteful to the young Cogan. After all, I'd lived in very meagre surroundings until my seventeenth birthday and the last three years had been a mixture of barrack room life and more recently, army married quarters, none of which could hold a candle to the lavishness of Jimmy McCreery's living space.

In 1982, I commanded the grand sum of fifteen quid a day. I figured I'd just seen Jimmy hand the lovely Chantelle somewhere in the region of four hundred pounds, a month of my wages. Of course, I know what you're thinking, you're of a mind that Jimmy had turned to drug dealing for a living. Well, the truth was, I was still young and a little too carefree to be that bothered. Tours of Northern Ireland had seen me grow up very quickly, but the danger you faced on patrol as a young man, also made you a little reckless in your downtime. I was at a very perilous point in my life. As a young, super-fit, highly trained Trooper, I felt almost invincible.

I'd also learned that married life was not all a bed of roses. Anne and I had been arguing a lot. But despite the rows, when I was away on tour, I longed to be home. However, when I was home, I couldnea wait to get the nod fer the next trip over the water. With Aptitude Phase under my belt, I knew I was headed for some turbulent times in the marital home. I was also fully aware that the boys in the Regiment had a rather shorter life expectancy than the average Para. So, with all that in mind, ye just have to forgive my young and stupid self. I reckoned that if one of my oldest and dearest friends wanted to buy me a curry and a pint or two, I didnea give a fuck where he got his money from.

Jimmy stepped back into the room pulling on a smart blue jacket. We'd always been of similar size and build, but I did notice some striking physical differences had occurred. He was now a good stone heavier than me, not that he was fat, just his body hadn't been put through the same things as mine the last months. Particularly the final days of Aptitude Phase, Test Week. When I look back, I wondered just how anyone could go through the demands of such a gruelling assessment. The final tests consisted of five marches of twenty k plus. Each were conducted on consecutive days so that by the time you got to the last endurance march, you were already on your knees. They upped the weights you carried too, from eighteen kilos on the first tab, to twenty seven kilos on the final 'long drag.' This ultimate endurance test is sixty four kilometres long, in any weather the Beacons can throw at you, and must be completed in twenty hours. With sixty pounds of kit in your Bergan plus water, food and a rifle, it was just about the hardest thing I could imagine, yet here I was, I'd done it and was ready for the jungle.

Jimmy may have been a few pounds heavier, but there was no hint of the blue Scottish tinge about him. His skin was tanned from a recent holiday or from one of those new-fangled sunbeds everyone was crowing about. In fact he was the epitome of health. I figured that if indeed Jimmy had become a young entrepreneurial drug dealer, he obviously wasn't indulging in his own product.

Another difference was our respective haircuts. Mine was a very unfashionable number one crew, whereas Jimmy had a glossy mullet that he stood combing in the mirror.

"Where we going?" I asked him.

"The Shenaz on Granville Street, ye ever been?"

"No, pal. Ye never ate curry in our house. Jeezo, my Dad would have thrown you out the door. He thought he was cosmopolitan having English sausage rather than square slice."

Jimmy had a giggle at that. "Aye, I remember that night when ye came home fe the chippy with curry sauce on ye supper and he had a wee fit."

I felt a smile on my face. It was good to talk about my old man.

"Ye right there, pal. I had to stand out in the yard to eat it…. In the piss-ing rain too." I stretched my arms above my head. "No, my liking fer Indian food came fe a pal in the Army. We had this boy in my barracks, Abhi. He was a Sikh, massive bloke, built like a brick shithouse and brave as a lion. Fuckin' nutter. He used to bring stuff back that his Mam had cooked fe him. He got me hooked. King prawns, lamb tikka… tell ye what, pal, my stomach's rumbling."

"Let's get off then," said Jimmy fixing his hair one last time. "I'll call us a cab."

"I've me motor downstairs, Jim, no worries."

He pulled his face at that. "Aww, I was hoping we could have a wee drink or three… D'ya have to be back or somethin'?

I shook my head. "Naw, I've another day yet."

"Well then, what's up with ye? Ye can crash here no bother," he pointed. "And I promise I won't spoil the party this time."

I looked into Jimmy's face. He smiled at me and I knew it was genuine. "Tell yer what, it's great to see ye, pal," he said.

* * *

The black cab dropped us at the Shenaz. It was one of the oldest Indian restaurants in Glasgow, first opened in the mid-sixties. As I stepped inside, the wonderful aromas wafting from the kitchen made my mouth water. The one thing about tabbing twenty kilometres a day is, you are always starving hungry, and as we were ushered to a window table, I already knew what I wanted to eat.

Three pints of Stella Artois and a mountain of excellent food later, Jimmy and I had covered most of what had happened to him since that fateful night at The Barras.

Jimmy had done a foreigner for this guy, Pete James. A face I only vaguely knew but who had a reputation as a coke head and gambler. Jimmy had fixed Pete's motor for him, but he couldn't pay. In the end Jim went round to Pete's gaff with the intention of giving him a slap. Instead he took a kilo of cannabis resin as payment.

Now, other than smoke it all, Jimmy had no idea what to do with his compensation, until he bumped into one of the boys that hung around on Possilpark's street corners each night. Jimmy discovered that these wee boys would gladly take the said resin off his hands and more if he could get it.

He doubled his money within the week, and the rest, as they say, was history. He was half owner of a small club in town that washed his money. Had the stunning Chantelle warming his bed and drove a Jag. He made it all sound so easy.

Just before nine o'clock, Jimmy asked for the bill. As it arrived, he stood so that he could again slide his hand into his jeans pocket and remove the now infamous wad of notes.

As we were perched in the window seats and I had my back to the street, I barely noticed a dark shadow standing outside on the pavement. I certainly didn't see the sawn off.

The glass separating us from the street exploded into thousands of razor sharp shards and I felt my skin tear around my neck and scalp as the minute pieces lodged there. People were screaming and there was total panic in the restaurant. Jimmy had been blown off his feet and was lying on his back clutching his chest.

I dropped to my knees beside him and pulled his hands away from the injury so as I could get a better wee look. There were at least three entry wounds and looking at their positions, all had pierced Jimmy's chest cavity. I'd seen a similar wound before. I was first on the scene when a young kid had been shot by the UVF, just off the Falls Road. That proved fatal.

Jimmy was gasping for breath, his eyes wild. "Don't let me die here, pal, eh?" he managed. "No here."

"You're not going to die, ye daft bastard." I said, not knowing what his prognosis would be. I stretched up, found a bunch of clean cotton napkins and applied some pressure to his wounds.

Looking up at the carnage in the rest of the dining area, I saw that another victim had been hit, this time a young woman. Somehow, I managed to catch the eye of one of the staff.

"Tell me there's an ambulance coming?" I barked.

"I called, sir," he said.

I looked into Jimmy's eyes. His pupils were dilated. "Hold these to yer chest, mate," I said, and shuffled through the broken glass towards the injured woman. As I reached her, I could see that she had taken a pellet to the face. It had entered her cheek and was lodged somewhere at the back of her throat. Her husband or boyfriend was in full shock and just sat by her, holding her hand, muttering gibberish. Finding more napkins, I turned her into the recovery position and applied the makeshift bandage.

Mercifully, within minutes, medics arrived. Jimmy's right lung had collapsed, but they managed to get some oxygen into him. Once they were stabilised, both victims were on their way to the Infirmary.

I sat pulling bits of glass from my head. One of the ambulance crew had stayed behind to tend to the many diners with minor cuts and shock. She strode over to me, had a quick look at my neck and said, "Maybe you should nip up to casualty and get those looked at, eh?"

She was right of course. "Aye," I said. "I will hen."

"I'll give you a ride up there," said a deep voice with an Edinburgh lilt.

I looked up to see a rather burly detective dressed in a beige raincoat sitting at the next table. He had a heavily lined face and a shock of pure white hair. His eyes were dark as coal and he examined me closely. As a young Catholic lad, growing up in the west of Glasgow, I'd always distrusted the Police. They were notoriously sectarian and best avoided, no matter what foot ye kicked with.

"I can get myself there, pal, no bother," I said.

"I'm sure ye can," said the cop. "It was just a friendly offer."

I nodded and kept my mouth shut. But the guy wasnea done.

"What regiment?" he asked. "I mean, ye are a squaddie, eh? I can see that fe here."

"The Shiny Two," I said, using 2 Para's nickname.

The cop knew exactly what I meant. He nodded and rubbed his chin with his hand.

"So… what's a fine upstanding member of Her Majesty's military doing sharing a table with a scumbag like Jimmy McCreery?"

I stood. "Why is a member of the Police asking *me* questions rather than out looking for the guy who just shot two people?"

"Touché," said the detective. "Did you get a look at the gunman?"

I shook my head. "Nothing much more than a shadow. I'd say above average height. I got the impression he was a white guy, but I couldn't be sure."

"You got a name son?"

"Cogan."

"Big Celtic fan then, eh?"

"None of your fucking business," I said, and made to leave.

As I reached the door, the Detective called out. "Hey, Cogan," he shouted. "People get judged by the company they keep."

I gave the cop a look. "That's why I'm leaving."

* * *

It took until just after two in the morning for me to be seen, have the remaining shards of glass tweezered from my head and neck and be issued with some antibiotic powder to slap on twice a day. After some gentle persuasion from yours truly, I managed to find out where Jimmy was. He'd left theatre and was in recovery under armed guard.

So he was alive.

I called a cab and made my way home. As I gently pushed the front door open, I could see a light on in the back parlour. My Dad sat at our kitchen table, stripy pyjamas buttoned to the neck, dressing gown over his shoulders. He hugged a cup of what smelled like coffee.

"Yer late, son," he said quietly.

"Aye, sorry Dad," I said.

He studied me a moment. "What ye done to yer neck?"

"Ah," I said. "Been a bit of a night to be fair. Remember Jimmy McCreery?"

My Dad pulled a face that I'd seen many times when he didnea care for his company. "Aye, Bernie's wee boy, used to live by us."

"That's him, well someone shot him through the window of the curry house we were sitting in."

"Jeezo!"

"Aye. He's still in the hospital. I just caught some of the glass, is all."

My Dad sipped his coffee and shook his head. "Sit down a minute son, I want to speak to ye before you go off again."

I did as I was asked. My old man ran his hands through his thinning hair.

"Desmond, ye need to think on a wee bit more these days. About who ye knock around with, I mean. It's very easy to get caught up in the wrong crowd."

"Come on, Dad. I'm not fifteen anymore."

"I know, I know, yer a grown man with yer own life, and I'm proud of ye son. It's just, well, lads like Jimmy are bad news. His mother talks to your mother and I hear all the tales. McCreery's nothing but a low life drug dealer. Okay, he's survived this one and it looks like you struck lucky too. But one day he won't be so fortunate. All I'm sayin' is, you will put yourself in harm's way often enough. You'll see enough danger, enough blood. Ye won't be needing to hang around with gangsters for excitement that's fer sure. Believe you me, son, you'll face enough enemies in your life, and you'll stare down the barrel of a gun more than most."

He reached across our tired worn table, the place I'd eaten, drank, laughed, fought, cried and danced. Never a man to show his feelings, this was a rare display of affection. He slid his hand across that scratched mahogany top and took mine in his. "Desmond," he said. "If ye going to go son… go in style, not sitting next to Jimmy McCreery eating that terrible food."

"Ye still don't like the curry then, eh, Dad?" I smiled.

"Shocking," he said, lifting himself from his chair.

"Goodnight son."

Twenty five years later, Ardkilly Ridge, The Republic of Ireland.

Rick Fuller's Story:

I was pushed below by the big Yunfakh goon. Past the first room I'd encountered, through a second door and down a further set of metal steps into what looked like a provisions store. The boat rocked gently. We were still in the estuary and not yet out at sea.

"Kneel," said the guy, arm outstretched, Glock firmly pointed at the back of my head.

I did as I was told, all my training flooding back. The gates to the past, wide open. The old Survive, Evade, Resist, Extract training, was finally about to come in handy.

"Hands on your head, interlock your fingers."

I felt the cold metal of a set of cuffs being applied to my wrists. The guy then yanked my arms above my head and fastened the cuffs to a metal bar driven into the hull of the boat. I wasn't going anywhere, unless those limpets were detonated, then I was going down with the ship, no danger.

"Can I have some water?" I asked, doing my best to look the beaten man.

It wasn't that I was thirsty, it was just that I wanted to know what this guy's intentions were. After all, there's no point in feeding and watering a bloke, if you're going to drop him in the Celtic Sea ten minutes later.

The goon grunted, slipped upstairs, out of the door and returned moments later with a cup of water.

I wasn't food for the fish then.

I took a good couple of gulps. "Thanks," I said, and noticing the boat was still stationary, tried my luck. "Why aren't we moving? Can you tell me?"

The guy snorted his derision. "You ask too many questions, Fuller."

"Sorry," I said, allowing my head to fall.

The guy dropped onto his haunches and gave my forehead a rough slap to get my attention. My poor beaten prisoner act was having a different effect than I'd hoped. It's intended to save you some physical punishment, not encourage it. The blow was nothing too painful, but I could tell that the big lad was itching to dish some out. There wouldn't be much I could do about it either. In the position I was in, all I could hope for would be to tuck my knees up, drop my chin on my chest and kiss my arse goodbye.

I looked into his face but a split second later, dropped my eyes again, instantly submissive. He gave me a second slap. Harder this time, right across my cheek. He was a big old boy too, strong as a fuckin' ox.

"Look at me," he said quietly, cocking his head inquisitively.

I slowly raised my face to his again and this time, looked him in the eye.

A big mocking smile spread across his face. He had a huge square head, all pig eyed with a Desperate Dan chin. "Where is the big brave Rick Fuller?" he said. "Where has he gone? Who is this slithering weakling that has replaced him?"

My mind worked overtime. There was no doubt that guy was Yunfakh, he had the tattoo, and fitted the type without a doubt. But he was just a big lump, he was definitely not the brains of the outfit.

My capture, this whole debacle had to have been an elaborate set up. Inside information had been accessed at the highest level.

Just look at who were involved. The CIA, MI6, the IRA and Yunfakh, the most powerful organised crime syndicate ever to come out of the Arab world. Someone who had access to all those agencies and criminal enterprises had conspired to ensure that it was me that did the deal alongside Finbarr O'Rourke, and that it was me that would be on that beach with those AK's. Al-Mufti had paid dearly for that to happen, and it wasn't just about three hundred grands' worth of old PIRA arms either. I mean, look, the Yanks had just paid our team a cool million dollars just to save a Senator's blushes. There was a much bigger payday for whoever had organised this little party, and it wasn't in those old crates. Al-Mufti and his boss, Khalid Kulenović had the resources to make that kind of transaction happen, and I was very keen to find out what that was. However, first I had other more pressing problems.

Whatever Square Face was, who exactly he worked for, and where he fell in the pecking order, he wasn't finished with me. He grabbed a handful of my hair and snapped my head back. "Where is the hero?" he sneered. "Where is the star of Her Majesty's Special Air Service?"

He made a low guttural sound and gobbbed straight in my face.

Well, if the foul bastard had been a few inches closer, he'd have discovered that Mr Fuller was alive and well. My teeth would have been locked onto his nose whilst I kicked fuck out of his meat and two veg with my Timberlands. As it happened, he wasn't, and all I could do was wipe my face on the arm of my shirt whilst he stood up and walked upstairs to the door.

"Coward," he said and slammed it shut behind him.

The boat continued its gentle rocking motion. Whoever was doing the sailing was simply ticking the engines over and keeping her steady. Either he was in no hurry as the vessel was in blackout, or we were waiting for someone else to arrive, the latter concerning me even more. The trackers Sellers had fitted inside the AK crates had been discovered and removed. Just how our team of happy clappers knew about those only added to my conspiracy theory. Either way, there would be no easy way for Des and the team to find the boat in the dead of night.

I was also concerned about Theo 'Marvellous Marvin' Varese, who would no doubt be trying to call the shots on how to proceed, now that I was indisposed. I trusted him as much as I'd trusted Mason Carver during the Todd Blackman investigation, and look what happened to him.

Moments later, my thoughts turned back to my imminent future as the big Yunfakh guy lumbered back into the room. This time, however, he had company, in the form of a slightly built man. He looked to be in his sixties with small rodent like features. I would have put him as Libyan or Moroccan. As it turned out, he was an Afghan and a fully-fledged member of the Taliban.

I was having a fucking bad day.

"Are you comfortable, Mr Fuller?" he said in an accent that had been moulded in the best Universities any money could buy.

It was, of course, imperative that I didn't lose my rag, didn't turn up the heat in any way, so I looked towards my shackled wrists above my head.

"I have pins and needles in my hands," I said quietly, allowing my head to fall, resting my chin on my chest as if exhausted.

"Yes, of course, that is natural under these circumstances," said weasel-face, pushing thick glasses up his nose and peering at me. "But I assure you, Mr Fuller, these are not life threatening symptoms."

I nodded and wondered if the guy was a doctor.

"However," he added, "you should be aware, that it is my task to deliver you to my great friend, Abdallah Al-Mufti, with whom, I believe you have had a long and difficult relationship." He pursed his lips. "Therefore, I cannot see this ending well for you."

The plot grew ever stickier, but I played the game and kept my counsel. After all, there was no point in mentioning that Abdallah's only son, Siddique had fallen foul of an angry Scotsman and a six inch nail. He'd find all that out in good time.

"That was a long time ago, when I was in the Army," I said. "I was just following orders, just like any soldier."

A thin smile flickered across Weasel's face. He removed his glasses and polished them on the tail of his long shirt. "I've heard this said by your kind many times, Mr Fuller, 'following orders.' However, these thin words do not bring our brothers back that you and your friends have murdered."

The glasses were returned to his considerable nose.

"Now, Abdallah is a wise and generous man, who has supported our brothers in many conflicts, and many countries where the infidel has chosen to interfere. He has quietly gone about his business, raising money for the cause, helping the downtrodden and the invaded."

I wanted to say, 'oh yeah, he's a fuckin' pillar of the community. A drug supplying, arms dealing, murderous bastard.' But, of course, I kept my mouth shut.

Weasel hadn't finished his uplifting portrayal of my favourite Arab.

"I first met him in my homeland when I worked as a doctor... in Bagram. Do you know of this place?"

So he was a quack after all. I shook my head, giving nothing back. I'd heard some of the stories that had come out about the airfield there and the detention centre, but I'd never had the pleasure. That said, I had the feeling the guy liked the sound of his own voice and was going to tell me all about it anyway. Dr Weasel was warming to his task.

"Bagram is the site of the strategic United States Airbase. The runway was built in 1976, by the Soviets, before they ran home with their tails between their legs. But it was the Parwan Detention Facility that was my responsibility. The detention centre was a place of torture and depravation, Mr Fuller. It was I who tended to some of the terrible injuries inflicted on innocent civilians by your comrades in arms, the Americans. Bagram made

Guantanamo Bay look like a five star hotel. Men were chained to ceilings and walls and beaten to death. They lay in their own excrement, starved of food and water, unable to pray to their God."

He took a breath and the thin smile returned. "So, Mr Fuller, you now understand why your pins and needles are of little consequence to me."

Lauren North's Story:

Despite the body armour doing its job, my whole body ached from the rounds I'd taken back on the road to the port. However, I was still able to hold a gun, and as Varese opened his mobile to make the call that would send Rick to the bottom of the sea, I lifted my Colt to his temple and pulled back the hammer. In the confines of the small cabin, the click of the ratchet sounded like a bomb going off. It was a standoff that nobody wanted.

Des was instantly in Varese's face, snarling like a pit bull. The American was younger, bigger and stronger than the Scot, but none of that was going to help him this day. Mitch had instinctively pulled his Magnum and had it pointed at me, but Sellers had been equal to his movement, and her own weapon was aimed at the big American.

"Oh dear," she said in her finest English Rose accent. "Do you know that the French don't have a word for stalemate?"

Des' nose was almost touching Varese's, but he addressed our latest recruit. "I believe they use 'impasse,' hen."

The Scot slowly pulled his own weapon from his belt and pushed the barrel into the American's gut. "And they dinnea have their own word for predicament, either eh? And this is one big fuck off predicament, Marvin."

Varese was sweating, his eyes darting between Mitch, and the three people he'd supposed would all lay down and do as they were told.

"I suggest you put down your weapons," he said, swallowing hard. "I was informed that you were professionals, that you were soldiers. Where's your discipline?"

Sellers was not one to mince her very cultured words. "Ah, Americans and discipline. Remember when you declared war on terror, and invaded Iraq? Well, I served in Basra and Baghdad and witnessed what passed for discipline in your army, Marvin. Quite frankly, it was about as good as your modern foreign policy decisions. And that, is probably because your chaps tend to jerk their knee every time there is a little problem… just like you now, darling."

"I have orders," he blurted." I'm party to information that…"

I didn't think it was possible for Des to be any angrier, but he turned the hostility up another notch and hissed in Varese's face.

"I will gladly slot you here and now and drop you in the sea for the fish if you even think about triggering those mines… Am I clear, son?"

Mitch piped up. "Mr Cogan, I don't figure that… "

Des didn't turn or look away from Varese's eyes. "You dinnea need to figure anything Mitch. It's not your place. Ye know I like ye, but don't put me in the position of having to make a choice between you and Rick Fuller."

Varese blinked, swallowed again. "Look, can we all just calm down here?"

"Give me your phone," spat Des. "Now."

Varese reluctantly handed over the set. Des threw it behind him, and it clattered to the floor. "Now your weapon," he said, eyes wide.

"Come on, Cogan. Be reasonable," said Marvin.

"Ye want to see me when I'm unreasonable, son," said Des, and curled his lip. "Weapon… now."

The American handed over his gun. The moment he did so, Mitch holstered his own Magnum and the atmosphere took a turn for the better.

"I think you can let Mr Varese sit down now, Cogan," said Sellers, instantly commanding the situation. She eyed Mitch. "And I trust we can allow you your weapon without being murdered in our beds?"

"You can, Ma'am," he said.

"Good," smiled Sellers. "Now, as the craft carrying Fuller is sailing in total blackout, they will be moving very slowly, therefore it is unlikely that they will have made it to the mouth of the estuary." She turned to Marvin. "How fast does this thing go? I take it you know what you are doing?"

Varese was still sulking. "Maybe thirty knots, once we set sail."

Another smile spread across Sellers' face. It was far from genuine, but it was there, nonetheless.

"Then let's get on with it, shall we? If we make the mouth before them and drop anchor, engines off, we may hear or see them leave."

Varese didn't move.

"Quicker than that, Marvin," she said. "Or shall I let Cogan here keep his promise and we end up sending your relatives a cod in the post?"

Varese stepped over to the controls and started the engines. He looked over to Mitch Collins and bared his teeth. "I won't forget this one, Marine," he said.

Rick Fuller's Story:

The boat continued to rock gently, the engines ticking over, it was like being in a holding pattern, waiting to land. I couldn't be certain, but I figured we'd travelled less than a mile. Something or someone was afoot.

Dr Weasel had returned to the upper deck, leaving me with Square Face. He sat on a wooden box and stared at me. I continued my poor downtrodden prisoner act and kept my head down.

"You have a wife, Fuller?" he asked.

I stayed silent.

"Children?"

Again I ignored him.

"Yunfakh is my family," he announced. "Abdallah is our father. He is all seeing."

I studied the guy for a second. I wanted to say he was a weirdo and I didn't give a fuck.

Instead. "I need the toilet," I said.

He sneered. "Then go."

"I'm not well," I said, looking all sorry for myself. "And if I did that, the smell would be terrible."

It was a trade-off. If I'd been in a cell or some other room where he could have closed the door and walked away, I was sure that he'd have left me to soil myself, but he didn't have that option. He wandered up the stairs muttering something in a language I couldn't identify. Minutes later, he returned with a wooden pail. He shuffled over and dropped it by my side.

I waited, wondering what his next move would be. I could see his mind working overtime. He didn't want to uncuff me, but he sure as hell didn't want to pull down my pants and wipe my arse either.

"I'm getting desperate," I said. "Sorry, but you'll have to help me."

He turned his back and bawled up the stairwell. "Josip! Josip! Come down here." There was movement above and eventually I heard the sound of footsteps. A guy I'd seen up on deck during the handover appeared. He carried one of his newly acquired AK47's.

"He needs to shit," said Square Face, grimacing as if he could already smell it. He drew his SLP from his shoulder holster and rested it on the box he'd been sitting on. "Cover him," he said.

Josip did exactly that, brought his AK up into the aim and slipped off the safety. Square Face strode over, keys in hand.

"Sorry," I said, shrinking away from his bulk. "But I do have a stomach upset."

Square Face shook his head ruefully, and gave me a look that told me I was in for another slap or two the moment we were alone again.

Now, here was the calculation, and I say this because before most moments of conflict, the victor is the one who thinks things through before the bullets start flying. Of course, on the odd occasion, there is no time to think and whoever is the fastest on his or her feet comes out on top, but not this time. All my training told me to take advantage of any hope of escape as soon as possible, and that is just how I saw this moment. I knew as the big goon leaned over to release my cuffs from the bar driven into the wall, that his body would temporarily mask me, giving at least some element of cover from Josip's AK. I would, of course, still be bound at the wrists, but at least I'd be free to move. Square Face's SLP was a Glock 19, a model that doesn't require the shooter to disengage a safety, and it sat, in plain sight not ten feet from my position. The thought of spending time aboard ship with slap happy Square Face for company, didn't appeal. Neither did the prospect of being the prisoner of Abdallah Al-Mufti and being nailed to a cross for a few days. I reckoned that a 7.62 in the chest, was preferable to rusty nails in the wrists and feet, any day. I'd never been frightened of dying, but, given the option, it would be nice to go quick and clean.

The bottom line was, if I had any chance of escape, I was going to take it, come hell or high water.

As the big lump leaned over me, I tucked my feet under my backside, ready to move. He gave me a suspicious look. I did my best to look apologetic, shrugged my shoulders and explained, "I need to stand up, so you can pull down my trousers."

He pulled another face that told me he didn't care for that prospect and pushed the key into the lock.

The second I felt the cuffs release, I grabbed the wooden bucket sitting at my feet by its lip, powered it upwards with all my strength and smashed it under his chin. He grunted and staggered backwards, almost falling back into Josip who mercifully decided to stop his buddy falling into him rather than take a clear shot at me.

I rolled forwards using my cuffed hands as a pivot, and a split second later, was up on my feet and within touching distance of the Glock. Grabbing at the weapon, I saw that Square face was still staggering about, disorientated, but Josip had finally got his shit together and was swinging his weapon around towards me. I threw myself to my right, hit the floor hard and dropped behind a pile of crates. The boy let go with his AK47 and just as in countless other close quarter battles I had fought in, the report of the weapon turned me instantly deaf. There was no time to worry about my ears or if the thick wooden boxes would stop the hi-velocity bullet, so I just gritted my teeth, popped out of cover, opened up with the Glock, and hoped for the best.

Now, the Glock 19 Gen5 in my hand had the standard thirteen round mag. It wasn't my favoured weapon, but I'd always liked the fact that the shooter didn't have to completely release the trigger before firing a second shot. My first two hit Josip in the shoulder and throat. His legs buckled and he went down without firing again. Suddenly, Square Face was clear headed. However, he wasn't as big and brave as he'd been earlier when I was chained to the wall. I saw fear in his eyes. He was about to run.

Unfortunately, there was no time to wallow in our reversed roles. I just put two nicely grouped rounds in that big fat head of his and felt instantly better.

This, too, was short lived as the shouts and movement from above told me that I was about to have more visitors, and they weren't bringing me tea and cakes.

The boats engines went from tick over to silent and I figured that every last man and his dog was about to give me a talking to.

My next choice was in which order to recover the items I needed. Did I go for the key to my cuffs, or Josip's AK?

Key.

I turned and put four more rounds up the stairwell. They clattered against the metal steps and rails and ricocheted off up towards the boys thinking of coming downstairs to read me my horoscope. That gave me precious seconds. Square Face had dropped the keys as he'd fallen, and I scrambled across the floor and scooped them up. Moments later, I was free. AK tucked in my shoulder, Glock in my belt.

One thing was for certain, no matter how the next minutes panned out, no matter how many came for me. I wasn't going to be captured again.

Des Cogan's Story:

We'd been on the move for thirty minutes, but, despite Victoria's hopes to move quickly to the mouth of the estuary, as we too didn't want to adver- tise our presence, progress was slower than she'd hoped. Now, unlike my captured comrade, I'd learned the value of patience in my later years. Days of sitting in holes in the ground waiting for the enemy to arrive had taught me so much. However, with Rick taken and a seemingly endless blackness surrounding our craft, I felt not only fear for my best friend's safety, but im- mense frustration.

There had been no sign of the target boat, or any other craft for that mat- ter. The moon occasionally poked out from behind heavy, low cloud cover which made navigation momentarily easier, but each time it dipped back behind the solid rain filled banks, we were plunged into total darkness and I fell into an ever deepening melancholy.

Then.

"That was gunfire," snapped Lauren, taking a break from biting her nails, obviously feeling the pressure as much as my good self. "Kill the engines a second, Marvin… listen up."

The American did as he was asked, but glared at her, still smarting from our earlier rebellion.

Lauren was indeed correct. Moments later the unmistakable sound of small arms fire, followed by some bigger calibre stuff cracked through the night, masking the gentle lapping of the water against the hull of our boat.

I stood on deck and searched the inky blackness. "I cannea see anything, hen," I said, rueing our lack of NV kit. Mitch came alongside me as we heard more shots. We both strained to see anything resembling a craft. Suddenly, there was a flash of light and a corresponding crack.

"Muzzle flash," said the American. "That's dead ahead, sir, and that shooting can only mean one thing."

"Aye," I nodded, feeling my spirits rise. "It means he's free, and he's fighting."

Mitch pursed his lips and nodded.

"That's gonna be tough, Mr Cogan. Confined spaces, stairs, it's as bad as it gets."

I turned to the big fella. He was already checking over his Magnum.

"Well they don't come any tougher, Mitch, and there's no one better at close quarter work than Rick. While the shooting goes on, he's still alive. That's all that matters, son."

As if to prove my point there were more exchanges and I definitely heard shouts or cries ahead. I called to Marvin. "Fire her up, pal. And keep her steady on this course, easy does it, we're close."

Sellers sprang into action. "Okay girls and boys, kit up. Marvin, steady as we go, as soon as we have a visual, aim this thing for their midships and give it some gas."

"Nice to hear you have a plan, Sellers," he said flatly, increasing the engine's revs. "Do you have a plan for me? Or do I get to fight bare handed?"

She turned and studied our pet CIA man for a moment, then nodded at Lauren. "Give him his gun, darling." Then, to the American. "Just be a good boy, Marvin and we'll get along swimmingly."

She climbed up to where Mitch and I stood and handed us an AK each together with a couple of spare mags.

I took my rifle and loaded it. "If I didnea know any better, Sellers, I'd say you were enjoying yourself."

She peered ahead, her beautiful long raven hair blowing in the breeze. From somewhere in her clothing she pulled out an elastic band and tied back her locks. She then turned to me; eyes cold. "You know as much as anyone how this feels, Cogan. You can't let it go. It runs in the blood." Finally, she smiled. "Besides, I like to keep my hand in."

"We can see that, Ma'am," offered Mitch, racking his AK.

She turned and gave the American a knowing wink. "I'm used to being in charge, Collins… and don't concern yourself with your colleague. I'll handle him. Just concentrate on getting Mr Fuller back in one piece, eh?"

Mitch nodded his gratitude. "Ma'am," he said.

Then, seconds later. "There!" she said sharply. "Come on Varese, give it some licks."

Rick Fuller's Story:

As I'd anticipated the boys upstairs quickly got their shit together. Fortunately, as they'd done so, I'd had time to fashion a makeshift barricade from crates and pallets and had myself tucked in nicely. The stairs were covered, but to make life slightly more uncomfortable, there was a further door on the far side of the room. I had no idea what or who may be behind it, or indeed, even if it could be accessed from the upper deck. However, to keep me interested in proceedings, one of the boys above was feeling brave and kept pointing his AK around the door at the top of the stairs and letting go on fully automatic. It was more annoying than life threatening, but there was always a chance that a stray could find its way in my direction.

As my biggest concern was lack of ammunition, just half a clip in the AK and nine shots in the Glock, I waited patiently for him to make the mistake of sneaking a peak, and sure enough, after three bursts and no response from yours truly, he popped his head around the door to survey what damage he'd done. I caught him with a single shot just under his right eye.

Jesus, those 7.62's make a mess. He slid down the stairs with half his head missing. I jumped out of cover and relieved him of a spare mag and felt instantly more comfortable.

The loss of another crew member seemed to trigger all manner of arguments above. There were raised voices, including Dr Weasel, who I presumed was under strict instructions to keep me alive until his boss could nail me to the nearest cross whilst slaughtering a goat or three.

I had other ideas, and things were about to improve further.

There was an almighty bang and the boat lurched to one side, sending me crashing to the floor and boxes of God knows what falling on top of me. Then I heard the gunfire. Short controlled bursts, big calibre. It had to be Des. Just had to be.

Within thirty seconds, all was quiet. I stood up and listened. Then, I heard Des shout, 'clear,' as he dropped into the first small room at the top of my stairs. As he opened the second door leading to my room, he must have been able to see the guy with half a head at the bottom. The Scot wasn't about to take chances.

"Rick, where the fuck are ye, ye bastard?" he shouted, always the gentleman, but staying sensibly out of sight.

"Down here doing all the fucking work," I said.

He manoeuvred his wiry frame down the narrow steps, his AK smoking from use. I stood in the centre of the room, three bodies around me.

He gave me a broad smile. "Getting you out of the shit is becoming a fucking habit." he said.

"Glad you could make it," I offered. "Did you enjoy your cruise around Ireland whilst your best mate was being slapped about by half of the Baltic States?"

He smiled again. "It was very pleasurable, despite the need to have a serious word or two with one of our American cousins."

"Really?"

"Aye, we'll have a chat about that wee jobbie later." Des made his weapon safe. "We're all good up top, no casualties. However, we have one prisoner."

"A prisoner?" I said. "What's he look like?"

"Small dude, big nose."

I nodded. "As they say in your neck of the woods, pal… you fucking beauty. Just the man I want to chat with."

Des was about to turn and go back up top, but I held up a hand to stop him, pointed at my eyes and then the closed door at the far end of the room, the one I told you about, the one I'd never seen behind. The Scot gave me a knowing look, drew his BAP, and we made our way quietly over.

Des lifted a boot and smashed the door open. I was through first and stepped right, the Scot was in behind and left.

"Clear," he said.

The room was indeed empty, other than for two items. A three legged stool and a polished wooden coffin.

"The Captain?" offered Des.

"Only one way to find out," I said, doing my best to lift the lid. After two vain attempts, I turned to my mate. "Would you believe it's nailed shut?"

"I've seen a few dead blokes in my time, pal," said Des, checking the lid for himself. "But I dinnea ever recall one opening the lid of his own casket.

Bit creepy if you ask me. Like one of them horror movies where the dev-il jumps out, eh?"

I shook my head and smiled, happy to have my pal back alongside me. A bit of banter always went a long way to calm a sticky situation. He stepped out of the room. Moments later he returned with a small jemmy and hun-kered down next to the rather expensive looking coffin, Des eased each nail upwards until the lid was free.

Once the last one was out, he looked up at me, holding the lip of the cas-ket in his hand.

"If fucking Damien jumps out of here, pal, I'll be swimming for it, I'll tell yer."

It wasn't anything to do with a horror flick, indeed, there was no body at all. Rather than a corpse, packed inside the casket were dozens of rectan-gular packages wrapped in thick plastic and bound with packing tape. Des pulled his old service knife and carefully cut into one.

He raised his eyebrows and looked at me. "Well, isn't that a wee turn up fer the books, eh, pal?" he said.

I stood next to him. "Oh yes, you can say that again… Nail that shut, pal, and keep this to yourself, eh?"

Des began the task of hammering the nails back in place and my thoughts turned to that big payday I was talking about earlier.

As I kept watch at the door, I heard footsteps treading the stairs. It was Marvellous Marvin Varese.

"All clear down here," I shouted.

He stopped in his tracks. There was a look on his face that I couldn't quite read. Guilt? Suspicion? I couldn't tell. One thing I did know was I trusted him about as much as a wounded lion.

"Okay," he managed. "Good to see you in fine health, Fuller. We were worried about you for a while there."

"I'm sure you were," I said.

Lauren North's Story:

I watched as Rick dipped his head and stepped out onto the deck. His shirt was drenched in sweat sticking to his body. There was a slight swelling around his left eye, as if he'd been punched, but other than that, he looked well. Actually, he looked good enough to eat. He dropped an AK and spare magazines onto the deck and wiped his face with both hands. Just to see him alive and well caused tears to form and I felt them dribble down my cheeks. I thought my heart would burst.

He caught my eye briefly, but there was no smile, just a nod of acknowledgement. That, I suppose, was all I could hope for.

Mitch was covering our prisoner with his AK. He was a small Arabic looking guy and he lay face down on the deck, his hands tied behind his back, legs crossed.

Rick stepped over to him.

"Hello Doctor," he said. "Well, this is a turn up for the books, eh? Care to tell us where you were headed?"

"Ana la 'aerif 'aya shay," said the guy.

"He doesn't know anything," explained Sellers.

Varese, who had been remarkably helpful once he'd realised we had control of the target vessel looked over to Victoria. "You speak Arabic?" he asked.

Sellers pulled her hair from her ponytail and shook it, looking every inch a sex goddess. "I'm not just a pretty face darling," she smiled, and walked over to our prisoner.

"Hal taerif ma hu altazaluj ealaa alma?" she said, leaving the rest of us with blank expressions.

The guy began to shout what sounded like insults. I didn't understand, but he was obviously pissed off.

"What did you say to him, Victoria? I asked.

Sellers shrugged and gave me an impish grin. "I just asked him if he knew what waterboarding was, darling."

Rick lifted his foot and planted his boot firmly on the neck of our small friend. He leaned in until the guy began to choke. His voice low, threatening.

"Now, I am well aware that you speak perfect English matey, so let's not fuck about. You've already told me that you are bosom buddies with Abdallah Al-Mufti, which is enough for me to slot you here and now."

He lifted his foot and the guy took in lungful's of air. Rick dropped to his haunches. "Care to enlighten the group where you were taking me? Or shall I let our very capable Ms Sellers wrap a towel over your face and play, let's drown the man from the Taliban?"

"Ana la 'aerif 'aya shay," repeated the guy, and spat on the deck.

Sellers let out a long breath. "Right," she said, rubbing her palms together. "Cogan, North… find something weighty to tie to the corpses and chuck them in the drink. Fuller, find us a decent sturdy plank, some towels and a bucket, will you?"

Varese had been suspiciously quiet during the proceedings, but on hearing Sellers begin to bark her orders, he held up a hand.

"Whoa there, Sellers. Let's not get ahead of ourselves here. Firstly, if you hadn't noticed, we have left the island of Ireland. If you recall, the deal was that I would take charge from here on in. Secondly… "

"Secondly," said Sellers. "I've changed my mind on that one. Woman's prerogative and all that. The moment that you decided to try and blow this boat sky high with a team member aboard, you sort of played your ace, shot your bolt."

Rick's head twisted around so fast, I thought it may spin off his shoulders. He glared at Marvin.

Sellers noticed, but ignored the issue, cocked her head and looked at me. "Can you think of any more idioms to describe Mr Varese's lack of composure, darling?"

"He flies off the handle?" I offered.

"Ah, yes, nice one, Ms North. Yes, he does, doesn't he?"

Varese's face was thunder. "You can joke all you like there, Sellers, but when Whitehall find out about your treachery and deceit, there'll be hell to pay. And if you think I will stand idly by, whilst you play fast and loose with the Geneva Convention, you can guess again."

Rick's face was ashen with anger.

"And where in the Geneva Convention does is stipulate that it's okay to drown me, you cowardly fuck?"

Sellers turned down her mouth.

"Mmm… good point, well made, Fuller. By the way, are you currently employed by HM Forces?" she asked.

"No," said Rick, lifting the boat's gangplank from the end of the deck and resting one end on a chair. "Why? Does that mean blowing me to bits doesn't fucking count."

"I wouldn't have thought so, darling, but you miss my point," said Sellers. "Cogan, what about you?"

"Retired," said the Scot, rolling one of the dead players into the water. "I'm a pensioner, would ye believe?"

Sellers found her smile again.

"So, the only military employee aboard, is Mr Collins over there, and as the Bush administration only banned waterboarding on detainees, by military personnel, it would seem that he alone would be exempt from such barbarism. However, that ruling does not apply to anyone else, even you, Varese so… don't worry darling, I reckon the interrogation of our Taliban friend here, by any means we see fit, shouldn't offend your sensibilities."

Big Mitch shrugged his huge shoulders.

"You do what you like to the dude, Ma'am," he said. "Me and the Taliban go way back."

He then shuffled over to help Des with another body seemingly unconcerned about our prisoner's fate. Rick disappeared below and returned with a wooden bucket and a towel.

Varese was at his side in seconds. "You can't really be serious about this, Fuller. Come on man, you were a soldier once. This is torture. Let's just get this guy, and this boat back to dry land."

Rick began to tie a length of rope to the bucket. He changed the subject to one closer to his heart.

"So, Varese, I understand you tried to blow this crate to pieces with me in it?" he said eyeballing the American.

Marvin was resolute. "I was following my orders, Fuller. This cargo was not to reach its destination without our tail. You knew as much. That had always been the plan."

For the first time, Rick looked across the deck and deep into my eyes. "Lauren, how long did you search for me, before this fool tried to fire the mines?"

I just shook my head.

He turned back to Marvin. Rick had that look about him. The one that told you to stay away, steer clear.

"Is that right Varese? You didn't even try? Now, let me think. Why might that be?"

Marvin's bald head shone in the moonlight; he was sweating again.

"It was hopeless. I couldn't risk…"

Rick curled his lip. "But you didn't even try. So, I'll ask you again. Why was that, Marvin?"

He walked over to the prostrate Arab prisoner and gave him a swift kick in the ribs. The man cried out and cursed him. Rick turned.

"Because, you see Weasel here? When he had me all trussed up below deck, ready to deliver me to his pal, Al-Mufti, he seemed a real brave boy, just like the square faced goon with a couple of rounds of nine mil in his head. He was a fuckin hero too. Especially when he had me chained to the wall. Now, under normal circumstances, when a man makes decisions like the one you elected to do, I would usually question that person's courage. Was it down to lack of guts?"

Rick got in close. Varese looked very uncomfortable.

"You know what, Marvin, I don't think so. I don't believe that a Silver Star winner and veteran of dozens of covert operations behind enemy lines, is the fucking squeamish type. I think there may be something that you're not telling us."

He ran a hand through his hair, his face incredulous.

"Let me take a wild guess at what happened after I was taken. The moment my guys got back to your boat and gave you the good news, you immediately tried to detonate those mines," Rick pointed at Des. "But this wee Scotsman here threatened to slot you if you did. Am I warm?"

"Fuckin' eejit," muttered Des as he disposed of a third corpse.

"I figured that one," said Rick. "So, just as Sellers here has eluded to, you seem to suffer from overreaction under pressure. Not a trait that I would expect to find in a man of your reputation. Which brings me back to my earlier point."

Marvin glared at Rick. "I was given orders. And unlike some here, I follow them, to the letter. There is a bigger picture, Fuller. A picture that you don't need to know about."

"Really, you don't say," said Rick, eyebrows raised.

"Something stinks," said Des, washing blood from his hands.

Rick gave Varese a thin smile. "My Scottish friend has always been able to spot a gang fuck when he sees one."

Marvin's tone was suddenly and unexpectedly conciliatory.

"Look, Fuller. We're on the same side here. We just work in different ways. Think in different ways. As I said, the priority now, is to get this cargo back on dry land, contact HQ and take stock."

Rick shook his head. I could almost hear his mind working overtime.

"Doctor Weasel here knew all about me. He knew I'd be waiting for this very boat. He knew I'd be delivering those AK's. How do you think he knew all that, Varese?"

"I don't know," said Marvin.

Rick pointed in the American's face.

"But you do know more than you are saying and I'll bet a pound to a pinch of shit that the reason you don't want us to interrogate our big nosed friend here, is because he knows that very same shit... and that's why, I'm going to tie him to that fucking plank."

Rick Fuller's Story:

Doctor Weasel was fastened firmly to his board. Des was sitting at the stern smoking his horrible pipe. I reluctantly joined him as we watched Varese bitching about his lack of authority and trying to persuade Sellers not to go through with what we were about to do. He just wouldn't shut the fuck up.

"Do ye think the Yank is in on this?" asked Des, blowing smoke over his shoulder, and thankfully away from my face.

"I don't know, pal," I said. "When you deal with MI6 and the CIA, nothing is straightforward, eh?"

"Where did the intel come from that the AK's were bound for Yunfakh use?" asked Des.

"Ask me one on sport."

"You think Cartwright will tell you?"

I shrugged my shoulders. "I reckon there's another bigger puzzle to solve."

"Oh aye, ye mean the box down below?"

"I reckon there is close on a hundred kilos of charlie stuffed inside that coffin, pal."

"Jeezo."

"Exactly. And where the fuck was that going?"

"Maybe the wee boy with the big conk will tell us."

"Maybe," I said. "And maybe that's just why Marvin is so touchy about how we obtain that information."

Waterboarding was nothing new. It had been around since the late seventies. It's a form of torture where liquid is poured over a cloth covering the face. The subject, in our case, Doctor Weasel, is immobilised on their back at an incline. You then pour water into the breathing passages, causing an almost immediate gag reflex and creating a sensation of drowning.

The trick is, to pour just enough, or you kill your prisoner, dry drown the boy. Either way, it's extremely painful, causes harm to the lungs, brain damage from oxygen deprivation, and other physical injuries, including broken bones, if your boy struggles hard enough.

It is most fucking unpleasant.

As I sat and watched Varese argue his corner to the point of ad nauseum. I still couldn't get my head around the man. On the road to the port, when the shit had been flying, he'd fought like a lion. It was as if he needed to get us to our destination at all costs, but as soon as I was taken, something had changed. He'd been like the worst kind of Rupert. It was 'by the book and hang the consequences,' and that worried me on a job like this. I needed him gone. Out of my hair.

Varese was a problem, I didn't trust him. But it was the drugs stored in the hold that worried me even more. Drugs, especially in that amount, meant big trouble.

I turned back to Des, my head spinning with information. "Why would you be transporting weapons and drugs on the same boat?"

The Scot lit his pipe again. "Ye wouldnea. All yer eggs in one basket like. Too risky."

"That's what I thought, pal."

The Scot blew out another long plume and tapped his pipe on the rail to empty it.

"Ye know what I think, Rick? I reckon the AK's were bound fer the Continent, but the coke is meant fe the UK. And I reckon, the buyers were, or still are waiting close by. This boat was never going to enter the open sea with all that gear on board."

"You could be right there Des. The boat pulled away from the coast then sat in some kind of holding pattern. It's possible they were waiting for another craft. But I know one thing. Some very powerful people will want their charlie back. And until we get it off this boat and out of our hands we are all in the proverbial brown stuff."

"Aye," said Des stuffing his pipe back in his pocket and eyeing Marvin again. "Greed is a terrible thing. When that kind of money is at stake, it makes good folks do bad things."

"It does indeed."

"You think he knew it was aboard all along? Is he on the take like Mason Carver?"

I shook my head.

"I couldn't say, but I bet I know a man who can."

I rubbed and cricked my neck; it was creaking and cracking like an old sideboard. Then I stood and stretched the pain from my back. I was definitely getting old, feeling my age, my body complaining at every juncture.

As I stood there in the darkness, the breeze in my face, the aches in my muscles paled into insignificance as I was overcome by another, greater pain. At that moment, I longed for a little normality, the tender touch of someone who cared about me for who I was. I yearned to step away from the violence and the betrayal, to find compassion, kindness, maybe even love.

Looking across to Lauren, I knew the answer to all of that lay with her. She stood close to Sellers, staring into space. How did I feel about what she'd done? I knew how angry I was, but I also realised that during those awful moments on the road to the handover, as she lay motionless, slumped across the wheel of her car, that there were more important things in life than a man's pride.

She looked over and there was a hint of a smile. Despite everything, her injuries, the fighting, the lack of sleep, she looked beautiful. I nodded and her smile broadened. There were no words required.

Pushing thoughts of predictability and passion from my mind, I couldn't help but feel that Des was right. The reason the Yunfakh boat had made such little progress, was that Doctor Weasel and the crew had been waiting to offload the contents of that coffin below, maybe a meet at a nearby cove, maybe another boat. We needed answers, and quick.

On the other hand, Marvin was not only a liability, but he was getting right up my nose with his constant whining about the rights and wrongs of drowning the good Doctor. He was fast becoming a pain in the arse. So, I decided he was better out of the picture.

If I was right, and we were due a visit from some very big hitters in the nose candy world, the last thing I needed was someone I couldn't rely on aboard. However, even though he'd tried to top me, I still didn't have him down as a traitor. No, there was more to this story than another bent CIA agent. Varese was not only a tough cookie, but a follow orders at all costs, type of guy. Someone at the very top chose him for this task just because of that.

As for the problem at hand, as weird as it sounds, I half hoped that the intended buyers came calling. I had method in my madness, believe me. Those drugs amounted to a five million pound payday for Al-Mufti and I was extremely curious to find out who they were destined for.

The boat that Mitch and Marvin had hired was still tied alongside us and that would put any would be drug dealers off. So, I decided that I could kill two birds with one stone.

"Varese," I shouted. "Tell you what, why not give it a rest, eh? If you are so against our methods, why not jump on your boat now and take it to the RV? That way, we won't offend your precious principals and I can get some peace."

I expected a full on rant about how his seniority was being undermined. Instead, he looked around him and studied all the faces of the team

When he saw no support, he turned to big Mitch.

"Collins?" he asked, grasping his final straw.

"Sorry, Sir," said the big American. "But I'm of a mind to help Mr Fuller here."

Marvin strode over to me, chest all puffed out, doing his best to save some face.

"You're making a big mistake here, Fuller. This mission is over. The trail to Al-Mufti and Yunfakh is cold. I say we take both craft back to the RV, call the job in, and await further orders. You can't risk losing this cargo."

I looked into his eyes and tried to read him. Whatever was going on in that shiny head of his, whatever the cock up with the intelligence, one thing I was certain of, Marvin was desperate to make sure the contents of this boat stayed in his hands. Did he know what was down below? On a scale of one to ten? A solid fucking eight.

Pulling my Glock, I pointed it straight at his chest.

"Just get aboard, Varese," I said. "This mission is over for you."

"You wouldn't dare," he hissed.

"Oh yes, I would," I smiled.

There was a moment or two of defiance, but he got the picture, and with his cruiser unleashed from our craft, he reluctantly stood behind the controls and began to edge away. I heard him fire the engines. The black water foamed white behind the boat, and moments later he was out of sight.

Des stood alongside me. "Did you tell him about the charlie?"

"Nope. But that doesn't mean he didn't know, eh?"

"True, pal. Either way good riddance, I reckon."

I shrugged. "Fuck him. Let's see what our good Doctor has to say, eh?"

Lauren North's Story:

I watched Marvin guide the boat away from our craft and disappear into the night. Within minutes, silence had returned, and Rick rekindled his interest in our prisoner.

"Gather round chaps," he said. "Now, this is Doctor Weasel, a self-confessed Taliban member, who speaks the Queen's English almost as good as Sellers here. His plan was to deliver me to his good pal Abdallah Al- Mufti. Someone on our side of the fence has been a naughty boy and sold us down the river and I'm sure we'd all like to know who that is, eh?"

The guy stayed silent.

Rick wasn't done.

"In addition to the spy in our camp and the location of the said, Al-Mufti, there is also the pressing little matter of some unusual cargo down below. I wonder what our friend here would be doing with a coffin full of cocaine? Say five million quid's worth?"

"That's one hell of a party, darling" said Sellers, her face full of surprise.

"Tell me about it," said Des. "And I'm really interested to know if our friend Marvellous Marvin knew it was down there when he was about to pull the plug on this wee boat."

I felt my stomach turn.

"Maybe Varese was right though guys. Maybe we should get back on dry land. I mean, what if someone is out there right now waiting for that shipment. They'd have to be pretty serious players, wouldn't they?"

Des racked his AK. "So are we hen. Bring it on, I say."

Rick checked the Afghan's ties and dangled the bucket into the water. "Let's have the cloth over, Sellers," he said.

As I looked out to sea, just a few hundred metres to the south of our position, I saw navigation lights and instantly felt that my worst fears were about to become a reality.

"I don't mean to worry you guys, but we have company," I said.

Rick looked up and threw the bucket to the floor. "Sellers, Des, Mitch… sort yourselves out. Lauren, stuff a rag in Weasel's mouth and kill the lights. We may just have a customer for our coffin."

The Scot and the big American didn't need any further encouragement, they began to tuck themselves in and check over their weapons. One thing was in our favour, with all those AK's and ammo in the hold, we wouldn't be short of firepower.

Rick walked over to Sellers, it was obvious he respected her, and I couldn't help but notice the way she looked at him. Despite our precarious position, my green eyed monster reared its head.

"How do you want to play this?" he asked her.

"There's only one way, darling," she replied. "Reel them in, then pop them off."

He nodded and smiled at her and I felt another twinge of jealousy.

"That's what I thought you'd say," he said.

I could hear the other boat's engines burbling away in the distance. This was not some pleasure cruiser approaching, this was a big fast vessel, something to outrun the coast guard, or any other nice folks that may want to interfere in their business transactions.

I knew that Rick had been part of a few of these dodgy deals in his time, providing security for both buyers and sellers. Not something he was proud of, but he couldn't turn the clock back, and as things stood, his wealth of experience in that department wouldn't do the team any harm.

"You think it's them?" I asked him.

Rick shrugged and checked over his rifle. "What I do know, is even when a deal is worth thousands of pounds, everyone gets a little edgy until the transaction is completed. With somewhere in the region of five million at stake, these boys are going to be properly on top."

He reached out and held my chin between his thumb and fingers, looked deep into my eyes, and said. "So keep that pretty head down, okay?"

He walked back to Sellers leaving me with a stupid grin on my face.

"What do you know about boats?" he asked her.

She smiled, not taking her eyes off the approaching vessel.

"Your boyfriend punts you along the river in one, then buys you a nice lunch."

Rick pulled a face. "Can you start this one or not? Get us ready to move if we have to?"

"Of course Fuller," she said. "Just my idea of a little joke."

He shook his head. Sellers stepped to the controls and fired the twin diesels, revving them hard.

Our boat had two large spotlights on the cabin roof, with controls that allowed you to manoeuvre them from inside. I found the power switches. "Shall we light them up?" I asked.

"Go for it," said Rick, then shouted to the team. "Standby… on me."

I hit the switch and the ocean turned from black to emerald green. The craft in question was cruising straight for us.

"Fucking hell," said Sellers. "Now that is what you call a toy."

"It's a Barracuda," said Rick. "I've only ever seen one in pictures. Forty feet of bulletproof beast. Two six hundred horsepower engines. Designed right here in Cork…"

"Are we getting a visit from James Bond?" shouted Des over the engine noise.

"Maybe his evil twin," said Rick pushing spare mags into his jacket. "But whoever it is, we've been easy to spot for some time. That thing has sonar, thermal imaging and night vision surveillance. If they'd been hostile, we'd have known about it by now."

He walked over to the Scot and lowered his voice. "You got any morphine on you?"

Des pulled two field doses from his pocket.

Rick nodded. "Put the good doctor to sleep for a bit, eh? I have a feeling our visitors will value their secrecy."

Des walked over to the prostrate doctor and jabbed him twice. Within seconds he was away with the fairies.

The Barracuda's engine note fell, and the bow of the boat settled in the water. Seconds later it was the turn of the impressive craft to show us its lighting array and we found ourselves squinting against its many millions of lumens. There was the whirring of electric motors, and a pair of carbon fibre doors opened on the foredeck. More concerning for our little crew, was the evil looking gun that popped out from the hull below.

"Fuck me, it's Thunderbirds," said Des.

A cultured and instantly recognisable voice boomed out of an unseen PA system.

"In case you are wondering, Fuller, this monstrosity you see before you is a Barracuda XSV 17, and the weapon currently pointing in your direction, is a remotely controlled, gyroscopically stabilised 12.7mm machine gun, fitted with a 40mm grenade launcher."

"Impressive," shouted Rick to the, as yet unseen, Cartwright. He lowered his voice and turned to Des. "Told you it was Bond's evil twin."

There were more whirring sounds and a rear hatch opened. The elderly spy stepped into open view; his white hair blown by the night breeze. He wore his trademark Saville Row number but rather comically had been forced to add a bright orange life preserver by whoever crewed the boat.

He also looked very pale.

"Sorry about the show of force, old chap," he shouted. "But your old SBS pals wanted to play with their new toy. Besides, with that chap Varese aboard, it was a case of better safe than sorry."

"I can imagine," said Rick, seemingly as relieved as the rest of us, that the craft contained friendly faces. "However, he's just left with his toys and his pram."

Cartwright manoeuvred himself to the rail of the Barracuda. Sellers grabbed his arm and helped him aboard our creaking boat. Once on deck he immediately removed his orange vest, threw it petulantly onto the floor and gestured towards the state of the art machine alongside.

"Fucking Nazis," he said. "Don't know what has happened to selection these days. Forcing an old man into such discomfort."

The Special Boat Service crew remained inside their craft unseen, and I considered that was the way it was going to stay.

Cartwright hobbled towards a wooden chair fastened to the deck, totally ignoring our now unconscious prisoner, who was still strapped to his plank. He sat heavily and pointed at Rick.

"Please tell me that you have tea and fresh milk, Fuller. That and a damned good brandy, preferably an Asbach 21. You have no idea what it was like to travel around the coast in that carbuncle of a vessel and with those children as a crew."

"I imagine the lads gave you the full tour," said Rick, doing his best to hide his amusement.

"I feel like I've done the full ten rounds, I'll tell you." Cartwright took in his surroundings. "Where's Varese you say?"

"Taken another boat to shore," said Rick his conviviality dropping from his face.

"I see," offered Cartwright. "And the chap lying out cold on the plank at a jaunty angle?"

"Doctor Weasel," said Rick. "It's a name I've chosen for him, obviously. He's an Afghan, ex Taliban turned Yunfakh actually, was a medic or doctor at Bagram back in the day. That's if you believe his story. Good mate of Al-Mufti too, so he says." Rick cocked his head and eyed the old spy. "Funny how he was expecting me, eh?"

Cartwright pulled a face and waved his hand like the queen in her carriage. "All will be revealed, Fuller... just get me that tea. My stomach is churning."

Rick Fuller's Story:

Sellers found tea and milk. Unsurprisingly, there was no alcohol on board. I mean, heaven forbid, the mere thought of having a bottle of Jack in the cupboard would see the Weasel slung out of paradise in an instant. The hundred kilograms of cocaine nestled in the stores were okay though, no problems at all with that.

Cartwright sipped his tea, grimaced and set down his cup. "Close the door, Fuller," he said.

I did as he asked. We'd moved to the small room that I'd first been taken to and sat opposite each other. It afforded the old spy the privacy he desired. On the small polished table between us, lay the case containing the three hundred and twenty thousand euros that had been intended for Finbarr's back pocket.

Cartwright tapped it with a bony finger. "You chaps can't keep this, I'm afraid. Destined for our forensics department."

I shrugged. "It's hardly the pressing issue, is it? Not when there's five mil's worth of charlie in the hold and we've just lost any hope of finding Al-Mufti."

The old spy took another sip of tea and raised his brows.

"There is always more than one way to skin a cat, old boy. We're not done yet, although I have to say, the intelligence that the Benzoyl methyl ecgonine you refer to was aboard, came to us very late. Indeed. Far too late to inform your good self. Strange how it's become so popular, isn't it? The Incas chewed coca leaves to increase breathing in order to survive in the thin mountain air, you know?"

"Fascinating," I said.

"May I see the booty," said Cartwright placing his cup delicately on the table.

I blew out my cheeks. "It's in a coffin with the lid nailed shut."

"Really?"

"Yes."

"Most ingenious... Sigmund Freud was a big advocate of the drug, you know? And John Pemberton used coca leaves as an ingredient in Coca-Cola, not that it is present these days."

"Your lesson of cocaine history is riveting, Cartwright. However, what I want to know is, how did that little Taliban guy out there know that I would be meeting this boat, in this cove, on this day?"

The old spy sniffed. "There is a mole somewhere."

"You've always got a fucking mole somewhere."

Cartwright lay his hands on the table.

"It's a constant battle, Fuller. Unfortunately it goes with the territory, we turn one of theirs, and they turn one of ours. It's been going on since time immemorial. The informants identity is currently a mystery, but I'd wager it was someone above my pay scale."

"Mmm... Talking of traitors, do you realise that Varese tried to slot me?"

"Ah," breathed Cartwright, reaching for his cup. "So hard to get the right people these days. I would wager, his actions had more to do with the coffin full of fun, than the AK47's down below. You see, our good friends the Americans came up with the remotely controlled explosives idea during their final briefing. I did wonder why an organisation as corrupt in their thinking as the CIA were so concerned about a few boxes of old AK's. After all, they've sold millions of dollars' worth of arms to just about every terrorist organisation on the planet. No, I'd wager Varese would have been under pressure to ensure that casket didn't get delivered. Those old Russian rifles would have taken the back seat in his thinking. The folks above him wield significant power, you see, and blowing one of my operatives sky high wouldn't have concerned them one iota"

"And just who are these folks?"

"The powers that be, Fuller. You've been on operations before where the command is made up from two or more countries. It's always problematic. Damned Yanks have always been trigger happy."

"And you're not concerned that he's still out there and those mines are fastened to the bottom of this boat?"

Cartwright shook his head.

"Not at all, Richard. It's been dealt with. The capability to remotely detonate those devices has been disabled... hence the reason I'm sitting here drinking tea."

"Of course, so riddle me this, how did you know where we were and that things had gone pear shaped?"

Cartwright finished his brew and took a deep breath.

"Well, for a start, the trackers Sellers fitted to the IRA's Kalashnikovs are very clever little bugs. Once they are fixed to their target, they begin to transmit a traceable GPS signal. Nevertheless, the moment they are removed, they stop transmitting GPS and switch to audio mode. Actual live broadcast. The boys in GCHQ heard every word. Therefore we knew you'd suffered a … setback."

"That's one way of putting it. So why were the Yanks so desperate for the coke not to reach land?"

Cartwright rubbed his chin. "Hmm… that's politics for you. I haven't quite got the answer to that one yet. As soon as I know, so will you."

"So you're saying, Varese knew about the additional cargo?"

"It's possible… no probable… have you ever heard of lateral thinking, Richard?"

I had an idea, but as I knew the old git was going to tell me anyway, I stayed quiet.

"It's a manner of solving problems using an indirect and creative approach via reasoning that is not immediately obvious. It involves ideas that may not be obtainable using only traditional step-by-step logic… Something, I've noticed that you apply to almost everything."

"I'm all ears Einstein."

"Look, Fuller, Finbarr O'Rourke is the catalyst here, not Marvellous Marvin Varese. Finbarr had been working undercover for far too long. I knew that, and when you met him, I'm sure that you'd agree."

I nodded.

"Anyway, Finbarr came to us with the story that he'd made contact with these Balkan chaps and had brokered a deal to sell them the very weapons sitting in the hold right now. He was to buy them from his old PIRA contacts, turn a profit and that was that. Our initial interest was twofold. One, get rid of hundreds of automatic weapons from the island of Ireland, and two, track the passage of the cache to its final destination and pass on the intelligence to the relevant parties. Everyone's a winner. However, as you know, further information surfaced that these Balkan arms dealers were to sell their goods to Yunfakh, indeed directly to Al-Mufti himself."

"And where did that intel come from?"

"Finbarr."

"I'm starting to see a picture."

"Indeed, Fuller. There is no doubt that Finbarr O'Rourke was a thief and a tad eccentric, but I still don't see him as a traitor. The Balkan chaps passed on the information to him, and I believe he passed it to us in good faith. It was they who set the Yunfakh trap, and we fell for it. Now, I agree that there has to be another leak somewhere, someone who knew that you had travelled to Ireland. Someone who could confirm that their ruse had worked."

"Another mole? There are two?"

"Yes but, this particular mole is closer to you than you think. Look, Fuller, on board this very boat, is a large amount of cocaine, so large, that the Americans were prepared to kill you to ensure it never made its final destination. Then, there is your good self, a precious prisoner that Yunfakh has gone to a great deal of trouble to capture, not forgetting an IRA arms cache and three hundred thousand Euros in cash."

"Like Des said... Too many eggs in the basket."

"I concur with Mr Cogan and here is my lateral thinking. Our Taliban chap, you, and the weapons were bound for one location, and the narcotics, were destined for elsewhere, on a different vessel."

"You think the coke is payment for my head? It would make sense. If your mole is a Whitehall big hitter with underworld contacts."

Cartwright blew air down his nose and rubbed tiredness from his face.

"I'd be more inclined to suggest that the Euros were meant for that particular loose lipped traitor, possibly to be handed over once you were on dry land and in the hands of Al-Mufti. No, I have a mind that the cocaine was destined to pay for political influence. American political influence. Hence Varese's desperation to drop you, and it, in the drink, old boy."

He was losing me altogether.

"Okay. So where is this other vessel?"

"Again an enigma. Maybe the Barracuda scared them off? Possibly they heard your gunfire as they approached. Any of the above."

I shook my head. "So what now?"

"I start by finding out exactly what your good doctor knows. As for your good self, here is my suggestion..."

Lauren North's Story:

Rick finally emerged from his meeting. He looked suddenly tired and a little confused. The still unconscious Doctor was carried aboard the Barracuda, Cartwright gingerly followed him, and the craft turned north. Sellers set our boat in behind and we followed the impressive vessel at a steady pace. Rick had remained tight lipped about his lengthy conversation with the old spy and sat deep in thought throughout the whole journey.

I, like the rest of the team, let him be.

We made land at Rosslare, County Wexford. It's a large port with all the trappings of an international passenger terminus. Ferry operators run regular trips to Fishguard, Cherbourg, Roscoff and Pembroke Dock. Cartwright had pulled out all the stops and men in suits ushered us away to a small portacabin where we were given clean civilian clothes and a chance to freshen up. Our prisoner, however, was not so fortunate and I'd seen him being led unsteadily away in the distance. He'd been hooded and shackled by another far more churlish looking squad and bundled into the back of a black transit.

As we stood on the dockside, a smart, silent man gave Rick, Des, Sellers and me, tickets for the next ferry to Fishguard.

He turned and looked up to Mitch. "Mr Collins," he said. "Your people have requested that you make separate travel arrangements, come with me please."

The big American turned to the group. "Looks like it's really the end of the road this time, folks. I'm of a mind, I'm going home," he said with a smile.

I walked to him and wrapped my arms around his huge frame. "It's been a pleasure, Mitch," I said.

He gave me a playful squeeze, "It was all mine, Ma'am." Then, looking over my shoulder, "Mr Fuller, Mr Cogan, Ms Sellers. God bless y'all, now."

He released me, the suit gave him a nod and they walked away.

We all watched him go until he was out of sight. It was like losing a good friend, but at least, unlike our great ally and colleague, JJ Yakim, Mitch Collins was still breathing.

Rick stepped over and stood alongside me, "See that?"

I watched as a long line of vehicles began to board our ferry, "What?"

"The hearse."

"I don't understand."

"Oh, I didn't mention? The cocaine was hidden inside a coffin?"

"No?"

"Oh yeah, and there it goes."

"Cartwright is no fool, eh?"

"No, but I'm beginning to wonder if I am."

"Meaning?"

"Meaning he wants me to go back to my old life. Back to the mean streets. He wants me to find out just who that coffin was destined for. He believes those drugs belong to Yunfakh and whoever the buyer was, will know where to find Al-Mufti."

"You think we can do it?"

"I think so. But we need more information. All we can do right now is try and rattle some cages in and around Manchester's drug scene. Who's buying what from who? It's a dangerous game to play, but nothing I haven't done before. That said, I've been out of it for too long to know who the big players are. The boys at the top of the tree are hard to find. The drug scene is like a mobile phone, within two years you are out of date, out of touch. It's ever changing. One thing I do know though is that we'll be on our own. Cartwright will be working hard to make sure we are in the right place at the right time, but with at least one informant still out there, this job will be as dark as it gets."

I turned to him and looked up into his handsome face. There were more flecks of grey in his hair. He needed a shave. His tired eyes lacked their usual sparkle, they demanded sleep, but he made my stomach flip all the same. I desperately wanted to hold him, yet I was terrified he would rebuke me for what I'd done, for my stupidity, my infidelity.

Yet for all my trepidation, I felt my arms lifting until they draped around his neck. He let his head fall and I lifted mine to meet him. I felt his strong arms wrap around me as he drew me ever closer.

Lifting my palms, I held his cheeks. "I'm so sorry," I whispered.

He raised a hand and rested a single finger to my lips.

"Listen to me, Lauren," he said. "This is the last one. I know, I've said it before, but this time it's the truth. I don't know if Al-Mufti knows about Siddique yet, but he will soon and that will drive him on. He will never stop looking for us. Even if I'd turned this one down, we would always be at risk from a man like him. We would never be free. So this is it. The final mission. Find the buyer, slot Al-Mufti and walk away."

What Rick was saying was music to my ears. I knew that Des was thinking the same way. He desperately wanted to go back to Scotland and take Grace and Kaya with him.

I mustered all my courage. "And me?" I asked. "Me... and you?"

Rick swallowed hard.

"Over in Ireland, I killed a man by the name of Tommy Brannigan. It was him and his sons that were holding the AK47s at their farm. By pure chance, I'd found out, that he was the second of three shooters that murdered Cathy back in Hereford. Before I shot him, I told him that he'd killed me that day too, killed me as sure as any bullet could ever do. I told him that when Cathy took her last breath, mine went along with it, that I didn't live, didn't feel anymore, and that my tolerance, understanding, forgiveness... they'd all left me."

He gripped my arms and looked deep into my eyes.

"I told him the truth, Lauren. Told him how it felt to grieve, to lose. I've always asked myself, how could any woman love someone like me? Someone who can't give everything he has. Someone who is always holding something in reserve because he just can't bear to lose again?"

"But Rick... we can make it work. I'm sure we can. I love you. What I did was crazy and..."

He stopped me in my tracks.

"Lauren, for all my misgivings, for all my self-doubt, I love you too. Back there on the road, in the firefight, when I thought I'd lost you, my heart was breaking all over again. I held my breath so long I thought I may go with you."

He smiled and I thought I may burst.

"So, Ms North, it would appear that you are stuck with me."

Cartwright may have seemed generous when it came to our welcome on the dockside, however, our travel tickets were sail and rail, meaning a long and laborious trip back north.

Our team sat around a circular table in the Stena Lines comfy bar. Sellers and I opted for a bottle of white to share, Rick sleepily nursed an Evian.

Des eyed his ticket suspiciously whilst holding his second pint of Guinness.

"They're having a laugh here, pal, eh?" he said holding up the offending travel document. "Nine hours from Fishguard to Liverpool?"

That woke Rick up. He peered at his own docket. "Two train changes… fuckin' hell."

Sellers sipped what had turned out to be a remarkably decent Chablis.

"I take it we're babysitting the 'body' all the way to Manchester."

Rick shook his head and gestured towards a band of very serious looking suits several tables away. "No, the spooks have taken charge of the coffin, the AK's and the cash."

"How do you feel about that, Fuller?" she asked.

Rick shrugged and threw his bottle of water aside. "I feel the need for a beer or two… fuck it, we'll get a taxi home."

"That'll be a few quid," said Des frowning. "I'll bet it's a four hour drive at least."

Rick stood. "You can afford it, Desmond. I just negotiated us ten grand a day for this next job, so… what are you having?"

Des turned down the corners of his mouth. "Ten grand each?"

"Each," said Rick.

That made the Scot smile. "Well, if yer buying like, I'll have a Guinness and a wee Jameson's chaser."

I sat and watched Rick walk to the bar, shaking his head at his best friend. For the first time in ages, I felt comfortable and happy. One last job. One last push and we could think about the rest of our lives.

For the next three hours, we drank, laughed and took the piss. Rick kept catching my eye, and I figured I must have looked like the cat that had got the cream.

As the ferry docked, I switched on my personal mobile and it instantly began to vibrate. I checked the screen. Dozens of messages began to come through. The first read:

Where have you been? I miss you. Larry x

Des Cogan's Story:

I got back to my wee flat in Manchester just after nine in the morning, feeling a little worse for wear, I might tell ye. Pushing open my door, I was met by a carpet full of mail and the good news that my water had been disconnected due to a leak in the flat above. The life of a jet setting mercenary, eh?

I flopped on my bed and fell asleep in an instant. However, it was not to prove a blissful rest. Just before eleven, I was awakened by a fervent knock on my door.

This was most unusual, as I had no friends in Manchester, and other than a young lady who I'd had a brief and rather tiring alliance with, I didn't think anyone knew my address.

Peering through the spyhole I saw that my visitor was indeed Estelle, from our office. She looked rather flustered too.

I opened the door and she stepped inside without being asked.

"Finally," she said with more than a hint of annoyance. "I can't keep on like this y'know. Nobody answers their phone, no one is ever in. I mean, this is the third time I've been here, it's cost me a bomb in cabs, Mr Cogan."

She flopped in the single chair I possessed and took in her surroundings. Estelle Ryan was in her late twenties. She was a born and bred Mancunian, and despite trying to hide it during her duties as our much maligned receptionist, she possessed one of the broadest Manchester accents I'd ever heard.

She sounded like Noel Gallagher on acid.

"Where's all yer stuff?" she asked, noticing the distinct lack of furniture.

"This place was meant to be temporary, hen," I said. "But ye know how things have been lately. I've never got around to looking for something else."

She sniffed the air and pulled her pretty face. "Smells of damp, you need to get onto your landlord and get him to look at it."

I shrugged.

"There's been a leak, fe upstairs like. The water's off, I can't even offer ye a brew." I sniffed my armpits. "I cannea get a shower either."

She rummaged in a cavernous bag, pulled out a bottle of water and held it up. "I take it you have coffee?"

I nodded. "It'll have to be black I'm afraid."

She smiled to reveal perfect teeth. Estelle had fine cheekbones and beautiful almond eyes, but there was a hardness in them. Just before our last mission, she'd told me how she lived with her disabled mother and that she had a brother with a bad coke habit that got him in regular trouble with the cops. I didn't know for certain, but I figured that she was probably the only breadwinner in the household.

Taking the water bottle from her, we wandered to my small kitchen. Estelle instantly began to delve in my empty fridge and cupboards.

"You need a home help," she said.

"I'm not geriatric," I complained. "It's just that I'm never here, and I'll be honest, I've never learned to cook."

She found the kettle, plugged it in.

"What, not even a breakfast? Bacon and eggs?"

"I'll tell ye this, Estelle. No one got anywhere near my mother's kitchen, unless it was to clean it or wash the pots. Then I joined the army and there was ne need to learn, eh?"

"Suppose," she mused finding two cups, then changed the subject. "So is everyone back? Mr Fuller? Ms North? Mr Collins? And what happened to that nice lady, Victoria something?"

"Sellers," I said. "Aye, but I think Mitch has gone back to the States for a while. Victoria will be helping us out in the short term... Can I ask you something, Estelle?"

She looked up from her task and cocked her head. "Course you can, Mr Cogan."

"Why are ye here? In my house, I mean?"

She handed me my coffee. "Well, that's simple enough. I needed to speak to one of you, and you live the nearest."

"Okay, what is this about hen? What's so important that you come knocking on my door?"

In that instant, Estelle's confidence, that hard exterior seemed to fall away.

She took a large gulp of her drink and then a deep breath.

"I need some money, Mr Cogan."

"Okay," I nodded. "I'm sure we can give you an advance on…"

"I need more than that," she said sharply.

I put down my coffee cup and examined the girl again. She was smart. Her clothes were clean and tidy, but her shoes had seen better days, something that Rick had pointed out previously. She was naturally auburn but had dyed her hair blonde. However her roots showed through. We'd all been there, when there was too much month at the end of the money, but this was something different.

"You want to tell me what's going on, hen?"

Tears pooled in her eyes and I got that same old feeling that I always got around a crying female. I felt totally fucking useless.

I put my arm around her and led her back to the lounge and my solitary chair.

"Come on, eh? We'll sort it out, whatever it is."

Estelle found a tissue and wiped her eyes. She looked up at me and for the first time I saw fear in them.

"It's our Sean," she said, lips trembling.

"Yer wee brother?"

She nodded and did her best to compose herself. "He's in bother."

"With the cops?"

Estelle shook her head, "If it were the coppers that would be easy. He'd be locked up and it would be just me and me mam, simple. Easy life."

"So who is it?"

I could tell that even though she was sitting in my flat begging for help, she was reluctant to name names.

Finally, she said, "It's our Sean's dealer. The little prick thought he were being clever. Fucking hell, he's always thought he were clever, that one. Ye see Mr Cogan, a few weeks back, he had a win at the bookies, big for him, fifteen hundred quid."

Estelle wiped her eyes again, cleared her throat. "But instead of helping us out, I mean, after all, we could do with the cash like, he had a brainwave and went and bought an ounce of coke from his regular guy."

I nodded. "I'm with ye, hen. Go on."

"Well, he was all full of himself, was our Sean. What he was going to do, how he was going to become some big time dealer."

"Except he didn't?"

Estelle snorted her derision. "He put most of it up his own fucking nose. Look, I mean, that in itself wasn't surprising, but the silly bastard went back to his man, cap in hand with five hundred quid, and bought another ounce."

"So he owed them a grand?"

"It's the way they work, eh. Draw them in."

"Go on."

She ruefully shook her head and cleared more tears with a solitary finger. "Well, he did it all again, didn't he? Sold one, snorted two. And what cash he did have he was throwing around like water."

I sat on the arm of the chair. "How much does he owe them?"

"Five grand," she said." And not to his regular guy… to *his* supplier, Arti Jonas. Arti will kill him if he doesn't pay, Mr Cogan. Kill him dead."

Lauren North's Story:

I'd hoped for an invite back to Rick's apartment, but it wasn't forthcoming. I was desperate to hold him in my arms, fall into bed and spend the day making love to him. But he'd muttered something about business and pleasure and keeping a clear head. I wasn't surprised, I wasn't even that disappointed. I told myself there would be time for that. I was however, determined to deal with the problem of Larry Simpson.

But not before I'd rested my body.

I'd slept most of the day away, and in that time, many more texts had appeared. They all followed the same theme.

Are you avoiding me? X

Can we have dinner? X

Are you okay? X

Please call, I'm worried X

I was worried too. Larry the text pest wasn't the Larry I knew. I was, of course, aware that he'd taken a major knock, during our investigation into Todd Blackman's murder. He'd been suspended, and during that suspension, I'd made him realise that he could have prevented further bloodshed by helping us. This had weighed heavy on him. Larry was one of the good guys whose dedication to his job was paramount in his life. He'd played by the rules from being a teen and could see no other way of working. I'd tried to show him that sometimes, rules were meant to be broken and that life wasn't always black and white.

But, scrolling his messages, I understood more than anything, that not only had I attempted to change his philosophy towards the law, but I'd given him false hope. I'd allowed him to believe that we could one day be an item. It was time to play the game and be straight with him. I looked at my phone again and counted twenty seven texts and eleven missed calls.

Not good.

Despite this erratic behaviour and my reluctance to be seen in public with our pet Detective Chief Inspector, I wasn't a coward, and he deserved to be told what was happening face to face. Now I know what you're probably thinking, I'd made my own bed and all that, but everyone deserves a second chance. I knew I wanted to be with Rick, and Larry would get over it.

Wouldn't he?

I sat on the end of my bed, my wet hair wrapped in a towel, and again stared at the screen of my phone.

How do you play this one then?

I didn't have much time to think. The set rang in my hand, making me jump so much, I almost dropped it. It was, of course, Larry.

"Hello Darling," he breathed. "My word, you are hard to get hold of."

"You know me, always busy… How is Kaya and Grace?" I asked, doing my best to keep the conversation away from drunken sexual exploits and his recent stalking activities.

"They're good," he said. "Both at home. Kaya has some speech issues, but with therapy, should fully recover. We have a patrol at the house for the time being, but they can't stay there indefinitely. I could do with picking your brains, actually. We need to know what the threat level is likely to be."

He lowered his voice. "Why don't you tell me over dinner? I'll pick you up, say eight? I've booked a lovely table at Dimitri's. Dress nice uh?"

And he cut the call.

I sat open mouthed and scrolled his messages again.

Enough of this shit. Grow a set, Lauren. You've played far harder ball than this.

By harder ball, I meant with my ex-husband. I'd met him whilst working at Leeds General Hospital. I was a trainee nurse, just turned twenty one and about as naïve as you could get. He, on the other hand, was a junior doctor, handsome, full of confidence with all the right words in all the right places. I fell so hard, I didn't think I would ever get up. We had the perfect romance, and within two years, we were married. I looked forward to wedded bliss, a lovely home, kids, hot summer holidays.

Like I said, just about as naïve as you could get.

Our careers progressed, and he became a specialist, respected throughout his profession. To the outside world he was a good guy, Mr fucking perfect. No one, my mother, my best friend, Jane, no one knew he beat me. I spent more time covering my injuries than I did preparing his food. For weeks, he could be the model husband, attentive, loving, generous. Yet if things didn't go his way, he would become a violent psychotic.

And I don't just mean a one-off slap in the middle of a drunken row. I mean systematic punishment. Carefully placed blows and kicks. I even have the scars of two cigarette burns that are hidden by my hair.

Leaving him was the hardest thing I'd ever done in my life. He pestered me for two years. Everyone thought I was insane, that I was having a secret affair or something. People talked behind my back. What a bitch I was, leaving such a wonderful young man. After all, he had given me everything and I was just an ungrateful girl from a working class background.

I remember one day, my father came to see me in my little flat. He was a butcher by trade, rose each day at four in the morning, never home until five at night. He was my hero, he gave me everything and never asked for a single thing in return. All I had to hold on to during that time, was my father's trust and love.

I remember, he sat on my sofa and asked me what I was thinking of. Why was I dragging the family into the disgrace of divorce? Why had I become so thankless?

That hurt me more than any blow I'd taken, more than any kick or punch.

No, giving Larry the elbow, was going to be easy by comparison.

I stood and walked to my wardrobe.

Now, what to wear for the event?

* * *

Larry indeed collected me at exactly eight. He wore a pale grey single breasted suit, pink cotton open necked shirt, and brown leather brogues. As I slipped into the passenger seat of his Jaguar, he smelled and looked delicious.

I'd opted for the tried and trusted, LBD, but one that fell to the knee and sported a fairly conservative neckline. Not that Larry hadn't seen all that I had to offer, but I figured that as this night was going to end at the dinner table, it was best not to inflame his already red hot ardour.

Dimitri's Taverna had been serving Mediterranean dishes on Deansgate for over 15 years. Nestled in Campfield Arcade it was a lively establishment infamous for its Greek mezze. Inside was all traditional red and white checked tablecloths and vibrant timeless décor. On our mission to Corfu, I'd visited some lovely little eateries in the village of Arillas, and fallen in love with the Greek food and way of life. As I stepped into the doorway, I secretly hoped that I could return with Rick, maybe even visit the Greek Islands again, and spend a lazy summer there.

As I shook myself out of my daydream, I was pleased to see a live band setting up in one corner. At least if the conversation waned, I had some traditional Greek music to listen to.

We were ushered to our table by a very pretty Greek girl wearing a white Polo and black skirt. She announced her name as Maria and gave us our menus. As the band began to play, I was once again transported back to Corfu and its wonderful people. As I sat, my warm thoughts were also tinged with sadness as those same memories brought back images of JJ Yakim and how he'd given his life for ours over in Albania.

"Drinks?" asked our waitress.

"Water for me," I said with a smile. "Work in the morning."

Larry gave me a look. "Aww come on, darling. This is a celebration. Surely a wine at least?" He turned to our waitress. "Champagne, please, a bottle of Moet."

The evening was going to be difficult enough, and I had no intention of getting drunk. I smiled sweetly, "That's fine, Larry, I'll have a glass with you, but I'd still like the water."

The girl turned on her heels and we were alone.

"What are we celebrating?" I asked.

"All will be revealed," said Larry with an impish grin. He lifted his menu. "Now, what do you fancy? The food here is delicious and I'm ravenous." He gave me a lustful look, "For the food, and for you, Lauren.... Now, you must try the keftedes."

I scanned my own menu feeling ever so slightly like I needed a second shower, "I think, I'd like the Kalamarakia," I said.

He gave me another strange look. Stern, demanding even.

"But the keftedes are wonderful here. You *must* try them."

It was more of an order than a suggestion. Our eyes met and I nodded slowly.

"Okay… why don't you just order for the both of us?" I began to feel the way I used to when I dined out with my ex-husband. This was just his way, controlling, challenging, ever forceful. And more often than not, his mood would continue into the bedroom. And if that didn't satisfy his lust for dominance, I would end up with bruises to cover.

Larry smiled at my submission and rested both palms on top of his menu. "I'll do just that, shall I? … ah the Champagne is here."

The cork was popped, and the liquid poured. I took a sip and felt the need to talk business, anything but romance, relationships, or Rick Fuller.

"So, Kaya is recovering well, that's good news. Thanks for helping us out there."

Larry gulped his glass down in one and for the first time, I noticed a nervous twitch around his eye.

"Are you alright, Larry?" I asked. "You don't seem yourself."

He darkened and I instantly admonished myself for falling foul of my own advice.

"Yes," he snapped. "I'm fine, working hard as ever, you know trying to catch up after those fools suspended me. And for what, eh? Nothing, just so some overblown religious fanatic could get his next promotion."

"I just wanted to know about Kaya, Larry," I said, doing my best to steer him back to reality.

"The kid's fine," he sniffed. "Or should be with a little help. The mother was most uncooperative regarding the perpetrators though. I got the feeling that the matter had been dealt with… in house. If you know what I mean?" Once again, I got the hard stare. "You wouldn't know anything about that would you, Lauren?"

I had no intention in divulging any part of our little soiree into a Lancashire traveller's encampment, so simply shook my head and went to open my water. Larry shot a hand across the table and grabbed my wrist, not hard enough to leave his mark, but enough to get my attention. This was not going well.

"Please, Lauren," he said with the fakest smile ever. "I've missed you. Have a proper drink."

I locked eyes with him again. "I think you should let go of my arm, Larry," I said.

He did as he was asked and smiled again, sweeter this time, but it still didn't reach his eyes.

"Of course, sorry, I didn't mean to…"

"It's okay," I said. "Why don't you just order?"

With the food on its way, Larry seemed to calm down somewhat. The old affable, witty Larry was making an appearance. Over dinner, there was well over an hour of small talk. He asked his typical questions about my work and I, as usual, fobbed him off. There were a couple of veiled snide remarks about Rick, but all in all, it wasn't too difficult, the food was excellent, and I had begun to relax about what I was about to do.

Just before ten, the lights in the restaurant were dimmed and the bouzouki player from the band wandered over to our table and began to sing.

"Romantic," I said with more than a hint of confusion.

"'The song is called, 'An eisai ena asteri,'" said Larry. "It speaks of a man's love. He asks that if his woman is a star, burning bright, that she only shines for him."

At that, he left his seat and walked around to my chair. I still hadn't got the picture, but I was about to, in full colour. Falling to his knees, he removed a small box from inside his jacket and opened it to reveal a diamond ring.

"Lauren, you are my star," he said. "Would you do me the honour of being my wife?"

The whole room went up like it was midnight on New Year. Cheers, whoops, applause. The owner was over with a second bottle of Moet. There must have been a dozen women in that room, looking at me and thinking I was the luckiest girl on earth. A strapping handsome guy, on his knees, proposing marriage in the most romantic of ways.

I thought I would be sick.

Somehow, I managed a smile. He took my hand in his and slipped the ring on my finger. There were even more cheers from the crowd. The owner popped the Moet and the band burst into full swing.

Thankfully, just before I threw my meatballs all over Larry's pale grey number, he returned to his seat and the lights went up.

"That was quite a shock," I said, swallowing bile, unable to hide my surprise.

"I'm nothing if not spontaneous," smiled Larry. He reached across the table and took my hand. "I don't sleep around, Lauren. That night, our night together, was very important to me. It cemented our love for one another. This is the most natural step forward."

"Our love?"

"Yes, I love you. You love me, it's obvious. We should make the arrangements immediately, the church, and the honeymoon. Of course you will have to give up that crazy job you have. I mean, you can't possibly be around Fuller anymore. He's such a bad influence on you. You should go back to nursing. I can help you with that."

I pulled my hand from his and slipped off the ring. My head spun.

"Help me? Leave my work? Leave Rick? Marry you? Are you mad, Larry? Are you having some kind of breakdown? I don't love you. What happened between us was a drunken mistake, surely you must be able to see that? I like you. You're a handsome, intelligent, decent guy, but I'm sorry, this is crazy. I came here tonight to tell you that Rick and I are going to give our relationship a go. That I wouldn't, couldn't, ever see you again."

I stood. "I'm really sorry, Larry… Good luck… Goodbye."

Standing on the pavement trembling with emotion, I looked up and down Deansgate hoping to see a cab with its light illuminated. As I stood there, the crowds of Manchester filing by, I felt a strong push in my back almost sending me into the traffic. As I staggered, I was grabbed by the wrist and a napkin was thrust into my hand.

Larry strode away without a word.

I opened my fist and noticed that something had been written on the paper. I read the text then looked as Larry disappeared into the crowd.

'You'll be sorry,' it said.

Rick Fuller's Story:

I was so exhausted that I slept until late afternoon. Rolling out of bed, I pulled on my running gear, and tried to clear my head by taking a late run. I managed a little over 10k then stepped into my home gym and worked my back and biceps.

I always felt better after a workout. No matter how bad things were, I could always put things in order as I ran or worked my muscles. It seemed that the simplicity of exercise brought order to my life.

What Cartwright had asked me to do, was not only dangerous, but it could get us all locked up until Spurs won another title. The old spy believed that the coffin full of cocaine was destined for a major UK supplier and that no one but Al-Mufti himself would have been trusted to complete that deal. In Cartwright's thinking, Al-Mufti would have wanted to dispense with me and then complete the transaction for the charlie. Therefore we both agreed, that our enemy wouldn't be too far away, maybe even in the UK. However, his plans were now in tatters, and the Egyptian could only assume one of two outcomes. His drugs and guns were in the hands of the authorities, or my good self, a man who had tried to kill him, been hounded from the SAS in disgrace and worked for the most ruthless drug lords in England. Either way, he would not be a happy bunny.

Cartwright was very keen to let Al-Mufti think the latter. The Egyptian would come for me. Come to Manchester and take his revenge.

To make this little ruse work, the old spy needed a deep cover team, a crew full of experience in urban combat and an intimate knowledge of the UK's drug culture. A group of individuals with the bottle to take on the boys at the top of the tree and discover just who was waiting for that five million pounds worth of pure cocaine to be delivered.

That, of course, was us.

We would play our new role, muscling in on the mean streets of Manchester, breaking some legs, making some noise and letting it be known that the lack of happiness powder could be rectified by yours truly, but only for the right price and the right information.

I'd done it before. Joel Davies took me on because I made a show in the Hacienda one night. I'd shown him just how ruthless I was, and just how much he needed someone like me. The Davies' of this world were all the same. Once they got to the level of buying a hundred keys of charlie in one hit, it wasn't about the cash anymore, it was all about power.

However, this ruse was anything but simple. I say this because it wasn't just as straightforward as walking up to a well-known Manchester dealer and asking him if he was in the market for five million pounds worth of Brazilian marching powder. For a start, I'd lost touch with the really big players, certainly those with that kind of coin. To be fair, most of them were dead, and anyone in their right mind, and believe me, drug dealers at that level are very smart cookies, would smell an almighty rat. New faces, even those like yours truly with some previous, are viewed with considerable suspicion.

If Cartwright did his job right, Al-Mufti would be telling his buyer that he'd been ripped off, and that his coke was in the hands of a man called Fuller, a man with Manchester connections. It would only be a matter of time before the big boys came asking for their ball back.

Of course, if it went wrong, we were totally deniable, and if we got caught, Larry Simpson and his cronies would be laughing us all the way to Strangeways.

One difference to all the other jobs The Firm had recruited us for, was that this particular cunning plan, was put in place by Cartwright himself. Not even Whitehall would know about it. His concern over a high flying informant and his inherent distrust of the CIA, meant that this job was to be the most secret of them all. Until it came time to pay our bill, of course.

The old spy wanted us to turn the screw on the mid-level boys first. Tax them and cut the last of the stock to the street dealers, bleeding the city dry. You see, the cocaine business is like the car manufacturing trade. Ford don't have all the parts to make a car just sitting in a yard in the back. They have a supply chain that is on demand. Stockpiled car parts are an expensive commodity. Now, the boys that sell gram bags in your local pub on a

Friday night, don't have a couple of ounces of pure sat in their front room either. They buy from the guy above them on a Friday lunchtime, cut it, bag it and sell it. By Sunday, it's all gone up the good folk's hooters and the game starts again. Now the same applies to the Al Pacino type character that was awaiting Al-Mufti's very expensive oak casket. His last delivery would already be in the system, which meant his cocaine cupboard was currently bare and the party goers of the UK were about to be disappointed. With what I had in mind; we could make sufficient waves within days. Slap the mid ranking boys about a bit, nick what was left of their stash and point out that there was a new show in town. A new show in possession of a very large quantity of beak. In drug dealing terms, from zero to hero in less than four days. Whatever part of the country our big hitter came from, once Al-Mufti gave him my name, it wouldn't be long before things got really naughty. The buyer would have to save face, come looking, and, if we were really lucky, Al-Mufti wouldn't be far behind him.

The thought of going back to my old life didn't sit well with me. I, and anyone working with me would make enemies by the hour. From the little street rats riding BMX's, to the boys hiding behind electric gates with an army of security and paid muscle at their disposal. Still, at ten large a day, who were we to complain?

As I pulled on a new pair of Duck and Cover chinos, I began to feel that familiar tingle of excitement that only a new mission could give me. However, I couldn't quite decide how to sell the whole idea to Lauren. That, and which of my Thomas Pink shirts to wear.

Choosing the blue gingham number, I wandered to my kitchen, only to find the cupboards bare and the fridge full of out of date delicacies.

No sooner had I binned the contents of my chiller; I was saved from ordering takeaway by my phone. It was Des. The Scot had a similar predicament and wanted to meet and eat. That made me feel better. It would give me a chance to run my ideas by him, before we met the rest of the team.

Just before seven, my cab dropped me at The Rajdoot Tandoori. Des had always had a liking for Indian food. Apparently, his father wouldn't have anything spicier than a pickled onion in the house, however this had done little to dissuade the young Cogan from his favourite cuisine and he never missed an opportunity to visit the oldest Indian restaurant in town. The

Rajdoot had been around since Adam was a lad and served North Indian delicacies. It was located in a basement deep under Albert Square. The interior was a little brash for my liking, with lots of brass, wooden carvings and bronze statues, but its reputation for excellent food ensured the place was always busy.

As I dropped down the stairs, Des was sitting on an ornate sofa in one corner of the bar. He waved over and I joined him. Moments later a very efficient waiter strode to our position and took our drinks order. I'd had enough alcohol on the boat from Ireland to last me a lifetime, so decided on water. Des did not share my reticence and chose Stella Artois.

We were shown to a quiet table and over the course of the first drinks, I ran Cartwright's plan by the Scot.

"Sounds a wee bit hairy," he offered. "Look what happened when we nicked the last lot of charlie, we ended up chasing Stephan Goldsmith around the globe."

"This is different," I said. "And nothing we can't handle. We just have to make our presence felt straight away, be quick about it. Hang around too long and the cops will come on top. As usual, we won't have much in the way of protection from the long arm of the law."

Des nodded. "No change there, eh, pal? So have ye still got some contacts in the trade, y'know somewhere to start like?"

I shook my head.

"No, that is an issue, could take a day or two to rattle some cages."

Des nodded and then got down to discussing the visit of Estelle Ryan to his flat earlier in the day. That and her brother's predicament.

"And your thinking is?" I asked, feeling ever so slightly suspicious.

Des took a long drink and licked his lips, "Well... I kind of promised Estelle we'd look out for the kid, sort his debt. But with what yer sayin', why not use the boy as a way in? He knows the score and a few players. We're going to need a friendly local to get us inside. This boy, Arti Jonas that Sean owes the coin to, sounds just the level of face Cartwright wants us to turn over."

I shook my head and sat back in my seat. Knowing the business as I did, one thing was for certain, putting an outsider in harm's way, was playing with fire. Especially one that was connected to us.

"I don't know, Des. Sounds to me that the kid is a liability. Once he has a few lines up his nose, he'll think he's fucking Ronnie Kray. I've seen it happen loads of times, and those boys always end up dead. Trust me on this one, pal, do you want to be the one who tells Estelle her brother's been slotted? I reckon we can find this Jonas bloke without involving Estelle's brother. May take us a few days, but we'll get to him."

The Scot blew out his cheeks, took another sip and eyed me coldly. "According to Estelle, the boy hasnea got a few days."

He was right, of course. I'd never heard of this Arti Jonas, the face that Sean owed the cash to, but I knew how the game was played. Sean Ryan was as good as a walking corpse. I could see the method in the Scot's madness too. The kid's predicament was a place for us to start. Jonas sounded like a mid-level dealer. The boy could get us in close. We could turn Jonas over and our game could begin right there.

"Okay," I said, reluctantly. "Maybe Estelle has brought us a bit of luck for a change. This could be our way into the mix. Maybe it's an opportunity too good to miss. Where's this kid live?"

"In Longsight somewhere," said Des, looking over my shoulder and raising his arm. "But I took the liberty of asking Estelle to invite him for some curry. I reckon this is him now by the look of it."

I didn't turn around.

"Please don't tell me that he's wearing a fucking shiny tracksuit, or I might have to slot the fool myself."

He wasn't, but it was almost as bad. He wore skinny jeans of indeterminate make that sat so low on his hips, if it hadn't been for his Calvin Klein's you'd have seen his arse crack. On top he sported a Chemical Brothers t-shirt, a black puffer jacket with a Stone Island badge and a stupid floppy woollen hat. On his feet, were evidence of his recently discovered wealth in the form of a pair of Air Jordan XX2 basketball boots.

"Yo," he said as he approached the table.

I leaned over to Des.

"I won't forget this," I said, with a smile as fake as Sean's Stone Island number.

The boy pulled up a chair without being asked, sat and looked about the gaff.

"Sick place, man," he offered, sniffing loudly.

I offered Des another death stare.

The Scot just gave me his best, 'get over it,' look.

"Sean, I'm Des and this is my colleague, Rick," announced the Scot.

Sean made to fist pump me. I just glared at him. He drew his hand away and shrugged his shoulders.

"Whatever," he said, and turned and waved to the waiter. "Beers here, pal," he shouted pointing at the table.

"Not for me, son," I said quietly.

Sean looked at my Evian and turned again. "And a water for the girl," he shouted.

This was not going well.

I reached under the table and took hold of a handful of the boy's inner thigh. When the knee is bent and the weight is removed from the foot by sitting, no matter how toned or strong the leg muscles are, that part of the inner leg, just above the knee is always soft.

I applied just enough pressure to get the kid's attention, then spoke quietly, as Sean did his best not to cry out in pain.

"Listen to me, you little shit," I hissed. "Your big sister has come crying to us to get you out of the brown stuff, and into Arti Jonas' good books. As I understand it he's looking to chop off your bollocks and feed them to his pit bull. So..." I squeezed just a little harder. "Show some fucking manners."

The boy was bright red. He went to grab my hand.

"Touch me and I'll snap your fucking neck," I said.

Sean nodded like a budgie at a mirror. "Big sister? Oh yeah man, you mean Estelle. Okay, pal, sorry mate. Come on, you're fucking hurting me, eh?"

I released him and looked him in the eye. "You're stoned," I said. "You've been snorting your own shit... and don't even think of fucking lying to me, son."

"I just had a quick line, is all," stammered Sean, looking across the table to Des for some kind of support. "You know, just to take the edge off, like."

Des leaned over, his nose almost touching Sean's. I've seen a lot of menacing men in my time, but never one like Des Cogan. Face deeply lined by the countless hours spent in the driving rain, eyes as sharp as razors, wire in his veins.

His voice was low, intimidating, in fact, downright scary.

"Ye turn up here to meet men that ye hope will sort yer wee problem, and you show no respect," he said. "Ye come to share our table, to listen to our proposition, a proposal that will keep you alive and put money in yer pocket and yet, ye disparage us by yer childish behaviour."

Sean gave himself some space and wiped his nose with his palm. Despite his obvious predicament, the kid wasn't for backing down so easily.

"Look man, Estelle said you guys would help me out, right," he sniffed. "You know, front up some cash. Bail me, pay Arti off and I could pay you back, whenever. She never said anything about becoming a fuckin' priest."

I thought Des was about to slot the boy right there. His hand shot across the table. Grabbing Sean's right wrist and pulled the kid to him. Out of sight of the restaurant's customers, Des pushed his steak knife into the boy's ribs. Sean winced as the tip pierced his skin.

"Don't ye dare insult the clergy, son," hissed the Scot. "I could just gut you like a fuckin' fish right here and not lose a wink of sleep. Do ye understand me?"

Sean resumed his budgie impression. Des let him go and the kid sat heavily on his chair.

"Fuck's sake, man," he muttered. "Fuckin' nutters, the pair of you."

"What did you expect, ye wee jobbie," said Des. "A pair of Avon representatives? I mean, ye wouldnea be thinking that we would just help you out without anything in return, eh? This Jonas fella is going to slot you, son. You can't just pay him off and you're in the clear. You've disrespected him. He needs to show his strength, show his muscle. A man like Arti cannea be weak or he'll be eaten by the sharks. Every wee shite in Longsight will be trying to take his patch from him. Do ye get my drift, son?"

Sean swallowed hard and looked at us both in turn. "And what kind of stuff would you be wanting me to do like?"

"Take us to Arti's house," I said. "Get us in close. Inside his gaff."

Sean was wide eyed. "In close? Why would you…?" The light came on. "Aww, I don't know about this, man. I mean, Estelle said that you'd just front me the cash. I'll pay you back, honest."

I could see the kid's bottle going. There was fear in his voice, and we hadn't even started.

"Besides, man," he whined. "Arti's not a nice guy, he's got a temper and with all due respect, you guys look a bit long in the tooth to be taking him and his crew on."

I caught his eye. "Let me tell you how this is going to work son, then, you can make your decision. We are going to order some very nice food, and by the time the bill gets here, you will have plumped for one of two options. First, is you walk out of here and take your chances with the big fella, or second..."

Des jumped in. "Second, you arrange a meet with him, at his gaff, to pay him his coin. Then you keep him off his guard whilst we get in close and tax him there and then. We give you the five large for your trouble and everyone is happy."

Sean went pale. "You guys are fuckin' dreaming. Arti will have your balls... and mine for that matter."

"Your balls are already in the vice, son," I said. "Walk out of here and you won't last the week. However, do this little job for us and you're home dry." I grabbed the sleeve of his coat and managed a smile. "If you're a very good boy, you might even be able to afford a real one of these."

"Arti is going to kill you, Sean," added Des. "You know it, we know it. Even if you manage to find the money, your days are numbered."

The waiter walked over, pad in hand, smiling and efficient as ever.

"Can I take your order, gentlemen?" he said.

"Oh aye," said Des rubbing his stomach. "I'm starving."

"I'm not hungry," said Sean.

Lauren North's Story:

I hadn't slept well. I mean, would you have? What a fucking weirdo, eh? The more I thought about Larry's behaviour, the creepier it seemed. He was delusional. Last night had taken some planning, too. The ring, the song. I mean, it seemed everyone in the restaurant knew what was about to happen. Everyone but me that is. The napkin he'd written on sat atop my bedside table. It had drawn me to it several times during the night, and I'd read and re-read the words scribbled there. I have to say, they gave me chills.

As I pulled a brush though my hair, I couldn't take my eyes from it. As crazy as it seemed, those words haunted me.

Rick had called just before 7.00am to organise a meet at our offices. Apparently, he'd been having a meal with Des whilst I fended off Larry the wedding planner and, as a result, needed us all to get together to discuss our next moves.

I still didn't have my own car. The insurance company had written off my RS6 rather than repair it, therefore, until I had the chance to visit the showroom, it was public transport. I'd called a cab service and within minutes my phone vibrated to tell me the car was outside. Pulling on my jacket I made for the door, stepped into the hallway and instinctively checked I was alone. I then made sure my flat was secure and strode to the communal exit.

Walking into the garden and the morning sunshine, I fell straight into anti surveillance mode. I had to admit, I was spooked, and I just bet the bastard knew it.

A tedious and traffic filled forty minutes later, I arrived at our Piccadilly offices. As I stepped inside reception, Estelle nodded sheepishly.

I opened the conference room door to find the remainder of our team sipping coffee. Within minutes, the gravity of our situation became obvious.

"Let me get this straight," I said, eyeing Rick. "I know you said that Cartwright wanted you to return to your old life, but are you really saying that we are going to run a fake drug dealing operation? Have you gone mad?"

Rick ran his fingers through his hair. "Not a fake dealing operation, just making ourselves visible. We need the buyer of that shipment to come looking for us. For him to believe we have his charlie. I never said this would be easy, and I'll understand if anyone wants out."

I looked into Rick's face. "I never said anything about wanting out, but surely there has to be an easier way. What about our prisoner, the Doctor from the boat? What has he had come out with?"

Rick shrugged.

"I'm still waiting to hear from Cartwright. I'm sure as soon as he has anything worth telling us, we'll know."

Sellers took a sip of her coffee.

"Cartwright is out on a limb, darling. This is his game; he'll play it his way. He's concerned about the leak in intelligence. Moles slow up any process. You don't know who you can trust."

I sat back in my seat and rubbed my face with both palms.

"This is just crazy. Yunfakh already know about our team. They were all over us like a rash in Ancoats. It's obvious they have informants inside the security services. Look at Mason Carver. If they've infiltrated the CIA, why not MI6?"

"And that is why Cartwright is so keen to play his cards close to his chest," said Rick. "There are informants in all organisations, especially when there's big money at stake. Cartwright wants Al-Mufti and the buyer. Once he has those, he figures he'll have the traitor too."

"Fuller's right," offered Sellers. "All the major security services suffer breaches, and mark my words, Cartwright will want that mole. But he'll be equally desperate to find the buyer. The guy who was waiting for that boat."

"Why?" I asked. "What have MI6 got to do with catching drug traffickers?"

"The Irish connection," offered Des. "He'll be thinking that there's a terrorist connection there somewhere. Al-Mufti and the PIRA go back decades. Back to Gaddafi."

"Ha! That's just peachy," I said. "And the best plan we have is to stroll around town, taxing dealers, waiting for some gangster, or worse still, some terrorist, to come and kill us."

Rick stood up and paced the room. He tapped his temple with a finger.

"Right now, Al-Mufti has no way of knowing what happened to his cargo, or me for that matter. I personally don't think that the deal would have been completed at sea but that is all conjecture. However, neither player will yet know if it was the cops, the security services, or our team that spoiled the party. One thing is certain though, Al-Mufti won't make a move if he thinks the cops have me and his gear. No point."

"But if he thinks you have it," offered Sellers.

Rick pointed. "If he thinks I have it."

"We'll all be dead," I said.

Rick pulled a face. "Don't be negative, Lauren. Once we start to make waves on the streets, the word will spread like wildfire that I'm back in the game, and Al-Mufti and whoever his customer was, will believe that their product has been stolen by me... us. Look, I know it's a dangerous game, but it's the game we've always played. Al Mufti is being fed information from the inside, so even if we turned down this job, he'd find us eventually. He won't rest until he has taken his revenge. If we back off now, call it a day, it would play into his hands. He'll keep building his empire and wait for his opportunity, take his chances, simply pick us off one at a time. Now, I can't speak for us all, but I for one, have no desire to be looking over my shoulder for the rest of my days. This way, we are visible and we get it over with."

"Al-Mufti will take the bait, I'm sure of it," said Des. "The scam isn't that hard to believe, eh? He knows your history, knows who you've worked for. Besides, how many mercenaries do you know that would leave five million quid's worth of beak behind on some boat?"

Rick nodded. "Exactly. Now, the presumption is, that both the main players are in the country, or damned close. So, we must suppose that one or both parties will already have boots on the ground looking for their missing product. As you said, Al-Mufti knows of our Manchester connection, therefore, from today, this office is closed, and we go dark. The only time we go out to play, is to turn the screw on the locals. We'll be visible to all the right faces and the word will spread like clap in a whorehouse. Kostas Makris will provide all the papers should we need to skip the country for a while once the job is over. I've located us a place to work from, and we will all reside there from today. Our first target is a guy called Arti Jonas. We close him down, take what product he has off the street and begin to make our presence felt."

"And where in God's name, are we going to keep a hundred kilos of cocaine?" I asked.

"We're not," said Rick. "The drugs are already destroyed, along with the AK's."

"So we're the only drug dealers in Manchester, with no drugs to sell?" I said, unable to hide the incredulity from my voice.

"We actually don't need any, hen" said Des, standing and finding his lighter. "The trick is, to make the boys *believe* we have their gear and, at the same time, create a drought so folks are desperate to buy."

Des stood up and stretched. "Anyway, I think the plan is a winner, so if we're done here, I'll just nip and tell Estelle she's going on a long holiday."

Des Cogan's Story:

Whichever way you looked at it, this job was not for the faint hearted; if we cocked it up, it could end very nastily indeed. I knew that, so did the rest of the team. Cartwright would wash his hands of the whole affair and we would be left swinging in the breeze. Still, with a day rate that would outstrip most merchant bankers, I figured it was a risk worth taking, particularly if it concluded with Abdallah Al-Mufti dead in the ground.

I'd sat with Estelle and explained that we were closing down the business for a few weeks. I'd made the excuse that Rick and Lauren needed time together and that I had some family issues in Scotland. She asked about Sean, of course, and I'd made platitudes in that direction, without going into details. Then, I sat at her computer and began to book her and her mother three weeks, all-inclusive to Majorca, leaving just before midnight. She looked worried and rested her hand on mine.

"But I still need to keep an eye on Sean, Des. I'm so worried about him. And what about you, Rick and Lauren?

I assured her we would all be fine. More importantly, she and her mother would be safe.

We were going to go in hard, in an area of the city notorious for violence and drugs. Rick had rented a three bed terrace on Longden Road, Longsight. It was a grubby little gaff that had been previously occupied by a number of student types. I'd stayed in worse myself but had a sneaky suspicion that young Victoria was not going to be a happy bunny when she saw the place.

It was, however, tactically ideal, being close to the heart of the city and smack bang in Arti Jonas' drug territory. Once we gave that boy the good news, we would all have our hands full for the next few days, and that was before Yunfakh got a sniff. Me, as strange as it seemed, I couldnea wait. I knew I'd said it before, but one last bit of fun, a nice big payday, then some peace and quiet on the Loch.

With Estelle and her mum out of harm's way, I now wanted to ensure the safety and wellbeing of two more people, Grace and Kaya Yakim. They were probably the two most vulnerable people in my life.

Arriving at their home address I was instantly concerned that the police protection that had been promised was not in evidence. So much for our pet Chief Inspector, Larry Simpson.

Grace opened the door and gave me a tired smile.

"Oh, thank the Lord," she said, holding out her arms to hug me. As we embraced, she spoke into my ear, her voice cracking with emotion. "No one could tell me anything, I had no way of knowing if you were alive or dead."

Of course, there had been no time to tell Grace about the Ireland job, and some things are best left unsaid. "I'm fine, hen," I whispered. "How's the wee boy?"

Grace stepped back, yet held onto both my hands. She was tearful but managed to keep her composure. "Sleeping… He's… he's doing okay…so they say. I don't know how to thank you, Des. I can't believe what you did for us"

"It was a pleasure," I said.

She nodded and then suddenly appeared to realise that we were standing in the doorway.

"Oh, look at me now, how rude. Come on in, I'll put the kettle on."

I stepped down the hallway into the parlour. The place looked like a bomb had hit it. The usually pristine room was awash with piles of clothes. Dirty cups and plates littered the floor and coffee table and an empty bottle of Gordons was balanced precariously on the mantle. Our Grace had obviously been having a hard time of it.

She turned and gave me a guilty glance.

"Sorry about the mess, I've… well I've."

I put my arm around her, and she instantly buried her head in my chest and began to sob.

"Oh Des," she said. "Kaya can hardly talk, and when he does, he says some terrible things."

"Hey, hey… come on now, hen. He's had a bad time, eh? He's lucky to be alive, after what those eejits did to him."

She looked up into my face, wiped her eyes and swallowed hard.

"The cops, they said they didn't know what happened to those men, the ones who took Kaya. But this morning, that detective, Larry Simpson, well, he came over and pulled the guard from the house. He said the case was closed. I don't understand, Des."

"Did he now?" I said feeling for my pipe and heading for the back kitchen door. "Well, I can tell ye this, hen. You'll have no more bother from them boys, that's fe sure."

"So it was you," she said. "Wasn't it? You found Kaya, you saved him from those men?"

I stroked her face.

"It was a team effort, hen. And you'll have no more trouble, but Mum's the word, eh? That detective isn't to be trusted, ye mustn't tell him a thing."

Grace nodded and bit her lip.

"Of course. I mean, I couldn't bear to lose you too, Des."

I stood on the patio, indulged in my bad habit and made a mental note to speak to our Lauren about Mr Simpson.

Minutes later, Grace stepped out with two cups of tea. We sipped in silence for a while, then I broke it.

"You know the cottage I've put in your name?" I asked.

Grace smiled and shook her head in disbelief. "Yes, how can I forget, Des?"

I took on a serious tone. "Well, I want you and Kaya to go and stay there for a while. Just a week or two, maybe longer."

Grace was no fool. After all, she'd been married to JJ Yakim. She knew when things were getting hairy.

"What's going on, Des? Is it to do with my family? I mean, they've never been in touch since that night, not even to ask if Kaya was alive."

"No, hen. It's not about them, and the two men that took Kaya are dead. Like I said, that part of your life is behind you. They'll send no more."

She held her hand to her mouth, her eyes wide.

"They gave me no choice, hen," I lied. "So, in a way, Chief Inspector Simpson is right, that particular problem is dealt with. But this, well, this is another matter. It involves some very dangerous people that will stop at nothing to get to me, and Rick. That means anyone that I'm close to, would be a target for them."

She looked into my eyes for the longest time.

"And are we, Des? Are we close?"

I swallowed some nerves at that one.

"I think so. I hope so," I said. "But I need… *we need*, to be focused on the job at hand, not worrying about the safety of… of people we care about."

She nodded and there was a hint of a smile, but I could tell she wasn't convinced.

"Des… Kaya is already a very scared and disturbed little boy. He's lost his father and been through hell at the hands of those animals. He needs care. He needs to see people, a speech therapist. We're waiting for an appointment. I don't know if more change, more upheaval…"

"Grace, please, listen to me. I will make sure everything is taken care of. The place up north is beautiful this time of year. You will be safe and secure and won't want for anything. I'll make sure Kaya has the very best care available. I promise, just trust me on this one. Soon, this will all be over. After that…"

"After that, what?"

"Well, I have a house, about twenty minutes away from the cottage. I'll be living there as soon as this is over. If you decide to stay up there, start again, I can keep an eye on you both for as long as you need me."

She looked into my eyes again, and I thought I saw something in there, something more than friendship.

"That could be a very long time, Des."

Lauren North's Story:

"And just how do you feel about this little plan?" I asked Victoria, as I pushed more clothes into a holdall.

She shrugged her chiselled shoulders and continued to inspect my flat. "I've heard worse strategies. Some of the stories my ex came out with would make your hair curl."

I stopped my packing. "You mean the one who was killed… Simon?"

She let out a pained sigh.

"The one and only. Didn't the guys tell you; Si had worked with them in 22 before he went into the private security business?"

"No, they didn't. Is that why you came to us for a job?"

She nodded.

"Partly. And partly because I figured you might be involved in this line of work. You see, Simon and I had met people along the way, the black ops guys, always in the shadows. He constantly wanted some of what they were getting, and to be honest… so did I."

"The money, you mean. I suppose it is hard to turn down."

"That, and the excitement. Not having to obey any rules, not having a commander barking orders at you. The rush was just too great for him to leave alone. For some, it's booze or coke, for him it was the danger. And now, here I am."

I pursed my lips. "I think we all know that feeling, but you do realise that this is our last job? Rick says, after this one is over, we go straight, stand in the light and run our business as we'd always planned, back in the day when he first hatched the idea in a hotel in Abu Dhabi."

Sellers made a face.

"If you say so, Darling."

I cocked my head. My tone was sharper than I'd meant it to be.

"Do you know something I don't?"

"Whoa, paranoia girl. No, not at all. I'm the new face, remember?"

She sat on the end of my bed and tapped me on the bottom, playfully.

"Anyway, never mind all that. Are things alright between you and Fuller now? I'm not being nosey or anything, but I do recall the chat we had over in Ireland… you know, about the other guy?"

I looked Sellers in the face and sat alongside her.

"You are not going to fucking believe this," I said.

She grasped my hand in hers. "Want to talk about it?"

I leaned across my now bare mattress and picked up the napkin that still lay on the bedside cabinet. Gripping it in my fist, I took a deep breath.

"The other guy, he's a cop."

"Shit."

"Exactly. When I first met him, he was working undercover, trying to infiltrate our team. Believe it or not, he posed as my boyfriend."

"Now you are pulling the other one, honey."

I shook my head. "I found out, long before, well you know, before we did anything."

"Before you had sex, you mean."

"Yes, but… later on, after I knew who he really was, we badly needed information regarding a case we were working on, and I called his bluff and went to see him. Sort of payback for what he'd done to me."

"And he helped you out?"

"Yes, he's helped a couple of times, but it always went against his principles. It was always difficult for him. You see, he believed that Rick was some kind of gangster."

Sellers had a little giggle at that.

"Understandable."

"I suppose, yes. Anyway, once I got to know him a little better, Larry, that's his name, he seemed really nice. You know, a good, honest, reliable guy."

"Handsome?"

I managed a smile. "As hot as you like."

"And, more to the point interested?"

"That was the crux of it, I suppose. Like you said about Simon, there has always seemed to be something in the way of Rick and me. Then, when he left for Ireland without telling me, I did something really stupid."

Sellers put her hand to her mouth.

"You shagged the copper?"

I just looked into her face. She didn't need an answer.

"And Rick found out?"

A nod.

"Oh double shit," she said. "And I take it, our policeman is now smitten?"

I blew out my cheeks.

"Oh yes, the moment we got back into the country, my phone went mad with messages and missed calls from him; all the usual stuff, I miss you, can we go out? Are you okay? Lots of kisses and smiley faces, you know what I mean."

"I do."

I put my head in my hands for a moment, sorted my thoughts, took another breath and told Sellers the whole story of the previous evening.

"Now you are fucking joking me, darling," she said, pushing her hair behind her ears. "He actually proposed after one shag?"

I nodded.

Sellers couldn't stifle another giggle. "Well, you must have done something right, lady."

I handed her the napkin. She unfolded it, read the text and looked into my eyes.

"Ah, and he wrote this?"

I nodded. "He pushed it into my hand outside the restaurant."

"Who else knows about this?"

I gave her that look again.

"You *must* tell the boys. They need to know. We could have a nutter on our hands here, darling. A nutter with power too, someone with resources. We will be so close to the line on this job, the last thing we need is a nosey cop chasing you about all doe eyed and weepy."

I blew air down my nose. Was I overreacting?

"I don't know, Victoria. I mean, he was upset, hurt, embarrassed." I gestured towards the napkin. "That is just his temper boiling over."

"But what if it's the start of something more sinister? I mean, come on, darling, who in their right mind, sets up a proposal like that after one brief drunken dalliance?... What rank is he?"

"Why does that matter?"

"Does he have friends in high places, darling?"

"Not really, he's a Chief Inspector. Worked his way up I suppose."

ROBERT WHITE

"And you had no inkling of this kind of irrational behaviour before?"

I shook my head.

Sellers stood. I could see her mind working overtime.

"After the gypsy incident, you called two people. One I presumed to be, Cartwright. Then you called someone else, was that your man?"

"Larry Simpson, yes. It was Cartwright's idea."

Sellers rummaged in her jacket and pulled out her phone. She dialled.

"Ah, Cogan, just a quick one. Are the cops still at the Yakim house?" she asked.

"I see," she said. "And the officer in charge of the investigation…? Thanks… yes, I'm here now," she looked over. Her expression said it all. "We'll be along shortly, oh… and Cogan. Watch your back, eh?"

She closed the call.

"Security has been pulled at the Yakim's. Apparently on the say so of your boy. Grace and the kid are being moved up north out of the way."

"Probably best."

"You really need to tell Fuller the bad news," she said.

I nodded, put the last of my clothes in my bag and zipped it up.

"Let's get to the house, then. No time like the present."

Rick Fuller's Story:

I held the napkin in my hand and read Larry's message, once, twice. It didn't get any better. Then, I listened to the story that Lauren told; the restaurant, the proposal; all of it.

Des and Victoria sat in silence on the grubby sofa that the previous tenants had kindly left for us.

"And there's been no further contact?" I asked.

Lauren shook her head. "Not so far."

"But he did pull the police guard from Grace's place," said Des.

Lauren turned. "He was talking about doing that anyway. The Firm had their mitts all over the job. He knew there was nothing in it for his unit, that there would never be an arrest. Add to that, he was under pressure from the uniform command to free the resources. It may just be coincidence."

"Aye, and maybe not," said Des.

I pushed the napkin into my jacket pocket. "Either way, we have to make a start." I rested a hand on Lauren's shoulder. "Are you going to be okay?" I asked quietly.

She smiled and nodded.

"Good," I said. "Look, we can't ignore this, but we can't let it stop us either. We always knew that there would be a chance the cops would start sniffing around at some point, let's just be switched on regarding any surveillance, just keep up your usual routines and report anything you feel warrants it. Entry and exit to our little palace here will be via the back yard. The front door and windows will be screwed shut by end of play today. Now, I realise the place needs a clean… "

"Understatement of the year," muttered Sellers. "They've left us a really nice big present in the bog upstairs."

"I'll deal with that," said Des. "I'm a dab hand with a pair of marigolds and a bottle of bleach."

I nodded. "Good. I'll bring weapons and ancillary kit over from the lock up this afternoon and I've ordered four cots to go upstairs."

"One bedroom for the girls and one for the boys, I take it?" asked Sellers.

I nodded.

"Of course. But on a more serious note, this is a team job. Obviously, we need to work separately today, as we need cars, kit, food and to make this place secure and liveable, but from tonight, if it's possible, we all work together. If there is a meet planned, we all go. If we have downtime, we all have it."

"What about Sean? Is he on board?" asked Des.

"We're meeting him later in the Flat Iron, in Salford," I said.

"Sounds cosy," said Sellers.

"Cosy, my arse," said Des finding his pipe. "Ye need to wipe yer feet on the way out of that boozer."

"Bit like this place," added Lauren.

"Yeah, yeah," I said. "Okay, I'm going to meet Simon and get the SP on our target, Arti Jonas. Lauren, you and Sellers find us two vehicles, a small van and a 4 x 4, cheap and disposable. We'll RV back here at," I checked my Rolex. "1700hrs."

* * *

The girls called a cab and went off in search of our motors. I stood in the small back yard watching Des smoke.

"What d'ya think of that wee keepsake Larry left for Lauren?" asked the Scot.

I pulled the napkin from my pocket and read the script once again. "Could just have been a tantrum," I said.

Des didn't look too sure. "Is that what you really think, pal?"

I scratched my head. "No way of knowing for certain. If he's lost the plot, we'll just have to watch our backs a bit closer than usual."

"Sounds like we have a damn sight more enemies than friends right now," said Des, tapping out his pipe. "The cops, Al-Mufti, the buyer and half the population of Longsight could be on our case before we know it."

I looked my only friend in the face. "Going to be fun then, ain't it?"

* * *

I left the Scot scrubbing away at anything he could lay his hands on and went off to meet our pet technology expert, Simon or Egghead to his friends. I didn't think I could face another visit to his mother's house, home to half the feline population of East Lancashire, so I'd agreed to meet him in the Thirsty Scholar, the nearest bar to our lockup, which would be my second port of call.

I arrived at the pub to find the landlord, Martin the Mod, presiding over a totally empty venue. He gave me a slightly wary look as he poured my Evian.

"Friends not with you today?" he asked.

I looked about the deserted bar. "Obviously not, Martin."

He looked relieved. "That Jock mate of yours, looks a right handful," he said. "Especially once he gets on the Jamesons. I heard he used to be in the SAS."

"I wouldn't know anything about that, Martin," I said quietly. "But I do know what he does now."

"What's that?" asked The Mod.

"He minds his own fucking business," I said.

That sent Martin scuttling into the back to prepare the daily vegan menu. I could hear him muttering away to himself as he clattered about in the kitchen. I sat and waited impatiently for Simon.

Ten minutes late, Egghead barrelled into the bar, red faced and flustered. He had a laptop bag slung over his shoulder. In one hand he held a train ticket, and in the other, what looked suspiciously like a pork pie.

He stood in front of me breathing hard.

"Tell you what, Mr Fuller, them trains are not for the faint hearted. I get nervous when I go outside, see? All them people crammed into one place; well, it doesn't do for me if you know what I mean? I see all sorts of evil goings on in my line of work, Mr Fuller, and it makes me very anxious when I'm forced to sit next to someone who looks like a Taliban fighter and he's carrying a rucksack."

He took a large bite of his pie and waved the remnants at me. "Pork knocker, the Old Crone buys 'em from Bury market. First class."

I sniffed and did my best not to laugh.

"Firstly, Simon, not everyone of Asian extraction who sports a beard, is a member of the Taliban, and secondly, the landlord here will not take kindly to you eating your own food in his establishment, particularly as he's a vegan."

Simon took on the look of someone who'd just opened a year old carton of milk and sniffed it for good measure.

"Vegan? You've got to watch them fuckers, Mr Fuller." He lowered his voice. "They don't even eat eggs. Can you imagine that? I mean, I couldn't envisage life without double egg, chips and beans for tea, eh? What about you, Mr Fuller?"

Martin had heard the commotion caused by Simon's entrance, and walked cautiously over to our spot.

The Landlord's eyes were glued to Egghead's half-eaten pie. He pointed a bony finger at it, eyes wide. I didn't think anyone could look so offended.

"I'm sorry," he announced haughtily. "But I'll have to ask you to refrain from eating… that, in my bar."

Simon was not on the same page. A tech genius, with an IQ off the scale, he was the man you wanted when you needed to hack into the Kremlin's mainframe, however, social skills were not on his list of priorities. He pushed the offending pie into his coat pocket and jutted his chin in Martin's direction.

"You one of them stuck up vegans, then?" he said.

"I am a vegan," said Martin, equally ready for a verbal conflict.

"Thought so," said Simon. "You look pasty. You could do with an egg or three. Get some colour in them cheeks."

Martin stood, hands on hips. He gave me a sharp glance as if this was all my fault, then laid into Simon. "Listen… you ignoramus," he began. "Veganism is more than just a diet. It's a philosophy that rejects the commodity status of animals. Vegans do not eat eggs because their production requires the exploitation of female chickens."

Simon's voice went up an octave. He had, of course been brought up on a farm. From a young age, animals, the production of milk, eggs and meat, had been his family's livelihood.

"How the fuck can you exploit a chicken? A bird will lay eggs whether people eat them or not, you bloody idiot. And, for your information, a chicken is always female, and a cockerel is the male, sometimes referred to simply as, the cock... just like you."

"I'm going to have to ask you to leave," said Martin, pointing at the door.

Simon pulled his pork pie from his pocket and stuffed it all in his mouth in one go. He chewed slowly, crumbs of pastry dropping down his chin, his face inches from Martin's.

I'd seen enough.

"Right," I barked. "When you two girls have quite finished."

I grabbed Simon by his collar and marched him out into the sunshine.

Sitting on an outside table, I waited until my guest had finished chewing the remnants of his beloved pie.

Once he'd swallowed, I asked, "Are we okay now, Simon?"

"Folks like that get my goat," he said, wiping his mouth with the back of his hand.

"I can see that, but do you think it might be possible that we can get on with the business I mentioned to you on the phone, rather than arguing with the locals about the rights and wrongs of commercial food production?"

"Sorry, Mr Fuller," he said. "Is there another boozer you fancy? I could go a good pint. A nice ale will wash that pie down just grand."

At that, we walked under the arch, where just twenty yards along the cobbles nestled, The Salisbury. It was a traditional pub in every way, lots of real ale, pickled eggs, even more pies and cheery staff. At first, I couldn't recall why we didn't use it more often. It wasn't until Simon and I sidled up to the bar that I remembered. Every other drinker looked like an extra from Spinal Tap.

Feeling ever so slightly overdressed, I ordered our drinks and found a quiet corner.

Thankfully, Simon had calmed down and slurped quietly on his pint before opening his laptop bag, firing up his machine and connecting it to a small portable printer.

When he was happy all was functioning correctly, he turned to me.

"Now, I've done all the searches you asked for, Mr Fuller, and I have to say, that you appear to rub shoulders with some very nasty individuals. This Arti Jonas chap is a right one."

"Never met the guy," I said.

"Really?" said Simon. "Well, might I suggest that you avoid this gentleman if at all possible?"

"Thanks for the advice, Simon. However, I seem to recall that I am paying you handsomely for your hacking services and not advice on my wellbeing."

Simon shrugged, rubbed his palms together and began tapping away.

"As you wish, Mr Fuller... so Arti Jonas, real name Alajos Nagy, born in Budapest, Hungary. Lived with his mother and two siblings in Magdolna Street, Klinikak, a very poor and dangerous area of the city. Left his homeland in 2004 when Hungary became part of the EU and travelled here to Manchester."

"Looking for work, I presume?"

"Hmm," said, Simon. "We'll get to that. He did work several manual labour jobs in and around Salford, but it didn't take him long to become embroiled in the city's drug trade. He was first arrested early 2005 for possession of an offensive weapon, wounding with intent and drugs offences. His co-accused was another Hungarian male, Gage Molnár, who now uses the name, Tony Jacket. The pair were taxing another dealer, who lost an eye and suffered several stab wounds during the assault. The case never made it to court as the victim couldn't be traced."

"Dead?"

"As a Dodo, I reckon," said Simon. "Anyway, Jonas and Jacket then appear to have formed their own little gang in and around the Longsight area and quickly established themselves as medium weight cocaine providers. Neither have since been arrested, but there is plenty of intel to suggest that they are rising stars when it comes to Manchester's preferred narcotic. Neither the cops nor Interpol have a current address for either male, but trolling their social media platforms, I would suggest that they still live in the Levenshulme or Burnage area of the city."

"Any pictures?" I asked.

Simon pressed some more keys and moments later his printer whirred and clicked before spitting out the first sheet of A4. He took a quick glance to ensure it was the right shot.

"This is the Jonas mush, taken straight from his Facebook page."

The guy reminded me of the big meathead that spat in my face back on the boat in Ireland. He had a vast square ugly mug, tall forehead, piercing blue eyes and thin lips. In the shot, he was making his hard man face, and held a Hungarian made Vörös-Danuvia Pistol, or the VD-01 in his right fist. It was a bizarre looking semi auto having a cylindrical magazine situated underneath the barrel. A rare beast of a weapon, only 150 or so were ever manufactured, with production ending in 1998; but, with a 33 round capacity, it was a very handy and accurate little gun. However, its presence in the shot did make me wonder just how stupid you had to be to announce to the cops that you were in possession on an illegal firearm.

"And the second guy?" I asked.

There was further whirring from the machine, and seconds later I held the picture of Arti's right hand man. He looked to be of similar height and build, same large features and deep set light eyes, but, Tony Jacket as he liked to call himself, had a real nasty look about him. The lights looked on, but there was nobody home. That said, at least he wasn't waving a piece around.

"So they only have one arrest each? No convictions?"

"Ah," said Simon holding a solitary finger in the air. "Not quite. You see this mush Jonas, or to be more accurate, and use his real name, Nagy, served three years back in his home country for the indecent assault of a seven year old girl."

"So he's on the sex offenders register?"

"Nope," said Simon picking up his pint. "It would seem that the Hungarian authorities did not share this snippet of information with either Interpol or the British cops."

I let out a low whistle. "I'll bet he keeps that little dirty secret from the good residents of Levenshulme."

Simon nodded disapprovingly. "He wouldn't last two minutes, Mr Fuller, fancy gun or not. They'd have his balls in a basket."

I agreed. Sean Ryan would of course know how to get hold of this pair, no doubt, but just in case our pet cocaine sniffer got cold feet, it was always wise to have a backup plan.

"And you say, you don't know where to find these two?"

"If it helps, Mr Fuller, Jonas checks himself in at Murphy's Sports Bar on Stockport Road, quite a lot."

I slid two grand in cash across the table and Simon smiled broadly.

"Always a pleasure to do business with you, sir."

ROBERT WHITE

Once Simon had finished his beer, he packed up his kit, stuffed his cash in his bag and was off to take on his next train journey.

I sat in the bar for a while, had a ginger ale and studied the two pictures he had printed for me. I knew where Murphy's Sports Bar was. It wasn't far from the spot where I had been arrested by Larry Simpson's Serious and Organised Crime Unit. The same day Lauren had been taken by a New IRA Active Support Unit, consisting of Ewan Mark Findley, Kristy McDonald, and that delightful pillar of the community, Dougie McGinnis.

Murphy's sat in the area that used to be controlled by a Somalian called Maxi Touré. Between our little crew and Larry Simpson's SOCU, he was no longer in charge. It never took too long to fill a void in the drug world, and no doubt, the Hungarian boys had identified that gap in the market. Funny eh? That's exactly what we were about to do. Create that hole and fill the void.

Thirty minutes after Simon's departure, I stood in our lockup.

Now, I knew that the girls would come good with a small van and maybe something Land Rover size, but if you were a drug dealer with a few quid, you needed something with a bit of flash too, so I decided my 1988 Porsche 944 Turbo S could have a run out. I'd won the car in a game of cards not long after I'd made the trip north to Manchester. Finished in stone grey metallic with black leather trim, it was a cracking little motor. Not only that, unlike the Aston, at twenty grand, just two days wages, I wouldn't be crying in my soup if she got trashed.

With the Porker burbling away on idle, I loaded two suitcases with kit, starting with weapons and ammunition. For handguns, I chose all 9mm. First, was my personal weapon, the Sig Sauer 1911 Fastback. Then, I checked in Lauren's kit bag and found her preferred silver Colt SLP with pearl inlay grip. It had just a six-round mag, but she'd always put the little gun to good use, so in it went, along with her much loved ASP expandable baton. Sellers' own Rohrbaugh R9 Stealth Elite went in the case as I knew she loved the gun. Des could hit a gnats arse from a hundred yards with just about anything, but I knew he preferred the old school BAP, so that's exactly what he got.

For some extra firepower, I threw in two H&K MP7A1 machine pistols with suppressors, extended magazines and Elcan reflex sights. The weapon only fires its own bespoke ammunition and I'd been fortunate enough to acquire a very special job lot from the remaining members of the Makris family. VBR of Belgium produces a 4.6×30mm two-part controlled fragmenting round that increases the size of the wound cavity and doubles the chance of hitting a vital organ. Very nasty stuff indeed.

I dropped in eight boxes.

In the second case went four sets of covert body armour, shortwave personal comms, a set of NV binos and my trusty lock picking kit. The 944 sat down on its axels with all the extra weight, but as I negotiated the city centre, windows down, and Ray Bans on, I felt ready for anything.

I arrived back at Longden Road to find the whole team in attendance. The house smelled of disinfectant, but Des had done a great job and at least you felt like you could sit down without catching something nasty. He'd also built the four cots, so we had a place to sleep. Lauren and Victoria had spent just over four grand on two vehicles. A twelve year old Land Rover Discovery, fitted with a very thirsty but quick 3.9-litre Rover V8 and a six year old Ford Transit, sign written as a local builder's van… perfect.

With less than two hours before we had our meet with Sean Ryan, we had just enough time to go through the weapons and ancillary kit and grab a sandwich. We all sat in silence, and between bites of tuna mayo on brown, loaded magazines and checked and re-checked our weapon's moving parts.

Finally, we were done and I lay out the two pictures and antecedence of Arti Jonas and Tony Jacket on the kitchen table.

"So this is who Sean buys from?" asked Lauren.

"Actually, they are one rung up from his usual supplier," said Des. "The wee boy made the mistake of getting a little too big fer his boots and is in debt to these two, to the tune of five large. Estelle came to me and asked we sort his problem, lend him the cash, like."

"And you gave him another option," said Sellers.

"Aye," said the Scot, making for the kettle. "We want him to get us in close to this pair so we can make our presence felt."

"They look a right pair of darlings," said Sellers.

"Pair of pussycats," said Des. "But what the young Sean doesn't appear to grasp, is that even if he pays the boys, they'll still make an example of him."

"You mean kill him?" asked Lauren.

"Oh aye, ne bother," said Des. "And I'm not about to let that happen, eh?"

This was going to be a devil of a job and I knew it, but as I sat there in that poky terrace, I also believed I had the right crew and the right kit to make enough waves to draw out our enemies.

The game was well and truly on.

Des Cogan's Story:

We all piled into the Discovery, Victoria driving, Rick directing, with Lauren and I stuffed in the back. The old 4x4 needed a valet as much as the gaff on Longden Road had needed a clean. It smelled of wet dog and fags.

I opened a window for good measure. With the evening traffic, the drive to Salford would take forty minutes.

We were bound for an infamous boozer called The Flat Iron.

The pub had started its life as a hotel, called the Royal, but it never did well, being situated in one of the roughest areas in the city. In the late sixties, the hotel was re developed and The Flat Iron was born, designed to fit in with the more modern market area.

It was an 'early' bar, similar to those found in Scotland and Ireland, with an 8.00am licence. This did not help its reputation for being full of drunks and ne'er do wells. Folklore would have it that the local thieves would ravage the nearby market stalls to order. The receiver of those said stolen goods simply sat and enjoyed a pint or two in the 'Flatty', whilst waiting for his knock off items to arrive.

All in all. My kind of gaff.

However, I did feel that Victoria and Lauren would get far more attention than the average imbiber. Even though both had dressed down, they couldn't hide their beauty and lithe frames. I just hoped young Sean was on time and on message, and that our visit would be brief. If not, I could easily envisage things getting naughty.

As we stepped inside, all heads turned. If it hadn't been for the jukebox blasting 'Dirty Old Town,' you would have heard the tumbleweed. The girls went to find a seat and every male eye followed each step they took to get there. Rick and I went to the bar to order. One very rough looking boy with a face full of scar tissue and more busted knuckles than a blind cobbler was straight in.

"Not seen you before, lads," he growled.

"First visit," said Rick.

"What brings yer?" said the bruiser.

The landlady pulling our drinks must have had one ear on the conversation. She dropped my pint in front of me and looked over to our inquisitor.

"Play nice now, Billy," she said. "Let these folks about their business."

"Aye," I said. "Best ye do that, son."

He looked at Rick and me in turn, seemed to weigh up his options, and decided to leave well alone.

As I pushed the girls' drinks across the table, Victoria managed a smile. "Lovely," she said through gritted teeth. "You bring a girl to the nicest places, Cogan."

"I try my best," I said, taking a sip of a very well kept pint of Guinness.

Rick checked his watch. "The boy's late," he said.

I shrugged. "Give him a few minutes, pal. You were young once, eh?"

I could see Rick was uncomfortable. I knew it wasn't the pub, or the clientele. After all, we'd both been in worse places and all four of us could handle anything the locals could throw at us. No, I knew the reason he wasn't happy was that we were relying on an outsider, and one prone to snorting his own product.

"Five more minutes," he said with a grimace.

Thirty seconds later, in walked Sean. He wore the same clothes that he had on his back in the Indian. The same skinny jeans, the same floppy woollen hat. More importantly, he wore the same stoned expression.

"Fuck's sake," spat Rick. "Look at the state of the kid."

Sean was unsteady, eyes like piss holes in the snow. He stood at the bar; feet planted doing his best to fish a fiver from his tight trouser pocket. The boy looked over to our table and raised an arm.

"Yo," he exclaimed.

"I'm going to slot the fucker myself," said Rick.

We waited until Sean was served and made it over to our table.

"Sit down before you fall down, son," I said.

He waved an arm. "I'm cool, man. Honest I am."

Rick was on him in an instant. "What did I say to you? You're fucking off your face. You are no good to us. A waste of our time."

Sean was indifferent, the coke boosting his already cocky attitude. "Look, dude. That's what I'm here to tell you. I already said, your gig is not my scene, man. It ain't for me. I work alone, I'm a lone wolf, me. So if you could just see your way for the five large, y'know. sort us out, I'll pay you back soon as."

Victoria was unimpressed.

"As I understand it, Mr Ryan, this deal was non-negotiable. The money will not be forthcoming. For this arrangement to work, you had a task to complete and from then on, we would look after your wellbeing. However, from what I can see, you aren't fit to tie your shoelaces, never mind do our bidding."

The cocaine coursing through Sean's system was overpowering his common sense.

"Listen, babe… and you are hot by the way, I can look after myself. No one messes with Sean Ryan in these parts. Know what? I say me and you get out of this shithole, lose these donkeys and hit the town. What d'ya think, sweet cheeks?"

Victoria managed that grim smile again. "I'd say you were delusional, Ryan. A stupid boy who can't control his urges." She looked over to Rick. "Well, I don't know about you, Fuller, but I've seen enough. I say we re-group, re-think and leave Mr Ryan here to his own devices. You know what they say, horses to water and all that?"

I knew she was right of course. I'd seen this many a time, with boys who drank too much, never mind drugs. Every time they had a skin full, they thought they were ten men. That said, I'd made a promise to Estelle that we'd look out for the kid, and a promise is a promise.

"You need to keep your head down for a few days son," I said reluctantly. "Lay low, and we'll sort your problem."

The rest of the team looked at me like I'd lost my mind, but I had no choice. "You just tell us where to find Arti," I said, "And he'll have his cash by tomorrow."

Sean sat back in his chair and smiled. He really was playing the big I am.

"I told you, I ain't playing your game, Jock. I ain't no grass. I saw Arti earlier, man. He was cool about the dough, just as I said he would be. He'll wait for his cash, no problem."

Sean leaned forwards and lowered his voice.

"Listen, Jock, baby. I reckon me and you will get on just fine. You're a businessman, just like me. What d'ya say, Desmondo, you front me the five g, I turn it into ten, slip Arti a few quid to keep him sweet and then everyone gets a drink. What d'ya think? Bangin' idea or what?"

Lauren North's Story:

Maybe it was the subject matter. Maybe it was just that Sean Ryan was the most irritating young man I'd ever met, or maybe it was just because we were sitting in Manchester's answer to the Wild West Saloon, but I'd zoned out and was checking the comings and goings at the front door.

At some point since we'd sat down, a doorman had arrived, and he stood at the entrance giving all new arrivals the hard stare, flexing his muscles and checking the odd ID.

I watched him as two young lads arrived. Both were early twenties and despite the warm weather had their hoods up. Again, not that unusual in this part of town, but the doorman had been making all the other youngsters take theirs down on entry.

Not this pair. No ID check, no hard look, just a courteous nod and a step away.

Rick sat side on to the door, but Sean had his back to it.

The two new arrivals looked to our table and simultaneously lifted their hoodies at the waist to reveal a pair of SLP's. I went from zoned out to switched on in the time it took the gangbangers to take a single stride. Sellers instantly picked up the vibe too. She launched herself forwards and grabbed Rick by the collar, dragging him towards her. I threw myself to my left, pushing Des downwards as I did so. It all happened too fast for me to see what exactly the boys were waving about, but by the time they let go their first rounds, all our team were on the floor.

Except Sean Ryan.

The sound of any unsuppressed weapon being fired in an enclosed space is painful on the ears. Indeed, most of the Flat Iron's drinkers would have been instantly suffering from tinnitus. Both young hooded assassins opened up at close range and kept pulling the trigger until Sean fell. Then, one of the boys calmly walked over to his convulsing body and put two rounds into his skull.

The place was pandemonium, chairs and tables were knocked over. Broken glass crunched underfoot as drinkers clambered over each other to escape the violence. This was a tough area, and the Flat Iron was a rough pub, used to fists flying, however, a right hook is no match for a nine millimetre and the customers knew it.

The two boys turned, still holding their SLP's in their fists and walked calmly to the door. One gave the doorman a nod and he held back the panicking customers as the pair sauntered out into the evening sunshine.

I crawled over to Sean Ryan's body, already knowing the outcome, yet praying for a different one. As I did so, I felt a strong pair of hands grab me and lift me to my feet.

"He's gone," said Rick. "Leave him."

I nodded. "I know." I'd gotten used to witnessing violence and death, but it never got any easier.

"We all okay?" he asked the team.

"Aye," said Des.

"Tip top," said Sellers, sarcastically as she brushed broken glass from her jeans. She looked at me and nodded towards the exit. "I say, you and I go and get our car, whilst the boys ensure that bouncer over there joins us back at the ranch. We need a chat with that chap."

"Aye," said Des ominously. "I'm wanting a wee word with Mr Muscles, myself."

Des Cogan's Story:

I looked down at Sean Ryan's bullet riddled body, his blood slowly seeping into the purple carpet beneath him, and I felt true sorrow. The boy wasnea my flavour of the month, that was fer sure, but he didnea deserve what he got.

Things were not going too well for me. My head was all over the place and I was beginning to question whether I still had the mental capability to function under such pressures. Losing Ann, JJ, Maggie, Kaya's kidnap, they all weighed me down. I knew that there had been times of late, when I hadn't been in control, and that was a very dangerous situation for everyone in the team, not just yours truly.

I'd made young Estelle a promise to look after her wee brother, and now, as she was soaking up the Spanish sunshine, the dreadful carpet on the floor of The Flat Iron soaked up Sean Ryan's life blood.

I forced my eyes away from the boy's corpse and took a long look at the guy who had not only let his killers into the bar but aided their escape so casually.

He was a thirty something. A gym bunny. Not overly tall, with short cropped blond hair and a well-trimmed full set. He wore the bouncers uniform, black shirt, trousers, boots, and sported his SIA licence on an armband around his left bicep. All nice and legal, like. Except he wasnea, was he?

As the girls pushed their way through what was left of the pub's terrified punters, he eyed them with what appeared to me a mixture of appreciation and suspicion. Maybe Sean's killers knew where their target would be, but not who he was there to meet. One thing was fer sure, our bouncer pal, was about to find out a whole lot more about the company young Sean was keeping.

With the girls safely outside, Rick moved, edging his way towards the door, glass cracking under his feet. The bouncer was giving the odd drinker a casual shove towards the exit, not that anyone needed encouragement to leave. As I got closer to the door, I heard the first sirens. If we were going to do this, we needed to be quick about it.

"You have a word and I'll get in behind him," I said to Rick's back.

"No problem," he said.

I dawdled as Rick pushed his way forwards. He stopped right in front of the boy. "What company do you work for?" he asked, head cocked.

"Get yourself outside, mate," said the bouncer and went to push Rick towards the exit.

The boy was way too casual. Rick simply planted his feet and stood his ground.

The guy bared his teeth. "Are you fuckin' deaf, pal?"

He was about to try and push Rick for a second time but in dealing with the imposing figure of Mr Fuller, hadn't noticed me at all. I pulled my Browning from my belt and stuck the muzzle in the small of the boy's back.

"Now, dinnea fuck about there, son," I said. "You just follow my friend there outside and be a good boy. I'm just in the mood to put a couple of rounds in yer spine. They might just kill you, but then again, ye might just end up a cripple."

The bouncer was unmoved and twisted his head to look into my face. "You don't know who you're dealing with here, Jock," he hissed.

I eyeballed him and clicked off the safety. "Really? How about I dinnea fucking care?"

That did the trick and moments later the three of us were outside.

Surprisingly, it was pandemonium. The punters hadn't left at all, most were still on the pavement, talking on their mobiles. A few were even taking fucking selfies. The birth of the smart phone had given ghoulishness a whole new meaning. Mercifully, seconds later, Victoria pulled up in the Discovery and we bundled our new friend into the back.

"You won't get away with this," he said. "You're all as dead as that loser in the pub."

I tore his SIA licence from the holder on his arm and scanned it.

"Michael Forrest," I read out loud. I looked in his face, checked the picture on the licence. "You got a wife, Michael? Kids?"

"Fuck you," he spat.

Sellers put her foot down as three police vehicles sped by, heading back towards the scene. She looked in the rear view mirror at our prisoner.

"Best you change your attitude, darling," she said.

Twenty minutes later, Longden Road, had its first visitor.

Rick sat Forrest on a wooden dining chair in the kitchen, whilst I found cable ties.

"No proper cuffs, I'm afraid," I said, zipping the boy's wrists behind him and then looping another tie to the spindles of the chair.

Forrest grimaced as I did so.

"Sorry, sweetheart," I said. "Did that hurt?"

Rick gave me a nod and we joined the girls in the living room. We didn't have long to formulate an interrogation strategy, and there were a few doubters when young Victoria came up with her plan, but we all agreed, it was all we had. Five minutes later, Rick and I stepped back into the kitchen with a ploy to either kill or turn our visitor. His choice.

Forrest had been taking in his surroundings but was still surprisingly confident.

"Nice place you got here," he said. "I like what you've done with it. Now, when you two have finished playing the hard arse, let me tell you something..."

Rick punched Forrest square in the face. It was a huge blow with all his weight behind it. The boy lolled forwards, semi-conscious, blood pouring from his mouth.

We waited for him to come to his senses in more ways than one. Finally, he opened his eyes and spat a tooth out onto the carpet.

"You were going to tell us something?" said Rick.

The boy stayed quiet a moment; the sudden realisation of his situation etched across his face.

"Look, lads," he began. "I'm just a hired hand here." He spun his head and looked at me. "You were right before, Jock. I've a wife. Come on, I don't need this shit."

"Names of the two shooters?" asked Rick quietly.

Forrest blew air down his nose.

"Aww come on, man. If I tell you anything, I'm dead."

"What about Sean Ryan?" I asked. "He's dead… and you helped kill him. What about him?"

Forrest ran his tongue over his teeth, eyes closed, checking the damage. When he was done, he looked me in the eye again.

"The boy was a fool. He took the piss. Owed money and took the piss. You can't do that in these parts, pal."

"The two shooters?" said Rick, irritation creeping into his voice. "Names, and where to find them, tonight."

Forrest gave another snort of derision. "You think that you can go back into Salford tonight and take those boys on? Fuck off. You're dreaming. I told you, you don't know…"

The second punch was even harder. This time Forrest was out cold.

At that, Sellers popped her head around the door of the kitchen. She looked at Forrest for a moment, then smiled.

"Any chance of a cup of tea, whilst you're at it chaps?"

Rick shook his head at Sellers' indifference, ran his fist under the cold tap, then filled the kettle.

Victoria pulled up a chair and sat herself in front of our boy. This was her field and her plan. An army intelligence officer, battle hardened. She knew all about the psychology of interrogation.

Forrest began to come around again. He raised his head and squinted at Victoria, one eye beginning to close from Rick's second blow.

The boy was tougher than I thought he'd be. He actually managed a smile.

"You the good cop then, Ma'am?" he asked. "Cos that's what you are… or were, I'll bet… a Rupert."

Sellers stayed silent.

Forrest did not. He looked at Rick, and me, then back to Sellers.

"You're all ex-army ain't yer?"

Rick poured water into a teapot; I opened the fridge for milk. We both made the brews in silence before Rick handed Sellers her cup.

"Thank you," she said, taking a sip and setting it down on the worktop. "Now, Mr Forrest. From your last comments, I take it you served?"

"16ᵗʰ Air Assault."

"Impressive," said Sellers. "A Pathfinder?"

"What if I was?"

"I see. So… Kosovo, Sierra Leone, Macedonia?"

"Spot on Ma'am."

"Afghanistan?"

Forrest shook his head. "I was discharged before my unit were posted there."

"Discharged?"

"Medical," said Forrest. "I lost the plot for a while."

I knew how the boy felt.

"How long have you been in Civvy Street then?" she asked.

Forrest shrugged. "Four years, just over."

"And now you're a doorman?"

"I done all sorts, Ma'am. Labouring, warehousing, even tried telesales."

"Not for you then?"

Forrest shook his head. "I did alright for a while, but Lucy, my missus, well, she'd had enough. My moods, the depression, things weren't too good between us and she eventually kicked me out. I slept rough for a bit, until one night, two blokes tried to turn me over and I dropped 'em both. I got nicked and did some time."

"Oh dear."

"Actually, in one sense, it did me good. I got diagnosed with PTSD and got some help from the prison quacks."

"I sense a big 'but' coming."

Forrest turned down his mouth. "Well, you meet all sorts in those places, eh?"

"I can imagine."

Forrest shook his head.

"I don't think you can, but anyway. I was introduced to this face in Strangeways, big hitter… actually ran a business from the jail. A security company."

I tossed Forrest's SIA licence over to Sellers. She caught it.

"Big C Securities," she read.

"That's what it says on the tin."

"And you work for them directly?"

"Me and dozens of others. They run over half the doors in Manchester, but they've fingers in lots of pies, some legit, some not."

"And they gave you your brief tonight?"

"I'm wearing the badge, aren't I? Word was your boy owed a face from Burnage five large and he'd as much as told the bloke to stick it up his arse. All I knew was he was due in the Flatty and that the two boys were going to pay him a visit. I had a drink in it, ten percent."

"And you weren't to get in their way?"

"That's about it."

Sellers nodded, stood and walked out of the kitchen. I heard her talking with Lauren in the front room, then moments later she returned with a battery powered hammer drill in her hand.

She sat back down in front of Forrest, checked the chuck on the drill was tight and squeezed the trigger. The high pitched sound of the tool rotating even made me wince. It was like the worst dentist nightmare you could imagine.

"You are fucking nuts," said Forrest, eyes wide and suddenly much less confident.

Sellers blipped the trigger again for good measure. The drill screamed.

"Nuts? No... You see, Michael," she said. "People are often incredibly naïve when it comes to military officers, those of higher rank. For some ungodly reason, they have it in their heads that we are somehow more forgiving, or less ruthless than those who, shall I say, are further down the pecking order. This is not so. Even your associates that shot poor Sean Ryan tonight would probably baulk at drilling into your kneecaps. It takes a certain kind of human being to inflict that degree of agony and still feel absolutely nothing. So..."

She looked up at me, and then to Rick. I'd never seen anyone so calm.

"Stand on his feet, chaps," she said. "I don't want him kicking me in the lady garden."

"Ms North, if you please," she shouted.

Still in the living room, Lauren turned up whatever she was watching on the TV.

"Right," said Sellers. "That should cover the screaming."

She cocked her head quizzically.

"Now, Forrest. Last chance. You *will* tell us those names, either after the left knee, or maybe the right. I've never known anyone get past the first elbow joint though."

Forrest was sweating profusely. He shook his head.

"Come on Ma'am. You can't be serious. I served my country for fuck's sake."

Sellers pressed the trigger of the drill and it burst into life, the bit just millimetres from Forrest's kneecap. He began to struggle violently, but with Rick and me either side of him, our boots firmly on top of each of his feet and his wrists firmly bound, he had no chance.

"Please!" he shouted. "For God's sake…"

Like a well-oiled machine. Lauren stepped into the kitchen and in one swift choreographed movement took Sellers place.

"Good evening, Michael," she smiled. "My name is Lauren North. I'm not a soldier, nor have I ever served in any part of the military. I was a nurse, a sister to be precise and right now, I'm your stay of execution."

She clasped her hands together as prim as any costume drama extra and rested them in her lap.

"So, like it or not, right now, as we see it, this sorry mess is all your fault. Because of you, a young boy who we were counting on to assist us, is dead and as a result, you are on very thin ice. Therefore, as they say, I'm going to read you your horoscope. The offer I'm about to make you is non-negotiable. It is a once in a lifetime deal. Let's call it a life or death decision. I say this because, option one is, you carry on with your current stubbornness, Ms Sellers here drills into your kneecaps whilst I keep you alive long enough for you to tell us what we need to know, then we dump your sorry carcass in the Manchester Ship Canal for the fish to feed on."

Forrest curled his lip. He was a brave boy for sure.

"And option two, is I get my head blown off by some fourteen year old in a tracksuit before the week is out."

Lauren looked at Rick and he gave her the slightest of nods. The plan was about to work.

"Option two," she corrected. "Is you work for us."

I could almost see the boy's mind working overtime. He examined us all in turn.

"What the fuck is this about?"

Rick stepped in front of him, teacup in one hand, his other casually pushed in his jeans' pocket.

"So, now you know Ms North's background. As for me and my Scottish friend there, Mr Cogan, we both served with 22. Ms Sellers, as you guessed was a Rupert..."

"Steady, Fuller," said Victoria.

"Apologies... An officer," corrected Rick. "With the Intelligence Corps. Matter of fact, she worked alongside your mob for a while."

Victoria nodded.

"Yes, 152 DELTA Psychological Operations Effects Team, part of the PsyOps Support Element backup for 16th Air Assault Brigade in Helmand Province."

"I'm meant to be impressed?" said Forrest. "Seems to me, you're no better than them boys in the Flat Iron."

Lauren cocked her head.

"Wrong, Forrest... we run a legit CP business, amongst other things. Occasionally, we get asked to complete the odd delicate task for the powers that be."

"You mean black ops?" asked Forrest, suspiciously.

"Call it what you like," said Lauren. "For the next few weeks, our job is to rattle some cages here in Longsight and the surrounding area. You can help us do that. Front an op or two. Make a lump of money. Then, when it's all over, we'll give you some body guarding work, well paid jobs. You'd be tucked nicely away from prying eyes... Dubai maybe?"

Rick stepped forwards again.

"Look, pal. I know what it's like to fall off the perch. I left 22 under a cloud and came here to Manchester. But I've been lucky. I made some money and I'm alive to tell the tale. Look, think about it... a week's work, maybe two max... thirty grand cash."

Forrest looked around the room. "Have you any idea what and who you are taking on here?"

"We will take on all comers," said Rick. "But let's start with the two shooters. That should send Arti Jonas the right message, and we'll take it from there."

"You are fucking crazy," said Forrest. "They're all connected."

"If you are implying that I have mental health issues," said Rick. "I think all in this room would agree with you. Also, I'm fully aware of Jonas' antecedence."

The boy took a deep breath. We all waited.

"Thirty grand you say?"

Rick nodded.

"In cash?"

"In cash," said Lauren.

Forrest pursed his swollen lips.

"I don't have any choice, do I?"

Lauren shrugged.

Forrest shook his head. "I must be fucking insane too, but… okay, I'm in."

Rick Fuller's Story:

Once again, Des stood in the back yard smoking whilst I stood at arm's length. Through the kitchen window, he could see Lauren sorting out Forrest's facial injuries.

"You trust him?" he asked blowing out smoke.

I leaned out of the way of his plume. "More than I trusted Sean Ryan… much more. At least he's not an irritating little shit. Seems a handy lad, some combat experience, needs the money, and more importantly, isn't stuffing charlie up his nose every five minutes."

"So you're bringing him along tonight?"

I nodded, "Like I said, we all stay together if we can. Besides, I'd rather keep him in my sight for the time being, just in case I've lost my touch when it comes to a judge of character."

"You going to arm him?"

I shook my head.

"Not on this one, let's just see how he goes."

Des refilled his pipe.

"I can't quite place his accent. He's not a Manc that's for sure."

I shrugged.

"The Wirral, maybe even North Wales, I'd guess."

At that, the back door opened, and Michael Forrest stepped into the yard. I'd caused him some damage. His left eye was almost completely closed, and he had a good sized egg on his brow. His top lip was badly swollen, and he dabbed blood from his mouth as he walked over.

He'd obviously overheard me.

"I was born in Huyton, Liverpool, but we moved to Queensferry when I was small…. and the name's Mickey by the way. No one calls me Michael."

Des held out a hand and he took it. Then Mickey turned to me and we shook.

"Sorry about the mouth," I said. "Oh, and I wouldn't expect Victoria to be calling you anything more casual than Forrest... she's big into formality, that one."

"I've noticed," he said rummaging in his pockets for cigarettes. "We had a female Rupert in Kosovo. Hard as fucking nails."

Forrest popped a fag in his mouth.

Unable to hide my disappointment, I shook my head. Forrest just shrugged and looked to Des for support.

"I like a man with bad habits," said the Scot, defiantly lighting his dreadful pipe.

I took a couple more steps away from the evil smelling weed.

"So, the two boys?" I asked, as both my companions got on with their cancer regime.

"Cousins," said Mickey. "Davie and Stevie Melons. Manchester born and bred. They'll, work for anyone who will pay their fee. But, like I said, they're protected, they're in the Big C camp, just like Jonas. Word is, Arti didn't want to deal with this particular problem himself. He's trying to keep his head down for a while. Something to do with a big deal coming up. Anyway, he asked the Melons for a favour, you know, to sort out your boy, Sean."

Mickey took a long pull on his cigarette. He sniffed and dabbed his lip again.

"The kid could still be walking around, but he virtually told Arti to go swivel for his money. To make matters worse, things are apparently tight right now. There's a bit of a drought and cash flow is key. The kid signed his own death certificate. Within the hour, the deal was done to slot him. I got a call to say I'd been moved from my regular door, to the Flat Iron... you know the rest."

"Sounds like we need to take a look at this Big C lot," I offered.

Mickey looked me in the eye.

"In your dreams, Fuller. The place is all smoke and mirrors. Nice offices, pretty secretaries. You only ever get to deal with the legit faces of the company. For instance, I have all my papers in order. SIA licence, CRB check, the lot. I get paid through my bank, there's no cash in hand work, well, not officially. You never meet the real power behind the firm. Maybe a visit from a nameless face giving you the hard word and shoving a monkey in your back bin for your trouble. But those faces are never directly associated with Big C. It's like a parallel universe. These days, I get a call. Normally to watch for a particular crew walking into a venue to deal for an hour or two. I make sure they get in and out, all sweet like. When I get to my next job, there's normally a brown envelope waiting for me. I'll be honest, it never bothered me, just an extra tickle. I weren't too happy about the young kid though, but once they have you, well, you're in until they say otherwise. Know what I mean?"

I did.

"Anyway," said Forrest. "As I told you, the guy that runs the Manchester operation is actually doing a twenty stretch in Strangeways. You ain't going to believe this, but no one uses his real name. Even the screws call him by his street name, Jester. Funny really, he's just about as safe as anyone in his profession could be. The cons are all scared of him, and the screws are on a tickle to turn a blind eye. The word is that he is part of an even bigger crew that control other parts of the country, but that's just a rumour, I can't back it up with anything. When the Jester knew I was getting out, he gave me a number to call, a guy called Edward Fisher. He's the face of Big C, clean as a whistle, or so he would seem. Now, the moment you move to slot the Melons boys, you take on all this crew, and that is a very dangerous game, so what I want to know is, why? Was the kid related to you or something? I mean, otherwise, I can't see that little coke head being so important that you want to bring the wrath of the Jester down on you."

I took a good look at Forrest. He was younger than Des and me, by a good ten years. He was fit, well-muscled and despite his facial injuries, a handsome boy, and I could see from his hands, his damaged knuckles, that he'd dished a bit out in his time.

As a Pathfinder, an elite member of 16th Airborne, Forrest would have been trained to a similar standard to the boys in the Regiment. The Pathfinder Platoon Selection Course, known as 'The Cadre,' covers almost all UKSF Selection Course training grounds although, at just six weeks long, is much shorter. Pathfinder Platoon is made up of just forty men, an integral part of the 16th. The Platoon acts as the brigade's reconnaissance force, locating and marking drop zones. Once the main force has landed, the platoon then provides tactical intelligence and offensive action roles for the brigade. All this meant that Forrest was a tough boy, and I couldn't help but wonder what had sent him over the edge. Being medically discharged was a very difficult thing to cope with. The support for the men and women coming home from conflict was sporadic at best. Many, like Forrest, ended up on the streets, alcoholism was rife, as was the ridiculously high suicide rate. There were some charitable organisations who did excellent work, but it was no more than a sticking plaster for a much larger problem.

I knew all about mental disorders. You only needed to look in my wardrobe to see that.

As if to prove my point, I couldn't help but admire Forrest's Timberlands as I considered my reply.

"The boy was the brother of our secretary." I said. "She was worried about him, knew he owed money to the wrong people. We were going to pay his debt and he was going to front a couple of smaller jobs for us, a familiar face on the block always opens doors. Unfortunately, he was a silly boy and now, his job will be down to you. The powers that be want us to make waves, and quick. Once we start to make a bit of noise, they think our real target will come looking for us."

"Arti and Big C will do that, mate, but I'm guessing there's another face involved, an even bigger hitter," said Forrest.

"That's classified," said Des. "A need to know basis."

"Sounds like a gang fuck," said Forrest.

"Aren't they all? " I said. "So, slight change of plan, we take the Melons boys first, then Jonas and his sidekick."

Mickey raised his brows.

"Tony Jacket? Fuck me, you'll need to watch yourself there, he's a proper head case."

I shrugged.

"Yes, that's him, real name Gage Molnár, looks a bit of a handful in his picture, I have to say."

"He is," nodded Forrest. "But I'd still feel better if I knew who the real target is. I don't like being in the dark, especially if they are coming looking for me, too."

"Ye need to walk before ye can run, son," said Des. "Let's just see how ye get on, eh. Oh… and, for the record, if we end up confiscating any gear, it gets destroyed; nothing actually gets sold and none of our team use."

Mickey stubbed his fag under his foot. "Same here, never touched the stuff… Okay, so you don't want to tell me who the target is, but can I ask something else?"

"Ask away," I said.

"Who's picking up the tab?"

"The men in suits," I said.

Mickey nodded slowly, "And if we get lifted?"

I just looked him in the eye.

"Thought as much," he said.

* * *

The cousins lived in a block of maisonettes a stone's throw from Salford Crescent railway station. Salford was, of course, a city in its own right and had been a haven for gangland activities for more than a hundred years. But, where a long line of Chief Constables had failed, simple human need had begun to change the landscape, and the 'hood,' was shrinking. Along with large swathes of Manchester, Salford was being changed by education. Not the education of the poor souls born and bred in the City, scratching a living and doing their best to keep their kids out of the hands of the dealers, but the education of students from all over Europe. Salford University was growing and, with it, the need for student accommodation. This meant that privately owned rented housing was in great demand. The owners and landlords of these properties quickly realised that they could earn far more in rent if they replaced the underprivileged people of Salford with students supported by rich parents or large loans. And now, with newly built bespoke student halls to house even more middle class teens, Salford was becoming almost trendy.

Almost.

Davie and Stevie Melons did not reside in such an upwardly mobile spot and were well known faces. A couple of 'bad lads,' who had been systematically moulded into cynical hired killers, and all for the price of a couple of ounces of cocaine. That, and the street credibility they desperately craved.

We were all squeezed into our builders van. Mickey had driven us to our FOP (Forward Operating Point) and identified the target premises. Our plan called for just two of the team to make the entry and slot the shooters. Des had intimated he wanted to be at the sharp end on this one and he asked that I go along with him. The remaining members of the team would watch the street, Lauren on foot, Sellers and Forrest in the van. As Forrest was unlikely to need a weapon, I considered our new recruit could sit this one out, unarmed. It also meant that Sellers didn't have to watch her back if things went tits up and it turned out we'd made the wrong judgement about the boy.

In reality, that was definitely not the case.

I sat in the front passenger seat and checked over my Fastback as Des and Lauren pushed some comms in their ears. On my suggestion, Lauren also wore covert body armour.

A quick call to Egghead had ensured we knew the exact layout of the flat. The electronic transfer of 'a monkey', had seen him email us the council's original drawings for the gaff. However, Mickey was pretty certain that our targets had a metal cage behind their front door, a common addition to many gangsters' abodes, so our planned MOE (Method of Entry,) had to be the lounge window. It was a big single pane that would take just seconds to rake out. A risky strategy, but with the element of surprise, and with just two targets, I figured it was a banker.

With just seconds to go before we made our approach. We were joined by two very unwelcome visitors.

"That's fucked it," said Forrest, pointing out two kids on BMX's doing wheelies under the streetlight outside the block. "You won't even make the landing, Fuller. Especially with you being dressed the way you are."

I checked myself out and gave him a look.

"Like you said earlier, you're a stranger," he explained. "That... and everything you're wearing came from some designer outlet on Deansgate. The locals would spot you in an instant, and considering the Melons cousins have just topped a kid in broad daylight, everyone, including those two Sean Burns wannabes, might be a tad on edge, eh?"

He gestured towards the two new arrivals.

"And have you noticed they're both wearing colours? They're carrying for sure... At least it means the Melons are home."

"And your suggestion is?" I said, slightly irritated that he'd commented on my apparel.

"Well," he said. "If Sean Ryan was still breathing, I reckon you would have used him on this one, y'know, a Trojan horse. That's why I'm here, isn't it? The friendly face? I used to drink in the Lion just up the road, the Melons know me. And unless you intend to slot those pair of fifteen year olds outside the plot, we need another option. I reckon that's me."

I watched the two kids on bikes for a moment. Forrest was right, they were maybe fifteen at best. They wore the uniform of the street, hoods up, scarves covering the lower half of their face. I knew what those colours meant, too; I'd seen them dozens of times when I'd visited the Richards family on the Moss.

The Melons cousins were relatively small time but, in slotting young Sean, would be hoping to move up a rung or two. That said, even at their current lowly position, they obviously still felt the need to know if trouble beckoned. The two BMX bandits probably moved product around for them and kept an eye on their flat when they were home.

"Have you got anything with a suppressor?" asked Forrest.

I unzipped a bag at my feet and removed one of our MP7's.

"Nice," he said. "That will do the trick."

"And your plan?" I asked, unable to hide my rising irritation.

"I'll go knock on the door," he said.

"And the BMX boys?"

"I reckon I can blag two kids."

I gave Des a questioning look.

"I'm with Mickey on this one," said the Scot. "I dinnea fancy slotting a pair of wains, even if they are carrying."

"Victoria?" I said. "Do you have an opinion?"

She gave me a brief smile.

"Of course I do, darling. I think Forrest's idea is a possible, so long as I go with him."

She looked Mickey in the eye.

"That way, if he suddenly finds he has a conflict of interest, the job still gets done."

Forrest looked at Sellers, there was fire in his eyes.

"The job will get done, Ma'am," he said coldly. "It's me who's sticking my neck out here. Those two kids might not know me by name, but after tonight, it won't be long before I'm a wanted man in these parts."

"All in a day's work, Forrest," said Sellers, reaching for the MP7. "And just for the record, if this goes pear shaped, we revert to plan A... and I won't have the slightest problem slotting those two little shits outside to achieve that... understood?"

Forrest's face darkened.

"Understood, but you can't expect me to go out there unarmed."

I nodded to Des.

"Give him your BAP, mate... and your comms set."

Forrest took the weapon and pushed it in the back of his jeans.

"Tape your pressel down so the mic stays open," I said to him. "That way we get to hear what's going on, even if we lose sight of you. Sellers, will keep hers SOP, so we can talk to you."

"Roger that," said Forrest, and began to prep the set.

Minutes later, our two newest team members stepped from the van and began the walk towards the small block of maisonettes. Lauren turned her comms set to speaker so we could all hear their conversations.

"Hold my hand, darling," Victoria said to Mickey.

He did as she asked, and I saw her look at him.

"You're a bit short for me, Forrest," she said. "Shame that."

As the happy couple got within twenty yards of the target, I saw one of the two BMX boys pull out a mobile.

The cousins would soon know they might be about to have company. The kids then rode around the approaching pair in a large circle, having a closer look, doing their best to intimidate them.

Through the open comms set, we heard Forrest shout to them.

"Tell Stevie to open up. Tell him, it's an old mate of his from The Lion."

That seemed to do the trick and they stopped their spinning and returned to their previous position.

I'd always hated the watching brief. It wasn't my idea of fun, and as Victoria and Mickey reached the Melons' front door, I felt far more nervous than if I'd been standing there alongside them.

Mickey knocked and waited.

"We'll get them both in the same room before we make our move, darling," said Sellers quietly.

"Your wish is my command, Ma'am," answered Forrest.

The door opened and one of the boys stood there. As expected, he was protected by a metal grille. He held an SLP in his hand, but it dangled by his side, more a gesture than a threat.

"Alright there, man," said the boy.

"Alright, Stevie," offered Forrest. "We were just walking up to The Lion and I thought I'd nip in and see if you were both cool, see if you had any beak going spare for my bird here."

We watched as the boy unlocked the gate. He sounded very stoned.

"Hey man, you was on top tonight. We did that fucker good, eh. Arti will be buzzin' man."

"Looks like they're in," said Des.

"Let's just hope they don't recognise Victoria," said Lauren.

As if to answer her concern, the boy seemed to take a long and approving look at Sellers.

"You got good taste in chicks, man, come on in," he slurred. "Davie is just racking up some lines now. Bit of a celebration, eh?"

Seconds later the door was closed, and our team were out of sight.

We all three turned our attention to the open comms set.

Mickey spoke first. "You boys look like you've had a good night already."

"What happened to your eye, man," said Stevie.

"Aww, its nothin'," said Mickey. "A couple of City fans cut up after you boys did one."

A third deeper voice, who we presumed to be the other cousin, Davie, spoke next.

"Bet you sorted them, eh, Mickey?"

"You know me," said Forrest.

"Is one of those lines for me?" asked Sellers. "I do like a party."

"Knock yourself out, darlin'," slurred Stevie.

"What's she doing?" said Des. "Just get the job done, girl"

There was a rustling sound and a click as Sellers pulled her MP7 from her jacket and moved the safety to the fire position.

"Night night, boys," she said.

Through the comms set, we heard her MP7 spit out four rounds, two double taps. Then seconds later, two single shots as she made sure the job was done. From outside, the weapon was as quiet as a mouse.

"Shall we go now, darling," she said to Mickey. "Hold my hand on the way out, please."

Des Cogan's Story:

We all got back to Longden Road without incident. I put on the local news and flopped in front of the TV. Lauren and Rick got a late night brew on whilst Victoria and Mickey made sandwiches.

The news was full of the Flat Iron shooting, a very excitable young female presenter making the most of the gangland execution story.

Thankfully, our visit to the Melons cousins had yet to make the small screen.

Moments later, things took a turn for the worse, and none other than Larry Simpson came into shot. He was dressed to the nines, all shiny suit and perfect hair. I mean, I could see why the girls went for him, but he was a weird fucker, no doubt.

"Right now, I'm joined by Detective Chief Inspector Larry Simpson of Manchester's Serious and Organised Crime Unit," gushed the presenter.

"Boys and girls," I called to the kitchen. "You all need to see this."

Everyone filed into the small lounge. Sellers sat next to me and handed me a sandwich.

"Tell me that's not Lauren's man," she said, eyes wide.

I gave her a look, which she ignored.

"My, my, girl," she said turning to Lauren as she walked into the room. "He's a fine example of the modern male. I can see why…"

"I don't think anyone needs to know your thoughts on that matter… *Vicky*," snapped Lauren, obviously unimpressed by Sellers' lack of decorum. "Maybe we should all just listen and see what he has to say, eh?"

Sellers wrinkled her nose at the shortening of her name, and we all settled in to hear the cop's comments.

"Thank you, Natasha," he began. "I can give you a brief statement… An emergency call was received by police shortly after seven o'clock this evening, reporting shots fired inside the Flat Iron pub here in Market Way, Salford. Officers were immediately dispatched to the scene, including Armed Response Vehicles. On arrival, they found that a shooting had taken place inside the public house, and that tragically, the incident had resulted in the death of a twenty two year old male. We are aware of his identity, and he was known to us. However, as yet, we are unable to contact his next of kin, and until that time, we cannot identify him to you. The two suspects in this shocking and senseless incident are described as being white males, aged between twenty and thirty years old. They entered the pub shortly after the deceased arrived and shot him several times at point blank range, inflicting fatal injuries. Now, as a veteran of many of these kinds of incidents, I am fully aware of the reluctance of witnesses to come forward to the police, however, I can assure anyone who has information that may lead to the identification of the two suspects, that they will be guaranteed complete anonymity."

"Can you tell us, Chief Inspector," asked the commentator. "Is this murder drug related?"

Larry smiled at the camera, then turned to the woman.

"At this early stage, it would be foolish of me to speculate, Natasha, but suffice to say, it has all the hallmarks of a gangland murder... Thank you."

And with that, he was gone, leaving the presenter to waffle for a few moments more. Rick grabbed the remote and killed the set.

"Just what we needed," he said.

I shook my head.

"It disnea change anything, Rick. We always knew the polis would be all over this like a rash."

"I know," he said. "But with Simpson heading the investigation into Sean's murder, it will fall to him to take on the Melons inquiry, and with the history we have between us, that's not a good thing."

Mickey frowned and took a deep breath.

"What the fuck is happening here? Who's this cop? No one mentioned that we'd have the serious and organised on our backs from the beginning. We're taking massive risks, and for what?"

"For massive money," said Rick.

Forrest nodded slowly but went very quiet. Finally he turned to me. "Fancy a burn, pal?" he said.

I nodded, pulled myself from the sofa and we stepped into the small backyard.

"You did good tonight," I said. "Listen Mickey, don't overthink this, eh? Let Rick and me worry about the men in suits and the whys and wherefores of the job."

He lit his cigarette and took a long drag.

"I know what you're saying there, Des and I realise I'm just a hired hand, but I'm no fool. Arti Jonas, Tony Jacket, they aren't the targets here, you've told me that much. They're collateral damage. But I reckon this is something big that I've just fallen into and you can't tell me anything about it. Now, I showed my colours tonight, and from tonight my neck is on the line for a bunch of strangers who would have topped me soon as looked at me not eight hours ago."

He took another drag and then looked me in the face. He had sharp green eyes, but as he spoke, I noticed a change in his expression. One that I hadn't seen before.

"The Kosovo War ended on 11 June 1999," he said. "The Yugoslavs withdrew their forces from the province after a massive NATO bombing campaign. 40,000 Yugoslav soldiers were to be replaced by NATO troops, while 170,000 Kosovo Serbs fled for fear of reprisals. Pathfinder Platoon were ordered smack bang into the middle of the retreat. Our task was to find drop zones for the NATO air support and, even though the KLA were supposed allies of the NATO force, our instructions were to disarm any Albanian insurgents until things calmed down. The KLA were rife in the region, and I don't care who's side they were on, they were real nasty evil bastards."

"I know all about the KLA, son," I said, lighting my pipe. "And Albania fer that matter. I lost a good pal there. One of the best."

Mickey shrugged and continued his tale.

"We'd been on the ground for two weeks, camped just outside a small place called Staro Gracko. Just after dusk, British KFOR troops heard gunfire from the village and scrambled us. Turned out, the KLA had paid the locals a visit. You see, despite the evacuation, some Serbs had refused to leave their land. Staro Gracko was predominantly Serbian, but the surrounding villages were inhabited by Albanians who were pro KLA. Once we got on the plot, we found dozens of dead, simple farmers, who had been herded together and shot, some had been horribly mutilated and disfigured."

He took a long pull on his smoke.

"Me and my mate, Kev Willis, went to clear some outbuildings, and we found the women and kids inside. What they'd done to them... well, it wasn't pretty."

He dropped his fag under his boot. "I still see their faces, poor fuckers."

Mickey felt for his packet of Regal and lit a second.

"It was then that I had my first experience of 'the men in suits,' you talk about. These guys turned up, Americans, all shiny hair and pearly teeth, alongside people like yourselves... mercenaries. They worked for a group called L-3 MPRI, (Military Professional Resources Inc.)" He snorted derision down his nose. "You couldn't have made it up. The firm procured millions of dollars in private defence contracts and arms transfers. They had guys in Columbia, Africa. Jesus, people in high places didn't come into it. The word was, they'd been training and supporting the KLA prior to the arrival of NATO forces and as MPRI were already fending off a lawsuit from some Serbs who accused the firm of participation in genocide, they wanted to... 'clear things up,' in those fields and barns. Make your own assumptions there, Des. We were shipped out that night."

I listened to Mickey's tale, watched his face change, saw his pain. I knew he could see those images in his head as he recounted his experiences. I knew, because we all could, you never forgot, and some things, some faces, never left you, never gave you peace.

"I joined Two Para as a boy," I said. "Imagine me, a wee skinny Scottish kid from the Gorbals, brought up more Catholic than most bishops, posted to Armagh. I remember coming home on leave and an old mate of mine, getting all hot under the collar with me about my chosen career. We'd had a few beers and he started on about Bloody Sunday and all the bad stuff that had gone on across the water before my time. Now, I was a hot headed wee shite in those days, and things could have got out of hand between us, but they didnea. I put on my coat and walked home. I turned my back because folks that have never been there, don't and can't understand it. They think it should be a perfect world, with no fuck ups, no bad decisions. My old man always supported my career. He was proud of me, even though I suspect he got some grief about his boy's choice of regiment. He always told me, if you got involved in the politics of it all, it would eat you up, and he was right. I see it as black and white and leave the big picture to those in Whitehall. And this job? Well, this is a war we're fighting, Mickey, a war that nobody knows exists, but a war, nonetheless. And, as you said, there will be casualties, collateral damage, but we need to draw some people out, to bring someone out of hiding."

"And I'm still not allowed to know who this person is?"

I looked at the boy again and made my decision. He was right. He'd earned his stripes as far as I was concerned. The two wee boys on BMX's would be telling some very nasty folks all about how some guy that looked just like the bouncer from The Lion, had visited the Melons cousins flat tonight. Mickey's life had been changed forever. In that one instance, everything was now different. He could never have imagined that a crew like ours would come along, but here he was, and there was no going back.

So I told him. I told him all about Libya about Al Mufti, Yunfakh, the CIA and poor Todd Blackman. Then I told him about the Irish job, the AK's and finally, the coffin full of cocaine.

"So Al-Mufti thinks you have all that beak?"

"Aye, well if he disnea the now, he soon will."

"Fuck me."

"So ye see why we have to make these boys believe we have that gear?"

"But as you aren't actually selling anything, as you take these boys out, all you're doing is causing a shortage on the streets."

"In one, son. And when these boys start to lose customers, they'll come looking for the folks they believe have the product."

"Fuck me."

"Ye said that already."

Mickey thought for a moment. "I need to go home, pick up some gear, and I need to warn my ex missus."

"When's the last time you saw her?"

He blew out his cheeks. "Over a year, we don't speak, you know how it is, but I'd hate for anything to happen to her."

I did, but I also knew it was a bad idea.

"We have everything you need here, and I think she's best left alone. The cops will only ask when she last saw you. Better she can tell the truth. Better she can't implicate you."

"I was more worried about Arti Jonas and Tony Jacket."

"I reckon they'll be more worried about us mate. You don't know Rick Fuller, once he smells blood, he's like a shark, he just keeps swimming until everything is dead."

Lauren North's Story:

I slipped out of my jeans and pulled on pyjamas, the night's events still whirring around in my head. I considered that Forrest had turned out to be a good find. The last minute idea to try and turn him had been Victoria's. I suppose all that experience of counterintelligence work had paid off.

Rick and Des had only one plan in their heads, and that was to make him talk and dispose of his body. I suppose that's why there are different departments in the military. Either way, our new boy had done a good job.

The mission had started and once again, we were on the trail of Abdallah Al-Mufti. Despite my sometimes overwhelming desire to walk away from all of this, hand in hand with the man I had come to love, I still felt that adrenaline rush when the job got hairy and I understood just why, the likes of Sellers still sought that feeling.

She lay asleep not two metres away from me, seemingly able to switch off in an instant. The moment her pretty head hit the pillow she was out for the count.

The cots Rick had bought were narrow and uncomfortable, but, beggars and choosers and all that. Unlike Sellers, I lay there staring at the bare bulb that dangled from the ceiling overhead and it reminded me of my little flat in Leeds. In the early days after I'd split from my husband, I'd been so skint, I couldn't afford shades for all the lamps.

Having everyone in the same house was strangely comforting, yet as I pondered the day's events, my body tired, but my mind still very much awake, an overwhelming feeling of foreboding crept up on me and wouldn't let me be.

A myriad of dark thoughts swirled around my head, and I was unable to drop off. Sliding out of bed, I shuffled quietly towards the door and clicked off the light. Plunged into darkness in an unfamiliar room, I felt like a blind person without their stick or dog, arms out, feet slowly feeling the way. Finally, I made it back to my cot. As I sat, the screen on my phone lit the room.

My stomach did a little flip as I checked the message.

Call me, now. Larry x

Staring at the screen, I swallowed hard, gritted my teeth and deleted the text.

Fuck you, Laurence.

If sleep hadn't been forthcoming before, it was now an impossibility. I started by scolding myself in my head. First for my stupidity. Then my lack of morals.

Feeling ever so slightly like my mother, I moved on to the starkly disturbing changes in Larry's behaviour. His depression at being suspended, his genuine angst at the deaths of innocent people at the hands of Siddique Al-Mufti and finally, the shockingly embarrassing proposal and the dreaded napkin.

My phone flashed again.

I'm watching you right now. You look so pretty. Larry x

I thought I was going to be sick. My heart pounded. How could he possibly have found me? How could he know where we were? I rolled off my cot and walked to the bedroom window. My legs were like jelly, my hands shook. Reaching for the curtains, I opened them a centimetre and pushed my eye against the gap. The narrow street outside was deserted.

No one was in sight.

He's playing with your head, Lauren. Fuck him, there's nothing he can do to you.

Except, I didn't feel as confident as my thoughts. I shuffled back to my bed, sat on it for a moment, gave up all thoughts of sleep, pulled on a robe, and made for the bedroom door. If I was going to spend the night awake and feeling sorry for myself, I figured that I might as well do it with coffee.

I clicked on the kitchen light and filled the kettle. Forrest was sleeping on the couch in the lounge and his gentle snoring somehow made me feel slightly better. After what seemed like an age the kettle did its job, and I sat at the small table with both hands wrapped around my cup. As I took a sip, I felt my phone vibrate in my dressing gown pocket.

I asked you to call me. Larry x

Now, I've never been easily spooked, but as my phone began to ring, I felt a shiver down my spine.

I gripped the set, accepted the call, and felt my anger rise.

"What do you want?" I hissed.

"That's no way to greet your lover now, is it?" said Larry, calmly.

I couldn't help myself.

"One night, Larry. One fucking, stupid night. A mistake. Don't you get it? People do it all the time. They go out, drink too much and end up in bed with the wrong person. Grow up and get over it."

I killed the call, dropped my phone on the table and my head in my hands. Finally, I sat up, took a big breath and blew out my cheeks.

Get yourself together.

A good sentiment, yet as I brought my cup to my lips, I noticed my hands were still shaking. There was to be no let up. My phone flashed again.

Don't be cross. You need me more than you know. Larry x. PS. I like the top you wore tonight.

That did it. I thought my head would burst. I picked up and dialled.

"I see I finally have your attention," he whispered.

"What's this about, Larry? What do you want from me?"

"I want you to be my wife. I told you so. I love you. We are meant to be together."

"But I don't love you, Larry. I told *you* that, remember? And writing obscure threats on napkins won't endear me to you, either."

He was silent for a moment, then, "Things will be different once… once he's out of the way, you'll see."

"What? Who? You mean Rick? Are you threatening us both now? What has happened to you, Larry? You're just not functioning."

Again he went quiet, but I thought I heard a low pained sigh.

"Ah, but I am functioning, Lauren. I see everything so clearly now. Fuller lives by the sword, and so he shall die by it. He's up to his old tricks again, isn't he? I saw you all tonight on the Flat Iron's CCTV. Very sloppy work. There was a camera on the entrance. I suppose that you will say it was pure coincidence that you were present, but… I know better."

"So, we're not allowed to go for a quiet drink anymore, Larry? Is that it? We live in a police state? Did your little tape show us breaking any laws?"

"Wouldn't you like to know?"

"I already know, Larry. We went for a drink and two men came in the pub and started shooting… simple. You should be out looking for them, not harassing me. And on that point, if you ring me again, or message me, I'll make a formal complaint to your Chief Constable."

I heard him laugh down his nose. "No, you won't. You won't ring anyone or make any complaint because you are part of this."

"Part of what? Some junkie gets shot by other junkies in some random pub, and it's our fault?"

"Why did the doorman leave with you?" he said.

That threw me. He would have seen Forrest walking out of the door sandwiched between Rick and Des and he would have noticed that he didn't return. I had to think quickly.

"You mean Michael?" I asked, as calmly as I could.

"Forrest, yes. We know he works for Big C Securities."

"Did," I said. "That's why we were in the pub, Larry. To speak to him about a job. He applied for CP work, and now he's our employee. Nothing more sinister than that. He's an ex Para, just the kind of guy we like on our books."

"An ex Para with form," countered Larry.

"Look," I said losing all patience and warming to my tale. "Michael Forrest declared his conviction on his application. He's a good guy who needed a break. Now, if we're done?"

"Not quite," he said.

I waited.

"Where are you staying? You're not at home, I checked."

So he was stalking me after all. I went for the jugular.

"Don't ring me again, Larry, or I mean it, I'll complain to your seniors. Or worse still, I'll mention it to Rick, and that would be very messy."

"Is that a threat?"

"Do you want to take that chance?"

He closed the call.

I stared at the blank screen for a while, waiting for the next call, but it didn't come. Finally, feeling much better about the whole scenario. I poured what was left of my coffee down the sink, climbed the stairs to bed, and slept like a baby.

Rick Fuller's Story:

"So you told Mickey everything?"

Des stood munching on a bacon sandwich, looking out of the kitchen window, into the back yard.

"Not quite everything, pal, just enough to keep him in the loop. He's a good boy, mark my words, we've fallen on our feet there. Finding Mickey was a bit of luck, I reckon. I mean, he's streetwise, he knows the area and he's got urban combat experience. It's a no brainer."

I'd always trusted Des' judgement, and from what I'd seen of Forrest, there was no reason to stop now. He'd done the job we'd asked. He'd been calm under pressure and helped the team with a solution, so he was in.

My only issue with new people was one of their motivation. Someone had been feeding information about my whereabouts to third parties for months. Yes, there had to be a bigger fish somewhere and Cartwright knew it; but there was also a mole on our side of the pond, and new faces were always an itch that were difficult to scratch.

"Okay, pal," I said, tucking into my own breakfast. "Just keep an eye though, eh?"

"Ne bother," said Des. "So, are we going to stay holed up fe a while or what?"

I shook my head.

"No, mate, we're not. We go straight for Jonas and Jacket, take them and their product off the street. That will shake the tree. We need to move faster than I thought."

"Because?"

"Because, I think Abdallah may already be in the country... Look at this."

I scrolled my phone.

"Cartwright has sent me this via email overnight, copied from The Buxton Gazette, published yesterday. It's about the Transit we fired up on the moors. Some young hack by the name of Paul Willets, has been snooping around the crash site, and The Prince O' Wales in Ancoats."

"That Siddique was a cruel bastard," muttered Des. Still hurting from the loss of Maggie. "I'd slot him again in a heartbeat."

I nodded, understanding his pain.

That night, we'd cleaned the scene, piled the bodies of Maggie and Siddique Al-Mufti in the Transit and set it alight. Cartwright had been insistent, and I took some grief for carrying out his orders. Just as we'd thought, it had burned itself out on the desolate moors and was only discovered the following day. We knew the driver had taken a single round to his back and Siddique had a hole in his skull where Des had practised his DIY skills, but with a little interference from The Firm, those two small matters should have been overlooked and, let's face it, after a ferocious blaze like that, there wouldn't have been much left to examine. However, it appeared that Mr Willets was not so easily dissuaded. For a paper like the Buxton Gazette, this was big news.

I gave Des a sorrowful look and began to read aloud.

"The article is headed, 'Woodhead Bodies Mystery,' I said.

The Scot sat heavily on his chair. "Go on, pal," he said. "Get it over with."

I nodded. "It says: 'As a result of a painstaking investigation, this paper can now reveal the identities of two of the four badly burned bodies recovered from the fatal road accident on the Woodhead Pass. Victim one is Margaret Jane Bracewell, 43 years, of Ancoats, Manchester. The second is identified as Siddique Al-Mufti, a US national. It is understood that the ferocity of the blaze forced the coroner to make his identifications by the use of dental records.'"

Des raised his head.

"But Yunfakh members don't have..."

"Dental records," I finished. "I know that, so we have to ask, who's fed this Willets kid the intel?"

Des shook his head ruefully. I kept reading.

"'The cause of death in both cases is unknown, although the coroner stipulates that the victims had suffered serious injuries and therefore may not have been alive at the time of the fire. In each case, open verdicts have been cited. The identity of the driver and front passenger remain a mystery.'"

I cocked my head.

"Here is the interesting bit, he goes on... 'This case still leaves many questions unanswered. This reporter understands that until her untimely death, Ms Bracewell had been the landlady of the Prince O' Wales pub in Ancoats, and on the night of the fatal crash, two further incidents occurred at the premises. The first was a report of criminal damage, and the second, the building being left insecure. It is now understood, that the police arrived at the latter incident to find a forced entry and Ms Bracewell missing. There are also unconfirmed reports that bloodstains were found at the bottom of the stairwell leading to the landlady's accommodation, suggesting a violent struggle had taken place. A source close to the investigating team has also intimated that Ms Bracewell's body was found, not in the front, but the rear of the transit van, which begs the question, had Margaret Bracewell been abducted? And just who is Siddique Al-Mufti?"

"Aww fuck," said Des.

"There's more, mate... 'The Serious and Organised Crime Unit...'"

"For that, read our pal Larry," spat Des.

I snorted.

"In one, but wait for it.... The SOCU have issued a brief statement on the matter, it reads: 'Greater Manchester Police are currently liaising with the Derbyshire force regarding a recent incident involving a burnt out vehicle and the alleged abduction of Margaret Bracewell from the Prince O' Wales pub, Ancoats. Ms Bracewell suffered multiple fractures prior to the blaze and foul play cannot be ruled out. The SOCU are eager to speak to a man who had recently visited the premises and struck up a relationship with the victim. He is described as a white male, aged forty to fifty years, 5'8" tall who speaks with a Scottish accent. This man could be armed and dangerous and should not be approached by the public. Anyone with any information... blah blah.'"

Des curled his lip, unable to hide his temper.

"Some fucker is playing silly buggers," he said. "A quick chat with any of the regular drinkers in the Prince could have come up with that info."

I nodded. "But as the guy you slotted at the bottom of the stairs couldn't just get up and walk away, we have to presume that someone cleaned the scene. As it was half a job, my money would be on Siddique's men. Either way, Simpson has nothing. He's fishing. Anything to get to our team, or more importantly to him, Lauren. I reckon he just wants me out of the way, so he has a clear run at her. He's a lovesick puppy, nothing more."

"He's fucking dangerous," said Des taking a gulp of his tea. "He knows that the location of the pub is close to the Blackman murder site, and he'll have put two and two together. He'll be on our backs before we know it. He could drop the dime to that reporter and name me if he wanted."

"Naming you and finding you are two very different things, pal," I said.

Des knew that too. The thing about disappearing, is you don't have to travel far to do it. All you need to do is follow simple rules, like, use a car not registered to you, don't use your credit or debit cards, turn off the GPS on your mobile, that kind of thing. You only need to move a few miles away, keep your head down, ignore your old life for a while and you were incredibly difficult to find.

I heard footsteps from above. The girls were awake. Des stepped into the lounge and gave Forrest a wobble. "Brew, mate?" he asked.

I heard Forrest yawn. "Cheers, pal."

Ten minutes later we were all sitting around our small kitchen table. Forrest's face had bruised nicely. He must have been in some pain, yet he hadn't mentioned it once since I'd caused him the damage.

I gave the team the news about the Buxton Gazette and Larry Simpson's antics.

Lauren was the most troubled. Moments later, I found out why.

"He called last night, Larry I mean," she said. "Well, he messaged first, he was playing with me, trying to get under my skin, you know. He said he was watching me, when really all he was doing was reviewing the footage from the Flat Iron."

"Did he mention me?" asked Forrest.

Lauren nodded. "He asked why you left with us. I said that you were the reason that we were all there, that you'd applied for a job with our firm."

"And he swallowed that?" asked Des.

Lauren shrugged. "Hard to say. He can't prove otherwise at the moment."

Sellers sipped her tea. "Do you think he's lost the plot, darling?"

"Sounds like it to me," muttered Des.

Lauren pursed her lips. "Who knows? I'm not a psychologist. When I saw him that night in the Ostrich, the night Maggie was taken, he was stressed, no doubt. He'd been drinking heavily for several days, but I just figured that he'd be strong enough to come out the other side. Then, when we met the next time, he seemed fine."

"The night you slept together," said Sellers.

There was a collective intake of breath around the table at that one. Victoria was not noted for her delicacy, that was for sure. I felt my guts churn with jealousy. I was growing to hate the bastard. Any more of this shite and he'd have me to answer to. Lauren looked almost as angry as I felt. Des and Forrest suddenly found something interesting to look at outside the kitchen window.

"Come on," said Sellers, exasperated. "We're all friends here. You know, 'Let him that is without sin cast the first stone.' Jesus, if you weren't such a twat, Fuller, it wouldn't have happened."

Lauren gave Sellers a withering look. She then turned to me, her face full of pain and soldiered on.

"Then, of course there was the night of the proposal, and the napkin."

"The threat," said Des coldly. "That was a fucking threat."

Lauren nodded. "I agree with you now, Des, and last night he made a comment about Rick, too; something about, living by the sword. It was only when I told him I'd to go to the complaints department that he backed off."

"Anything else?" I said.

She nodded.

"I think he's been to my flat to look for me."

I found myself tapping the table with my fingers, my fury raging inside me. I did my best to keep my voice level.

"I need to make a call," I said. "Clear something up."

Stepping into the yard, I opened my phone and dialled.

"You know I hate mobile phones, Richard."

Cartwright sounded as if he was outside. I could hear birds chirping and the sound of children playing.

"Well, I'm sorry to spoil your morning outing in the park, but unless I'm very much mistaken, this job has taken a turn for the worse."

"Ah, you read the mail I sent you."

"Of course."

"It was a necessary evil, Fuller. We've had an issue or two this end, you see."

"What was a necessary evil? Why the fuck do you talk in riddles all the time?"

"Releasing the boy's name to the reporter, of course."

"So that was you? You gave Siddique's details to the press?"

"We created that leak, yes."

"Why?"

"Because …*our* initial plan is no longer viable, and time is now of the essence."

"What?"

"Doctor Hamid Shah was interviewed at length regarding the goods found in the hold of the boat in Ireland. It would seem that the vessel was indeed to be met by a second craft that was almost certainly scared off by your gunfire. The drugs, and you, were initially bound for Belfast, where the transaction was to be completed between Al-Mufti and the buyer."

"So Abdallah is in Belfast?"

"Was, anyway, listen up, Richard. From there the cocaine was to be split into three consignments. The first to remain in Ireland, whilst the other two were to be transported to Glasgow and Manchester respectively. However, despite the spread of locations, Shah insisted that there is only one buyer. The cities are all controlled by the same person. This oligarch of the drug world has three head men, one in each location. He simply bankrolls the deals and takes his cut."

"And he is?"

"He didn't know his name."

"Really?"

"We believe so… Shah was only aware that this mystery man's three subordinates went by pseudonyms, nicknames. Mr Punch, Belfast. The Fortune Teller, Glasgow, and The Jester, Manchester."

That pricked up my ears.

"I know that name. The Jester. He's in Strangeways, doing ten to life. He's connected to a company called Big C Securities. They had a hand in the shooting of Sean Ryan and are connected to the guys we're targeting next, Jonas and Jacket."

"That's helpful, Richard. I'll make some enquiries with HMP Strangeways. However, you do realise, that young Sean was not called Ryan at all?"

"Really?"

"Sean Patrick Donahue, to give him his full title, Fuller."

"So why did our secretary, Estelle tell Des he was her brother?"

"Maybe you should ask your employee that same question, Richard. And with that in mind, the good Doctor was also questioned regarding Al-Mufti's intelligence gathering capabilities."

"And?"

"And as we suspected, the Egyptian has spies in our camp... as do you, Richard."

"I'm all ears."

"Again, he didn't know the identity of the person, or persons, but he believed it was someone very close to you. Someone who knew your movements."

"Sounds to me like he was keeping you dangling. Feeding you the titbits but keeping hold of the good stuff. Either way, Estelle's out of the country. Majorca, out of the picture."

"Nice, this time of year, I believe. Anyway, you know me, Richard. I was born cynical, and of course, anything is possible, but as the Doctor is no longer any use to us, it is a moot point. He suffered a fatal heart attack yesterday. The point is things are moving on a pace."

"So you decided to up the ante?"

"Exactly, Richard. With the current information in my possession, I had to inform the powers that be of our mission. They have decided that our plan is no longer of use. This operation is now being measured in hours rather than days. Hence the fake coroner's report naming Siddique, being leaked to the press."

"Well, that press release will have Abdallah and half of Yunfakh printing their boarding passes to Manchester as we speak."

"That was our sole intention, Fuller. Young Mr Willets was most resourceful. He moved very quickly to link the Ancoats incident with the vehicle fire. Al-Mufti would need to be in a cave not to have received that information."

"Okay, but now we have another problem this end. Larry Simpson is breathing down our necks. Or to put a finer point on it, Lauren's."

"This is indeed true, Richard. We didn't expect Willets to involve SOCU so soon. And, of course, your friend Chief Inspector Simpson was very keen to help the young chap by issuing him with Mr Cogan's description. A minor irritation, and one I'm sure you can deal with, but all the more reason to dispatch this matter with most haste."

"So, where do we go from here?"

Cartwright was silent for a moment. I knew the old spy well enough to realise this only happened in conversations for one reason. He was considering exactly what I needed to know.

"Fuller, old faces come back to haunt us more often than not. Now, as I said on the boat in Ireland, as soon as I knew exactly why the Americans wanted the vessel sunk, I would tell you. Therefore, I want you to think of the connection that is at the heart of all of your recent operations and what binds them all together."

"Drugs," I said. "Weapons and drugs."

"Partly, Richard. Drugs and the men that sell them are definitely a major contributory factor here. However, cast your mind back to poor Todd's murder. You met JE Blackman as I recall?"

"I had the dubious pleasure, yes."

"Of course, well… despite the setback of losing his son, you will be unsurprised to learn that his campaign to become president of the United States, is now in full swing. Campaigns like his cost a lot of money, Richard. Millions of dollars a week."

"You're not suggesting that JE is selling…"

"Not at all, Fuller, heaven forbid. No, Blackman comes from old money. He can afford to campaign from now until doomsday, however, his nemesis…"

"Khalid Kulenović."

"Correct, Richard. Kulenović is a self-made millionaire but does not have the kind of resources that JE Blackman has at his disposal. He quickly realised that he needed other income streams to enable him to keep in the race, hence…his allegiance to Yunfakh. Now, whilst we are on the subject of arch enemies, if you recall, it was Stephan Goldsmith who gave me the information about this new gang muscling in over the pond, kicking out the Italians, even the Albanians. It was he who told me how Yunfakh operated, how Al-Mufti was at the helm and exactly where the Egyptian's political loyalties lay. As you know only too well. Al-Mufti dispatched his son and a few handpicked members of Yunfakh to travel to Manchester, kill Todd Blackman and ruin JE's reputation, all whilst laying down the infrastructure to begin trading in narcotics here in the UK."

"When are you going to tell me something I don't know?"

"Your lack of patience is sometimes irritating, Fuller. So… the good Doctor Shah, was initially enmeshed between Kulenović and Al-Mufti to supply the Taliban and their Baltic allies with weapons."

"So the PIRA's AK's were helping to fight the good fight."

"Exactly, Richard. However, Doctor Shah intimated that more recently, he had been tasked with another role. As a result of the failure of Yunfakh to make any headway at street level in the UK, Al-Mufti decided to change tactics and attempt to sell large quantities of pure cocaine to already established dealers across the Union. Khalid needs cash for his campaign, and he needs it quickly. So, despite the setback of losing their most recent cargo, Yunfakh have not been dissuaded in their quest to see their most glorious leader elected by any means possible. According to our CIA friends across the pond, there is a new consignment of cocaine on its way. Indeed, we believe it is already in the country. I need you and your team to find out who the intended recipient is and terminate the transaction… permanently. Call it a favour to our allies."

"I'm sure they'll be forever grateful… and Al-Mufti?"

"Our understanding is that he has been tasked by Kulenović to ensure the deal is done."

"So you think he's here? He's travelled with the cargo?"

"Our intelligence tells us he left Belfast for England last night. He will complete the transaction personally, the titbit we dropped to the newspaper was simply a belt and braces exercise, to ensure that the deal was done in Manchester, rather than elsewhere. After all we can't have our Celtic cousins having all the fun, now can we? Your tactic of clearing the streets of product and destabilising the local trade was a good one, Richard, but now time is of the essence. We can no longer sit back and wait for our prey to come to us. You need to discover the identity of this modern day drug lord, before the new transaction is completed. Find him by any means possible. Scared people tell tales, Richard. Instil fear and you loosen lips. Strike terror into Mr Big's customers and find this man who controls three cities. Do this and be rid of your enemies forever."

I closed the call and stepped back into the kitchen. All eyes were on me. I rubbed my face with my palms and sat.

"Okay, as you all know, our initial strategy was to make it look like we had possession of the coffin, stake our claim and wait for the big boys to come to us, but there's no time for that now. Things have changed. We need to make some real noise."

Forrest screwed up his face.

"Hang on, Rick. We've already got this Simpson bloke properly on our backs. As soon as we start throwing our weight around, he'll be on us like a rash."

"I'm aware of that, Mickey," I offered with no small amount of irritation. "The fact that the cops would be involved was always factored into the equation, and yes, I agree, as Simpson seems to be obsessed with Lauren, it makes things," I fought to find the word I wanted. "…Delicate. But this job is changing by the hour. The Firm have already upped the ante and released a fake coroner's report naming Siddique Al-Mufti as a victim in a fatal car accident. It's made the local press. Abdallah will know his son is dead, and there's no way he'll believe it was an accident."

"Jesus," whispered Lauren. "He'll come for us now, won't he?"

"And that is exactly what we wanted," I offered. "Now Al-Mufti knows Siddique is gone, he will want to be right here where he knows our team are based, take his revenge and be on his toes before anyone knows he's been on British soil. However, he has to complete the deal that we foiled. There is a second consignment of cocaine already in the country. The CIA believe that the profit from the deal will go towards Khalid Kulenović's presidential campaign fund and want it stopped. We need a rethink. We haven't got time for subtlety. This deal can't happen."

Des pulled his pipe from his pocket. "I was never one for being subtle, pal."

Running my hands through my hair, I carried on. "Cartwright wants the recipient of this cargo out of the game, and fast. Apparently, he controls major slices of three cities, Glasgow, Belfast and here in Manchester. And, Mickey, guess what? His contact here, is the Jester."

"Who?" asked Lauren, a puzzled look on her face.

"He's the guy who put me in touch with Big C. The guy in Strangeways. No one ever called him anything other than, Jester. Not even the screws."

I nodded. "The Firm are already looking into his real identity, but as he's locked up, and Al-Mufti will want to do the deal here in Manchester, the hope is that our Mr Big will be visiting the city, and soon. With luck, we can find out where that deal will be done and spoil everyone's party."

I pointed.

"So, we start on Jonas and Jacket today. Find out what they know. Are they expecting a delivery? If so, who's selling? You know the script. Now, when I worked for Joel Davies…"

Forrest almost dropped his tea. "You worked for Davies? *The* Joel Davies?"

"In another life," I said. "Anyway, in those days, I always figured that the *accidental* death of a drug dealer would be treated with a little less gusto by the cops. So, Lauren, Victoria, scope out Murphy's Sports Bar on Stockport Road. Try and set up a small buy from Jonas. Oh, and by the way, he's a paedophile. He did time in Hungary for sexual assault on a little girl. I'm sure you can use that snippet to loosen his tongue."

"I already have a plan, darling," smiled Sellers.

"Good," I offered. "You concentrate on him. We'll look at Jacket."

Des found his tobacco. "I'm just in the fuckin' mood fe these wee boys."

Lauren North's Story:

Sellers pulled a white t-shirt over her head and flicked out the strands of hair that were caught in the neck.

"How are you feeling?" she asked.

"About the Larry calls, you mean?"

"Of course."

I shrugged. "Strangely better now that the whole thing is out in the open."

"And Fuller?"

I picked up the photographs and intel reports of Jonas and Jacket and waved them at her.

"The matter at hand is the important thing right now, Victoria. Not my love life, or lack of it."

Sellers turned down her mouth and nodded.

"Fair enough, I was just making conversation, darling."

We sat together at the kitchen table and spread out the papers between us. Sellers was scanning Jonas' antecedence report. It had been clumsily translated from its original Hungarian, but still made very disturbing reading.

"I can't see how this didn't find its way into the hands of the authorities here," she said. "In fact, I'm mystified that this animal has ever been released into the community. This psychologist's report is pretty damning. It clearly suggests that shortly prior to his discharge, he was still a danger to young girls."

There was little doubt that Jonas was a predatory paedophile. I read alongside Sellers, and my stomach churned. Prior to my specialisation in HDU, I'd spent three very disturbing years in casualty and had dealt with just about every injury you could possibly imagine, including those inflicted by adults on children. What Jonas had done to that little girl was as bad as anything I'd ever witnessed.

"He will still be a danger," I said. "No doubt in my mind."

"So, as Fuller suggested, there is more than one way to skin a cat," said Sellers. "I think it's time we went to buy some drugs."

* * *

Murphy's Sports bar wasn't as bad as I'd imagined. It looked to have undergone a recent refurbishment and there were big screens on just about every available wall. However, as with any licenced premises, what wasn't so easy to change was its location and the clientele.

The bar opened early, 10am, so had been trading for a couple of hours. Even so the crowd was thin and less than a dozen customers were scattered around the place. Three burly men sat at one table waiting for the start of a horse race. They all had betting slips laid out in front of them and gave Sellers and me a cursory glance before the more important business of gambling took their interest away.

However, these guys were not of interest to us. Our attention was drawn to two younger men sitting on a raised area towards the back of the bar. They were watching Sky Sports and drinking pints of lager. The pair were just the type of guys we'd expected to find in a place renowned for its dodgy patrons. Tracksuits, baseball caps, shiny white trainers, lots of ink. One gave his pal a nudge in the ribs and pointed us out. There was a snippet of leery conversation that I couldn't quite hear, but I got the impression that it wouldn't be too long before we had the pleasure of the boys company.

Indeed, I hadn't even emptied the neck of my bottle of Becks when they decided to make their move.

The taller of the two, a late twenties bull of a man, strode out in front of his mate, one hand clutching his Fosters and the other mysteriously stuck down the front of his tracksuit bottoms. He wore a wide smile that revealed a single gold tooth.

Seconds later, he swept a stool from under our table and plonked himself in front of us. His shorter, slimmer friend was seemingly less confident of his pulling prowess, and remained standing, mercifully *his* free hand, was at his side and not feeling his own privates.

"Alright girls," said bollock feeler in a thick Manchester accent. "What brings you in here then?"

Sellers was first in. I figured that she wouldn't be able to contain her derision, but I was wrong. She actually played her part with some gusto.

"We heard this place was full of handsome men," she said, giving her hair a flick for good measure.

I shot her a look, I mean, you could have a white stick, guide dog and sing like Stevie Wonder and the guy would still be as rough as a badger's arse.

The nut rubber puffed out his chest, turned to his pal, who in fairness was quite a good looking boy, and gave him a knowing wink. This appeared to be the signal for number two to join the fray and the guy sat, a little too close to me for comfort.

"Hiya," he managed, and gave me a crooked smile.

"Hello," I offered.

"Not from round here, are yer," said Gold Tooth, giving Sellers' trim figure the once over.

"London, darling," she purred, lifting her own bottle of lager. "Kensington, to be precise. We're here to invest in some property. The prices are far more sensible in these parts."

"Right," offered Goldie. "Well, I'm Freddy and this is my pal, Dave".

We both managed smiles, tapped our bottles against their pint pots but kept our counsel.

Freddy wasn't done. "So, you girls just taking a break, then? We're born and bred here, know this area like the back of our hands, we do. Maybe we could help you look around, yer know, show you where to avoid. Can be a bit rough in parts, if yer know what I mean?"

"Oh, we're done for the day, darling," smiled Sellers. "Actually, we were hoping to run into someone who could point us in the direction of some fun."

Freddy looked like he'd just won the lottery. He gave his pal Dave another obvious wink.

"Well, you've found just the two blokes you need sweetheart. Fun is our middle name."

I figured it was my turn, so leaned across the table to reveal a little too much cleavage.

"The kind of fun we are looking for comes in little plastic bags, sweetheart. You know what I mean?"

I thought Dave's eyes were about to pop out of his head.

"We know a guy," he stammered, finally tearing his eyes away from my chest and looking to his mate. "D… Don't we, Freddy?"

I thought I saw a flash of anger in Freddy's eyes as he looked to his pal. The bigger, more confident guy, erring on the side of caution when dealing with a pair of strangers, no matter how attractive they appeared.

"We might do," he offered, giving Dave a hard stare. "He'll be in later. Normally gets in around four-ish."

I made a show of opening my bag to reveal a wad of cash and a slip of paper yet keeping my Colt and ASP out of sight.

Making a show of scanning the note, I said. "This guy wouldn't be called Arti, would he?"

Sellers gave Freddy an alluring look.

"You see, Freddy, last night some chaps told us this Arti fellow drank in here. They were certain that he could help a girl out with what she wanted." She ran her hand across the table and gave Freddy's arm a stroke. "They said he was a big, good looking, muscular guy. At first, I thought that you might be him, darling."

Freddy sucked in his gut and swallowed the tale.

"Arti's a big lad alright, but he don't seem to bother much with the ladies. He's all business he is. I'll say this though, things are a bit tight right now, not a lot of beak about. Reckon there's been a big bust somewhere, eh? So you might struggle if you want any real weight."

"That's what the boys said last night," I offered. "All we could get was a couple of grams, and that wasn't up to much. But they gave us this guy's name and this bar."

I tapped my bag bursting with cash.

"We don't need ounces of it, but it would be nice to get hold of say five hundred pounds worth. See, we're having a party at our hotel tonight. Lots of rich folks, lots of girls. So, we need someone a little more... connected."

I gave him my best beam.

"If you helped us out, I'm sure we could slip you on the VIP list."

"It will be wild," added Sellers suggestively.

Freddy seemed to weigh up his options. I got the feeling that he didn't know Jonas too well. Indeed there was a suggestion in his eyes that he may even be a little frightened of our target. We just had to hope that the promise of a drug fuelled night back at our hotel would be enough for him to swallow that fear and give us what we needed.

He waved his mobile.

"I'll give him a call," he said.

Freddy stepped outside into the street and we sat making inane small talk with his pal until he returned.

He swaggered back into the bar minutes later. By the look on his face, the deal had been done.

"He says he can do you ten gram for five hundred, but you have to go to his gaff now, cos he's got business later."

Bingo.

Des Cogan's Story:

The girls had played a blinder and the game was on. Jonas lived in a three bed semi just on the edge of Burnage, a short hop from Longsight. It was a tidy gaff with a wee front garden and off street parking for one car. A white Subaru Imprezza held that space.

Rick and Mickey Forrest were tucked in the back of our builders van and I kept a watchful eye as we waited for the girls to arrive and do the dirty deed.

Our role was intended to be purely supportive. Lauren and Victoria had a plan for Jonas, and I had to say it was as ingenious as it was deserved. My only worry was that the Subaru wasn't Arti's and Jacket was on plot, too. Despite my confidence in the girls, from what I'd heard about him from Mickey, he would be a real handful.

With less than five minutes to run before the girls' arrival, the front door of the gaff opened and just the man we did not want to see stepped outside.

Tony Jacket, or to give him his real name, Gage Molnár, was indeed a big unit. His huge square shaved head sat on massive shoulders. He was a steroid boy, which suggested he would be extremely strong and aggressive, but it also meant that he would run out of steam very quickly as the lactic acid built up in his muscles, slowing him down and putting a strain on his heart and lungs.

He wore three-quarter length shorts, and flip flops on his feet. In his right hand, he gripped a large heavy looking holdall, in his left were a set of keys.

He blipped the alarm on the Subaru, and I saw the indicators flash. Moments later, he was in the car and the engine roared into life.

Rick clambered from the back of the van and sat alongside me. As Jacket reversed from the drive, he gave me the nod.

"No time like the present," he said. "The girls can handle Jonas. Let's follow square head and see where it leads us."

Now, in order to follow a target by road, any surveillance team would want at least three or four different vehicles at their disposal. Anyone with any sort of sense, particularly someone who was involved in crime, would be surveillance conscious, so with just our solitary and rather sedentary Transit to hand, we were on a loser from the start.

If our Hungarian friend hit the accelerator on the Subaru, we would simply be eating his dust in seconds. We would also stand out like the proverbial sore thumb.

That said, sometimes you need that wee bit of luck and it seemed that our little team were having just that bit of good fortune. Jacket not only drove like Miss Daisy but appeared not to have the slightest inkling what his rear view mirror was for.

We followed as much of the protocol as we could, dropping back and using traffic to mask our van, then as and when we dared, got in close so as not to lose our prey. By the time we hit the M60 and saw the Imprezza indicate to exit at the Stockport pyramid, Rick began to get our kit ready.

"Either this guy is blind, or stupid, or both," he said. "I don't know about you two, but I'm itching to know what's in that bag he threw in the back."

"Aye, pal," I said. "The only reason you drive a car like that at a steady fifty-five, is you don't want a pull. I reckon something's on."

As it turned out, I was about as right as I could be.

Lauren North's Story:

Sellers closed the call from Rick.

"The boys are tailing Jacket out of town, so we have a clear run at our boy. If Jacket turns for home, Fuller will call again."

I nodded, pulled Rick's Porsche 944 up outside Arti Jonas' residence, gave the throttle a blip to announce our presence and stepped out into the street.

Of course, we were expected and even before we could knock, the door swung open. Unusually for Manchester's finest drug dealers, there was no secondary security, no cage, and no bars on the inside. Maybe our target had seen enough of those back in his homeland, or maybe, as he lived in a relatively affluent area, such things would only increase his neighbours' suspicions. He towered over both of us, standing in his hallway, barefooted. Sellers had that look in her eye that told me she was actually going to enjoy executing our little plan, but I felt unusually nervous.

"You must be Arti," she announced. "Big strong boy, aren't you?"

The huge Hungarian seemed unimpressed by us, which was hardly surprising as we were both way outside his preferred age range. He suspiciously leaned forwards just enough to see along his street, checked no one else was about to spoil the party and grunted at us in heavily accented English.

"Inside," he said.

As we stood in his hallway, Jonas closed the door behind us. Yet didn't move. He simply stared at us each in turn as if assessing us for threats. The Hungarian had the strangest eyes I'd ever seen. His light blue irises were so pale, his pupils stood out like jet pin pricks. And they were set so deep in his large skull, his brows shadowed them giving him a strange and eerie appearance.

I did my best to smile and play my part as a posh girl looking to party, but if I was honest, he unnerved me in an instant.

I instinctively grabbed at my bag and felt the reassuring bulk of my revolver and ASP tucked neatly at the bottom. If Jonas decided to search us, we would have to change tactics instantly, but he didn't make a move. His underestimation of the fairer sex was about to be his undoing.

"Come," he growled. "Back room."

We followed him to a sparsely furnished dining area. No pictures on the walls, no chest of drawers, no homely additions, just a cheap round table and two chairs. However, sitting in one corner was a large old fashioned green safe and a weird contraption that looked like an industrial press of some kind.

Jonas stood by the table. "Money," he said. "Five hundred. Show me."

"Not one for small talk, are you darling?" said Sellers, holding Jonas' stare. "We have the cash here, my lovely, but despite the fact we are girls, we are not inexperienced in these matters. I'm keen to try the product before we part with the readies. So much poor quality stuff about, you see."

The Hungarian screwed up his face.

"I not sell bad stuff. Only best. Show money or fuck off."

Sellers shrugged and gave me a look.

"That machine in the corner is to re-press the pure stuff after these chaps have cut it, so, no guarantee of the quality. Let's be off, darling," she said. "We're dealing with fucking amateurs here."

Well, that answered my question about the press.

Jonas' eyes flashed and he bared his teeth. They looked strangely small in his wide mouth.

"Wait," he snapped and held up a huge hand. "Stand over there, in corner."

He obviously wanted to put space between us as he was forced to turn his back whilst he opened the safe.

Not so confident after all, eh?

He rummaged in the neck of his shirt, pulled a key from inside that had been dangling on a long gold chain, then opened the heavy door. I saw two blocks of compressed powder and a further clear plastic bag containing several smaller packets. In the bottom of the safe was also an item that we were particularly interested in.

A silver coloured laptop.

Now was our opportunity, with Jonas kneeling and his back to us, even across the room, we had him at a disadvantage. Sellers pulled her SLP from her waistband stepped over and pointed it at our target's substantial skull.

"Up… slow and steady there, big boy," she said.

Jonas was anything but slow.

He twisted his massive frame swinging a ham of a fist blindly behind him until he made contact with Sellers outstretched arm. The sheer speed and ferocity of Jonas' movement took Victoria off guard and her weapon was knocked from her grasp, clattering against the wall and falling to the floor down the side of the still open safe.

"Bitch," he screamed as he launched himself towards her. Jonas was more than double Sellers' weight and as his shoulder smashed into her midriff, I heard her groan in pain. She was thrown backwards, and she hit her head on the small round table as she fell. Within three seconds, we had gone from a position of control, to being in deep shit.

I struggled with the zip on my bag, cursing the fact that I'd been forced to close it to hide the contents, my haste slowing what should have been a simple process. As Jonas drew back his powerful arm and punched Sellers in the head, I could wait no longer. I took three steps forwards and kicked him square in the jaw. It was a peach of a shot. Any footballer would have been proud of it. It was a top corner screamer if ever there was one, but the bastard just shook his head, slammed his fist into Victoria's face a second time and then came for me.

He roared like a lion as he stood and towered over me, grabbing at my jacket and spinning me around like a rag doll. As he released me, I crashed into the wall, knocking the wind from me as I did so. However, I wasn't done. Not quite yet.

I pushed my hand into my now open bag and tried to find my pistol, but the first thing that came to hand was my ASP.

It would just have to do.

Weapon in hand, I thrust my arm out to my side and felt the tungsten steel baton lock.

I was in business.

Jonas snorted his derision at the small steel bar and made to grab at it, but I had my fighting head on. I'd dealt with big bulls of men before. On the streets of Dublin, in the fields of Albania and bested them all.

My first blow struck his outstretched wrist, and as I took a sharp step to my right, I swung again and caught him cleanly on the elbow of the same arm. If the bones weren't broken, the nerve endings would be screaming at his brain to tell him they thought they were.

He grimaced yet didn't cry out. But despite his silence, I could see he was hurt, and he held his left arm to his chest as he came for me a second time.

"I fuck you up," he snorted. Red faced and sweating.

I was on the balls of my feet, baton ready. "Come on then, fat boy, let's see what you've got," I said.

Once again, he launched himself, but now I was more than ready. Too quick, too nimble. He grabbed at thin air and I simply side stepped him, and swung the ASP in a wide arc, arm extended for maximum power and connected with the back of his head.

I felt a warmth on my face, and instantly realised that I was splattered with his blood. The baton was running with it, my hand covered. Somehow, he managed to spin his body before he slid down the wall, barely conscious.

Turning my attention to a very dazed Sellers, I lay my baton on the table, and dropped on a chair breathing heavily.

Jonas' legs were twitching, but he was going nowhere for a while. Even so, I pulled my Colt and covered him. As I did so Victoria gingerly sat up, rubbing the back of her head and touching her ever swelling left eye.

She looked over at our target, then to me.

"You need to wash that blood off, darling," she said. "No saying what this pervert has got."

I nodded.

"You okay? They were some punches you took."

"Bit fuzzy, but I'll live. Cocked up a bit there, eh?" she said, recovering her SLP from the corner.

I smiled.

"No one's perfect, Victoria. Nimble for a big lad, isn't he? Keep an eye whist I find the sink, honey."

When I returned, mercifully blood free, Jonas was still in situ, but he'd been sick.

"I think you may have fractured his skull, darling," said Sellers. "Watch…" she said as she addressed our target. "Who do you buy your cocaine from, Mr Jonas?"

"Fuck you," he slurred."

"See," said Victoria. "I would suggest he's concussed at best, otherwise I'm sure he'd be only happy to help us, eh?"

I pulled the silver laptop from the open safe and lay it on the table next to my baton. Once I had it fired up, I was met by a password pop up.

"Care to tell me?" I asked Jonas pointing at the screen, or shall I take a hammer to your testicles?"

"Fuck you," he repeated slowly.

"Like a stuck record, darling," offered Sellers.

"Hmm," I offered pulling out my mobile and dialling Egghead.

He answered on the second ring. "Always a delight to speak to you, Miss North, a real pleasure, just a shame it's not face to face like."

"I'm sure, Simon."

"How can I be of assistance?"

I looked over to our prostrate target.

"Well, I'm in possession of a gentleman's laptop, and he's reluctant to give me his password to let me look at his content."

"Really? And this gentleman's name?"

"Jonas."

"Ah, Mr Alajos Nagy, a fine upstanding individual if ever there was one, Miss. Well, try the obvious, 1234."

I did.

"No."

"Not so lucky, eh. Okay, try Alajos," he spelled it for me.

"No,"

"Hmm… Hungary?"

"Bingo, Simon, you are a star."

"No worries, Miss. I erm, I take it Mr Fuller will recompense me?"

"Of course, Simon." I said, and I closed the call.

Sellers was busy tying Jonas' feet together. "You could have guessed that yourself, darling," she complained.

"He just has a knack," I said.

"Nice work if you can get it," she offered, standing up and admiring her handicraft.

Jonas' wallpaper was innocent enough, a serene picture of a lake with sail boats doing their thing. Then I clicked on his documents only to find everything was in Hungarian. Closing that page, I hovered the mouse over his pictures folder, where we considered that we may find enough material to loosen his tongue.

Sellers stood by my side.

"I'm not quite sure I can do this," I said.

She nodded. "Look, darling, the big brute isn't going anywhere, why don't you have a look in his freezer, see if you can find me a bag of peas for this eye of mine?"

I looked up at her and managed a smile. She was a tough cookie that was for sure.

"Thanks," I said, and did just that.

When I returned, Sellers was still sitting at the laptop, her face pale, lips pressed tightly together. She looked like she may cry.

She shot an evil glance across the room to Jonas, then looked back at me as I stood, rooted to the spot.

"There are thousands of pictures," she said quietly. "Hundreds of videos."

I held out the bag of frozen peas, arm's length, not wanting to approach the machine, as if, somehow, I might be contaminated by it.

"I don't want to see," I said.

Sellers swallowed hard.

"It's bad," she said. "Like nothing I've ever seen."

"How old are they...?"

"From... from babies," she said. "Tots... to... oh God."

She stopped herself, shook her head, took a deep breath, and straightened her clothes as she stood. Somehow, Sellers the officer had returned.

"I can't describe it, darling, just can't, so let's deal with this animal and get on with our business, eh?"

Jonas looked in a bad way. The blow he'd taken to his head had obviously caused him some serious damage and he now bled from his ears. He sat on the floor in the same spot he'd fallen, legs tied in front of him, propping his body up with one arm, his back to the wall. He was mumbling, but it was in his mother tongue, so we had no way of knowing what he was saying.

Sellers hunkered down in front of him, grabbed at his forehead and slammed his already damaged skull against the wall.

"Two choices, you piece of shit," she hissed. "You name your dealer and where to find him, and I put a bullet in your brain, all nice and quick. Or I will call you an ambulance right now and leave the pictures of those kiddies on display for all to see. Hopefully, you'll live long enough for the boys in the nick to get to you. You do know what they will do to you in there, don't you? What do you say, sunshine?"

Jonas coughed and tried to bat Sellers away with his arm, but he had no co-ordination, no depth of vision. He was bleeding on the brain, and without treatment, dying slowly. She pushed his arm away like swatting a fly and gave him an almighty slap.

"What's it to be?" she spat. "You don't have time to think about this one."

He groaned and moved his head so he could look past Sellers to me. He did his best to focus.

"You… you don't understand," he whispered.

I was shaking with anger. I hated him.

"The innocence," he said. "I crave it. We all crave it, all our kind, and only the very young can give that gift."

The bastard actually managed to smile.

"They are my children," he said. "And I love them."

I pulled my Colt from my bag, took two steps forwards, put the barrel to his head and shot him at point blank range.

Sellers lifted herself away from his body and looked at me, inquisitive, head cocked. "That went well," she said.

"I'm feeling impatient, today," I offered.

She nodded.

"Fair enough, darling. Let's fuck off and give the boys a reality check."

Rick Fuller's Story:

As Lauren drove my 944, Sellers gave me the bad news about Jonas. The way things had gone was disappointing, but as I already had the feeling that as we had stumbled onto something sizable, it wasn't the end of the world. Besides, one less individual with the kind of sexual perversions that Jonas had, was hardly anything to lose sleep over. I would probably have done the same thing myself. Maybe even sooner.

Tony Jacket had driven to a small industrial estate off the A6. It was an isolated place, and the dilapidated, mostly empty units, were surrounded by thickets and mature trees, masking them from prying eyes. From what we'd seen, there were no residential properties nearby. In fact, the place seemed just like a nice quiet spot for a drug deal.

We'd dropped Des off about half a mile back, on the main drag and he'd set off, on foot through the undergrowth to find a good spot to watch the antics. We drove straight into the small estate and parked two units away, from where Jacket's Subaru sat empty, but idling.

All in all, we were tucked in nicely out of sight of prying eyes. Without being asked, Forrest began to kit up and prep the weapons. He, like myself had a feeling about this one.

I got back on the blower to Sellers and gave the girls the heads up.

"Don't drive in," I said. "Park just after the bus stop on the main road. Ten metres after that, you'll see a narrow path. Take that and skirt the estate until you see a unit with red shutters. We're parked just behind that. Keep your heads down. What's your ETA?"

It was ten minutes, so we sat and waited. Moments later, Des was on comms.

"Second vehicle arriving," he said. "Blue C Class Merc, two up. Both white males, big lads. Looks like someone is expecting trouble... standby."

Inside the van was cool, even so I felt sweat trickle down my back.

"Roger that," I said.

Des was back in an instant.

"Bingo, boys. Jacket has met these two at the front of the unit and he's just handed them a shooter apiece. At least we know what was in his bag now."

"Hardware?" I asked.

"SLP's, no big stuff, well not yet," said the Scot. "All three are now inside, out of sight... standby... Okay, the roller shutter is being opened."

Mickey dragged himself forwards, and handed me an MP7 and a spare mag. "This is coming on top, mate," he said.

I gave him a look. "Always one for stating the fucking obvious, aren't you, son?"

"Very funny," said Forrest, with a sarcastic smile, and passed me a set of body armour.

"Save it for Lauren," I said. "We only have four."

He looked at his own set, then into my face.

"The new guy takes precedence," I said.

Mickey turned down his mouth and nodded. "Nice one, boss."

At that he checked over my Fastback one last time.

"And don't fucking lose that," I said. "It has sentimental value."

"I don't think I've ever known anyone to be sentimental over a nine mil."

"Well, you have now."

He shrugged and got comfy in his seat. He was a calm one that was for sure. There wasn't a sign of nerves about him. Eyes clear, looking straight ahead, focused, sharp.

Des' comms crackled into life again.

"They're pulling the Blue Merc into the unit," he said. "One of the new boys is keeping watch outside. Standby... second vehicle approaching. Another Merc, same model, same colour. Three in this one, two more bruisers and a suit in the back... wait, wait... okay, Jacket is handing out more shooters, a pump and another pistol for the two new boys. The suit is out of the vehicle now. Very tall guy, pure white hair, shiny suit, he's in charge fer sure."

Forrest sat up at that. He spoke into his mic.

"Does this guy walk with a limp?" he asked.

"Standby," said Des. "... Aye he does, left leg is straight. But it ain't stopping the big fella barking at all and sundry."

Forrest turned to me, face dark.

"That just has to be the guy I told you about, the guy that fronts Big C Securities, Eddie Fisher. I think we're on here, Fuller. This could be the big one."

I had to agree, but I also knew that this was all too fucking easy.

My phone vibrated on the dash.

"We're here," said Sellers. "Just parked."

"Okay, come in the way I said, but take extra care. They have security here now and they are all armed."

"Of course, Fuller," said Sellers and closed the call.

"There's a wee bit of a barney going on between the suit and our boy, Jacket," offered Des. "The Hungarian fella is on the blower, something's up."

"Maybe, but am I the only one who thinks this whole setup stinks?" I offered.

Forrest shook his head. "This is just what we needed Rick. The gear is on its way, mate. I can feel it in my water."

I gave the boy a look. "I've been tracking Abdallah Al-Mufti for more years than I'd care to mention, son. One thing I know about him, is he never takes chances. And this is all a bit too simple. A bit too naïve."

Des Cogan's Story:

I lay on my belly, as close to the plot as I dare, with nothing but a few brambles and a dead squirrel for company. That said, I was in good cover and had an excellent view of the front and left side of the target. The four bouncer types that had joined Jacket all looked like they could do a bit, but they weren't weapons savvy that was fer sure. Particularly one guy with a blond crew, who checked over his SLP like he'd never seen a gun in his life. Tony Jacket seemed to be the armourer and had dished out the guns to each of the guys in turn. All except the man in the suit. Either he was already armed, or he'd chosen not to be. He had a stilted gait and was extremely tall, 6' 6" I'd have wagered from my lowly position.

He was however, calmly going about the task of preparing the ground for a visit. Nothing was more certain.

Two of his boys stood either side of the open roller door. One blue Merc sat inside the unit, boot open. The white haired suit jumped into the second identical Merc and pulled that alongside the first. It was at that point, that I noticed, both German marques had identical registration plates.

He popped the boot and gave another order to Jacket who nodded and disappeared from view.

I gave the crew the heads up.

"Pound to a pinch of shite the next car is a blue Merc, two up with the same registration plate… This is the split"

"I'd got to that, Desmond," said Rick. "But I don't fucking like this."

I knew what the big man meant, things seemed a little too straightforward, but sure enough, minutes later, there was movement and clone number three drew up outside the plot. The car was met by Jacket, who once again issued the driver and his pal with shooters. The moment they were tooled up, Grey Hair gave them their brief. As they disappeared deep into the unit, the boss man moved the latest C Class and the three cars sat in a sweet line, boots open, all bonny like.

So who's next? The buyer, or the seller? I asked myself.

Actually, the next person who came into view, had obviously been there from the beginning, even before Tony Jacket had arrived. At first, I could-nea believe my eyes, but there was no mistaking it. The blonde hair, dark roots, the way she moved. Standing in the doorway of the unit, in deep conversation with the big Hungarian, was none other than Estelle Ryan.

I couldn't hear what they were saying to each other, but what I did hear, was the safety of an AK47 being moved to the fire position, just behind my right ear.

Lauren North's Story:

We'd heard a car draw up somewhere close to the unit as we gingerly made our way to our builders van, our FOP (Forward Operating Point.) I opened the back doors and jumped inside. Sellers followed me and we sat in silence as we pulled on body armour and waited for further updates from Des. We did indeed wait, there were no further transmissions.

Rick was on it. "Des, come in."

Nothing.

"Des, give me one click if you're receiving me."

Still silence.

Our concern for the Scot, became the least of our worries, as moments later all hell broke loose.

The front and rear doors of the van were torn open simultaneously and in a split second, the muzzles of four automatic rifles were pointing at each of our heads. All of the men brandishing what were unmistakably AK's, where clad in combat gear, balaclavas, and smoke hoods.

We were caught and we had nowhere to go.

The men began to bark orders at us. It was all very professional and even though we were roughly handled, there was no unnecessary violence. This was a specialised and skilled team, not a rag-tag band of criminals or terrorists.

We were expertly searched and pulled to our feet, hands on heads. As we were pushed forwards towards the target building, one of the team got on his comms. He was a Scot. "All parties accounted for," he said. "No injuries. We're coming in."

Des was tagged onto the end of our sorry line of prisoners, but from what I could see, he, too, was in good shape. The short walk to the unit revealed just why the Jacket crew were so confident and so open in their movements. The entrance to the small estate was blocked by what, to all intents and purposes looked to be a police car with its roof lights flashing. A man and woman dressed in full uniform stood at the junction.

No one was getting in here unless they let them in.

"Nice touch," said Des from behind me.

"Silence," barked one of the crew.

We were marched inside the unit, past the three waiting Mercedes cars until we reached the back wall. The place was obviously some kind of storage unit for a garden centre or nursery. Tall metal racking filled with all kinds of pots and boxes occupied either side of the space, and dozens of pallets of what looked like fertiliser or compost were piled high off to our left. I noticed movement behind one such stack and could hardly believe my eyes.

Estelle Ryan was standing alongside Jacket. He had his arm around her shoulders. She looked me straight in the eye, face completely devoid of emotion.

I was beginning to piss off the crew's team leader. "Look straight ahead," he shouted.

I played meek and mild and did as I was told.

We were made to face the wall and were put into stress positions. These are designed to keep you both compliant and in various levels of discomfort. The boys would all have suffered this treatment during selection, but that was more than twenty years ago, and this time it was for real.

All I could see was a concrete wall, yet I was suddenly aware that I had someone standing very close to me. It was the smell that gave her away, the smell of a perfume I used myself.

"Hello, Lauren," said Estelle Ryan.

"Hello, Estelle," I replied, not moving. "If that is actually your name?"

"Yes, of course it is."

"You organised all this?"

"I can't take credit for what is going to happen next. My job has been to keep people informed of your whereabouts these last weeks, and to make sure you were here for the party today, that's all."

I went to turn my head, but a pair of strong arms set me back in position.

"Face forward," barked a different unseen voice. He too, like all the other crew members, was from across the border.

I took a deep breath.

"So… Yunfakh got to you and you sold us down the river. I hope they are paying you well, Estelle. I mean, Des would have given his life to save your brother, Sean."

"No relation, actually. Just a kid Tony wanted out of the way. He's a tad upset about the Melons boys, though. Proper little killing machines, aren't you? Wind you up, feed you a titbit or two and off you go. But you got sloppy, impatient. Maybe because you were being pushed too hard from the other side. I bugged your offices, you know? It was so easy. Quite exciting, really. I mean, after all, you left me to my own devices day in day out. It was you who told me Rick was in Ireland. Don't you remember? Then from the moment you all returned, it was easy. I played the damsel in distress; you discussed your plans in the back office and I recorded everything. Did you really think that my Tony would have led you here so easily?"

I snorted.

"Your Tony? That's rich. He just wants you for what you can give him. Information, so it can be fed back to the big players."

"The biggest," she said proudly.

"You're a silly little girl, Estelle. You've chosen the wrong side."

"Really?"

"Yes, really."

I changed the subject, "Is your square headed friend not worried where his best pal Arti is?"

I risked a glance in her direction and saw her face fall.

"I'll give you a clue," I said. "He's at home watching his kiddie porn… Well, that's not quite true as he has half his head missing, but the cops should be there by now, scrolling through his laptop and bagging up the coke in the safe. I'll wager your boyfriend's prints are all over that gear, Estelle."

"That's enough!" shouted a new voice.

I heard uneven footsteps and gathered that it was the guy with the limp, the guy in the suit. "Step away from the prisoners. No talking," he shouted.

I heard Estelle's heels click across the concrete floor, and I was left with the bitter taste of betrayal in my mouth.

Rick Fuller's Story:

So, Cartwright was right about one thing. We did have a traitor close to us. Sometimes life surprises you, no matter how experienced you are. One thing was for sure, this job had gone about as pear shaped as it was possible to be. And maybe Estelle was right, we were pushed too hard, too quickly and should have seen this coming. But you know what? A traitor is a traitor, and I knew if I got the opportunity, I wouldn't bat an eye at slotting young Miss Ryan.

As it turned out, I didn't have much time to stew on that little snippet, as within minutes there was a frenzy of activity.

One of the players was arriving.

I heard weapons being made ready and orders were barked. Our guard was doubled to two. All the team that had taken us were ex-military, no doubt. The boys watching over the Mercs and the front door, looked like bruisers, probably trusted Big C Securities employees, just like Mickey had been. But the team that snatched us, were well drilled, they had trained together and had practised those techniques.

However, who they actually worked for was another question.

I heard a big heavy vehicle, its fat tyres slowing on the tarmac outside the unit. Doors opened and closed and then the place was silent. Then I heard the stilted footsteps of the man that Mickey believed was Eddie Fisher. They sounded ever quieter as he disappeared from the inside of the building. He was about to meet and greet one of the two players. One of the two we were here to kill.

"Boss," I heard him say.

"Eddie," said yet another Scottish brogue. "Good job, pal. The Jester said you were a man to be trusted."

So, at least some of our intel was good, eh?

Those same footsteps grew ever closer and I could just tell that the new visitor's interest had turned to us.

"A bigger crew than we expected," said the Scottish voice.

"They were no problem," said Eddie smugly. "Your boy's were first class."

"Aye, quality is worth the money, pal. Where is Kenny, by the way?"

"He's with the rest of his crew, up at the entrance, waiting for our man."

"Good idea," said the Scot. "Never trust an Arab. That's what my old man said."

He was very close, now. He stank of fags but tried to cover it with aftershave. He was a heavy smoker and there was the slightest wheeze in his chest.

"Turn them around," he said. "Let's see what we've got."

I felt a tap on my right shoulder, "Turn," said the voice.

As I did so, I was met by three men. One of the elite team, who remained masked and hooded. Eddie Fisher, who was indeed a very tall and slender man with a shock of white hair, and finally, a small wiry man in his forties.

He wore a Ted Baker suit, dressed down with a polo from the same label. I had to say, I was very taken with his brogues and had to force myself not to ask him where he'd bought them from. He sported a tan and despite his bad habit, looked fit enough, but spoiled the whole look with a shocking haircut.

He approached me but remained sensibly out of reach.

"You must be the first prize in the raffle, eh?" he said, smiling smugly.

He raised his brows, "Mr Fuller, I believe. Richard Edward Fuller, once of Her Majesty's Special Air Service and now a dark operations mercenary for MI6. Am I right? What did you think of my little team, eh? Kenny's boys are tip top don't ye think? The best money can buy."

"We'll see," I said.

The guy wrinkled his nose at that, like a father would to a guileless child.

"Ye never know when you're beat, eh, pal? I like that in a man, and I have to say, you have caused me a wee problem or two recently. Still, all's well that ends well, and Abdallah will be eternally grateful for his gift… Next," he said.

Mickey Forrest was turned. Fisher was the first to speak. "Silly boy,

Mickey. What were you thinking? Didn't we look after you when you were on your arse?"

"One of yours?" asked The Scot.

Fisher nodded.

The smaller man stepped in. "We'll just have to make a wee example of you then, eh, pal? Treachery is a terrible thing... It must be stamped out. Now, let's have a look at the wee lassies."

The masked guard tapped Victoria, then Lauren on the shoulder. Both girls turned.

"My, my," said the Scot appreciatively. "I have to say, Fuller, you have excellent taste in comrades. But ye know what I think? I reckon you should have picked men for this wee job. Maybe they would have put up more of a fight, eh?"

Victoria gave him a beaming smile. "If you'd care to step outside, darling, find a patch of grass to roll around on, I'll show you who can fight."

"Oh, a feisty wee bitch, eh?" said the Scot, then gestured towards Victoria's swollen eye. "Looks like ye mouth has got in a wee bit of bother already, hen."

She touched her face. "Oh this little thing? Yes, your pal Jonas thought he was a hard man too, darling. You know, your paedophile chum? He won't be joining you today, however, he's... indisposed. Part of his head is missing. So, I'm all yours... if you want to try your luck."

"He wouldn't last five minutes," added Lauren. "With either of us." She sneered at our VIP, "Go on, try it, where's your bottle?"

"He's got no bottle, darling," said Victoria, the smile gone from her face. "You can see that from here. Small man syndrome."

"Cock to match, I'll bet," said Lauren.

Now, exactly why the girls wanted to get a rise out of our Scottish chum was beyond me. As far as I was concerned, we were in no position to make a run for it, or start a fight for that matter, but it was funny.

The Scot with the worst haircut since Kenny G, went close to purple.

"Fucking English slags the pair of you. Ye willnea be laughing when ye get handed over to the Yunfakh boys. They haven't had a shag in months."

He got just a little too close to Victoria and pointed his finger.

"Ye'll do some rolling around then ye wee…"

She was like a rattlesnake. Her right hand shot out and grabbed the solitary digit. There was the unmistakable sound of a joint popping and the Scot cried out in pain.

The guard closest to me lifted his AK, but Sellers had pulled the screaming Scot in close and he had no chance of making the shot. I slammed my elbow into the guy's face and made a grab for his weapon. This was not a time to be restrained. Selecting fully auto I sprayed the unit with 7.62. Indiscriminate, gut height.

Two bruisers standing by the Mercs, fell wounded, screaming in pain, and the rest of the brave boys from Big C, scattered like pigeons without letting off a single round.

Funny that, eh?

Spinning around, I took the second of our guards out with a single shot. He went down holding his throat. As he fell, I twisted back again, pointed the weapon downwards, and put two in the guy I'd taken the gun from.

I couldn't believe it, but we were in business.

Sellers had the Scot in a choke hold and was using him as a human shield walking backwards, dragging him kicking and shouting threats. However, he was finding out just how strong and determined she was. She rummaged in his suit pockets with her free hand, found an SLP and slotted Fisher where he stood. The third elite guard had moved to get in behind Sellers and take a shot, but Des dropped him with a single punch, stripped him of his AK and put a round in his skull.

The Scot gave me a look that I didn't quite understand, but I could see that he was extremely pissed off with something or someone. One thing I did know, however, was that when Desmond Cogan was in a bad mood, things were going to get extremely messy.

Tony Jacket had proved not to be as heroic as his appearance might have suggested and, he and Estelle Ryan were running for the exit. Des went after them, stopped beside one of the Mercs, set himself, and shot them both in the back.

Mickey Forrest had sprinted over to the two wounded Big C boys and collected a Remington pump and a revolver. He then calmly slotted them both where they lay and other than the choking noises coming from our prisoner, the unit went eerily quiet.

I knew it wouldn't last long.

"Weapons and ammunition check," I shouted. "Then on me… behind the Mercs, get tucked in."

Kenny, and the remainder of the elite team were rounding up the boys that had scattered and were regrouping outside, but they now had a major problem. We had cover behind the cars, and they would have to cross open ground to get to us. Lauren skirted around the dead bodies and collected spare mags. Her efforts also gave us two further SLP's.

We had firepower, position, and a very important Scottish guest.

I felt that good, I went over to him and asked him where he bought his fucking shoes.

Des Cogan's Story:

I couldnea believe my eyes. I mean, as I'd faced the wall, listening in, I thought I'd recognised the voice, but I told myself I was wrong.

Victoria Sellers was choking none other than my old pal, Jimmy McCreery. I walked over to him. He was still spitting mad and struggling. Sellers simply held her SLP to his head and shushed him.

"Let him go," I said.

Sellers gave me a quizzical look. "Cogan?"

"I mean it, Victoria, let him be."

She released her hold on Jimmy, stepped back and immediately raised her weapon into the aim.

"Just give me an excuse, small boy," she said.

McCreery stood rubbing his neck and his wounded pride. He glared at Sellers.

"This isn't over, hen. Not by a long way."

Then he looked me in the eye. It took him a moment, after all, it had been twenty five years and some. "Des? Des Cogan?"

I nodded.

He snorted. "Well, fuck me, ain't this a turn up fer the books, eh?"

Rick was straight in, "Who the fuck is this guy?"

I didnea take my eyes from him. "

This is John James McCreery, mate. We lived in the same street as kids. The last time I saw him…"

"The last time he saw me," blurted Jimmy. "Desmond here, was saving my life."

I shook my head. "I reckon you would have made it without me son."

There was a hive of activity going on outside behind me, vehicles being moved, orders being barked. I pointed at Jimmy. "And I reckon that's enough small talk, for now... tell me, fe old time's sake if ye like, how long before Al-Mufti gets here?"

"Any minute," he said, then holding his palms out, took on a conciliatory tone.

"Look, Des. We go a long way back, eh? Ye cannea win this one. Kenny and his boys will walk through your lot like a knife through butter. Abdallah with come with a crew, you'll be outnumbered four maybe five to one. The Arab won't leave here without his money or your pal, Fuller there."

"So what's your suggestion then, Jimmy?" I asked.

He looked about him. "Give yer man up to Abdallah, and the rest of ye can walk out. A free pass. Ye have my word. Fe what ye did fer me all them years back. Fer old time's sake."

I couldnea help but smile.

"Ye seem to have come a long way, since ye took that lump of resin as payment fer fixing yer man's motor, eh? Ye moved up fast. I mean, that's what got ye shot back in Glasgow. And now, ye have a slice of three cities, I hear. Three cities and yer own wee private army."

"I got that idea from you, Des. I read books on it. What were the best regiments for street fighting, house to house combat, ye know? Then I met Kenny. He's one of your guys, an ex Para. I gave him a lump of money and he did the rest. The best cash I ever spent. No one fucks with me, in fact, they don't even know I exist anymore."

I felt a wry smile spread. "Y'know when ye was reading all those books about the army, like, did ye read any chapters on tactics?"

"I didnea need to, Kenny he..."

"Ah, the mighty, Kenny. Well, Jimmy, let me point out a few wee things to ye. Right now, yer main man out there will be shitting himself. He's only got three or four of his own guys left standing. The rest are a rag tag mob of bouncers who shit themselves and did a Seb Coe towards Stockport as soon as the first gun went bang.

Al-Mufti's crew will be more concerned about keeping their boss alive and the coke safe than looking after you.

As for us, we have cover, we have weapons and ammunition, and we have you. Kenny can make as many barricades as he likes, but to get to you and the money, which I presume is in one of these motors here, he's going to have to cross that yard out there, and that, Jimmy, is fucking suicide."

As if to prove my point, a member of the elite team was skirting around one of the vehicles the boys had placed as a barricade, and Lauren picked him off with a single shot. He fell and didn't move.

"See what I mean, pal? We can do this all day."

I stepped in close.

"And if you ever suggest that I give up my best mate to that scumbag Al-Mufti again, I'll cut your fucking throat myself and laugh while you bleed out. Am I clear, son?"

He was.

I nodded at Sellers and pointed towards a small portacabin at the back of the unit. "You and Mickey find something to tie this fool up with and shove him in there."

She managed a smile. "Feeling masterful today, Cogan? I could get quite used to it."

I gave her a look and she and Mickey dragged Jimmy away.

Sidling up alongside Rick and Lauren, I checked what I had left in the mag of my AK. They were in cover behind one of the Mercs, watching proceedings.

"You have the nicest friends," said Lauren.

"Should've seen the rest of the boys in my class, hen," I countered. "Any sign of Al-Mufti?"

"The lead guy has just done one up towards the entrance," said Rick. "I reckon he's here, and I can't wait to see him."

He looked over to the back wall, "With that in mind, are those fire doors secure?"

"I'll check them the now," I said. And off I went.

Lauren North's Story:

I looked out at our enemy's makeshift barricades. A mixture of vehicles and old pallets. Kenny and his men seemed to be preparing for some kind of last stand.

"Do you think, they'll try and attack us?" I asked.

Rick had his AK to his shoulder, elbows on the bonnet of the Merc. As he took in all the movements outside, he nodded.

"They don't have any choice. But they won't try it until Al-Mufti and his men are in position. He'll take control of proceedings."

I took a deep breath.

"This really is the last one, isn't it, Rick? I mean, from now on, it's me and you?"

He looked over at me and smiled. "I promise," he said. "But we have to see Al-Mufti dead, or we can never rest."

Right on cue, two of the bouncer types that had taken cover behind the barricade opened up in our direction and small calibre stuff clattered around the cars and bounced off the concrete floor.

Rick returned two short bursts and dropped one of them.

Des appeared at my side.

"Those fire doors are secure, and they'd take some opening. They'd need explosives to do it quickly and I can't see Kenny risking that with his boss in here."

Rick fired another burst and dropped the second bruiser.

"No, but Al-Mufti won't be quite so precious about it. If he can walk away with me, the money and his coke, he's on a winner. There's no honour amongst thieves, pal. If Al-Mufti's crew have grenades or C4, they could fight us on two fronts, and we could be in the shit again."

"Aye," said Des, thoughtfully. He turned to Mickey Forrest. "Hey, pal.

Can you drive a forklift?"

Mickey's scouse heritage was suddenly evident in his accent.

"I can drive a shitty stick up a dog's arse, Desmond."

Whilst Rick, Sellers and I kept the boys outside busy with the occasional pot shot, Des and Mickey began moving pallets of fertiliser and compost around the unit. First, they blocked the fire doors at the rear then made two u-shaped stations either side of the Mercs, which gave anyone inside the makeshift bunker, great cover.

When they'd done, the boys dropped in either side of us.

"No one's getting in those back doors now," offered Des, "And I reckon those wee bunkers we've made will take a grenade. Each of those pallets is a ton at least.

"Good work, pal," said Rick.

We tucked ourselves in and waited. Outside seemed strangely quiet. There had been no return of fire, no movement. The minutes ticked by and I began to feel a deep sense of unease.

"What are they waiting for?" I asked.

"It'll be dark in an hour, hen," said Des, searching for his pipe. "They'll come then. You'll see."

Des Cogan's Story:

I rummaged in my pocket for my makings, only to realise that I'd had them taken from me when Kenny's boys had so expertly searched me.

Keeping my head down, I ran over to the portacabin that held our prisoner. If my memory served me well, Jimmy had always smoked.

I opened the door to find him trussed up like a turkey in the corner of the room, wedged between a small desk and the wall.

He glared at me as I walked in.

"Ye picked the wrong team, Des," he said, as if trying to make his point all over again.

I rummaged in his pockets, found a pack of Embassy and his lighter, sat on the floor next to him and lit up.

"I haven't got a choice, Jimmy," I said, blowing out smoke. "I cannea choose a different team. I've always been on the same side. That's been the difference between me and you ever since we were wains. You decided which road you wanted to walk. But I could never have taken that path, see. It wasnea in me."

I held out my cigarette so he could take a drag. He took a pull and nodded his thanks.

I flicked ash, took another lungful and eyed him.

"That night you were shot, I came to the hospital to see ye."

"Aye?"

I nodded.

"Aye, I did. They took me in an ambulance. I needed some work myself; I had some glass in my neck and I couldn't risk an infection as I was about to go to jungle training."

"Aye, I remember ye sayin' somethin' about that."

"But I came to see how ye were, anyway, just so I knew ye was alive. The cops had you under guard, wouldn't let me in the room like, but at least I knew."

I took another pull.

"See Jimmy, that visit to yer gaff in Glasgow opened my eyes. The nice flat, the pretty girl, the wad of cash. I was young but I wasnea stupid. I mean, I'd already figured what ye was up to. I knew ye were dealing. But if I'm honest, back then, I didnea really care. All I wanted was a few beers and a curry with my old pal, eh? I just hadn't realised quite how big your operation was, until ye got shot, that is."

Jimmy smiled at that.

"I got shot over two hundred quid, Des. Ye dinnea need to be big time to get yersel topped in my game. Every dog and his dick thinks they're Al Capone. But yer right, I was on the way up, even back then."

We shared some more of the Embassy as I thought back to that night.

"When I eventually got home, my old man was waiting up fer me," I said.

"Fuck, I'll bet he was pissed off with yees. How is he by the way?"

"He's gone, Jim, quite a while back."

He nodded, "I'm sorry, Des."

I wasn't sure if he was. Even so, "Thanks," I said. "... Well, he was sitting at our kitchen table and, as was his way, he was a wee bit worried about me."

"And ye told him what happened?"

"Aye... I did, and he gave me some advice. He said that because of the path I'd chosen, the team if ye like, that I'd face danger more often than most, that I'd stare down the barrel of a gun more times than I would remember."

I stubbed out the cigarette on the floor.

"Of course, he was right. But he said something else that has always stuck with me."

"Aye?"

"He said, not in so many words, but he said, you choose who you die alongside."

"I don't get yer drift there, Des."

I stood up.

"He said, it's better to go in style, die next to a fighting man, rather than next to someone like you Jim. Which is why, I'm going back out there, to stand alongside Rick Fuller, and help him kill every last soul that's against us."

He stared straight into my eyes.

"And me, Des? Will you kill me, too?"

I nodded.

"If I have to pal. If I have to."

I scuttled back to the line of cars and sat alongside Mickey Forrest. I handed him Jimmy's pack of fags and lighter.

"Cheers, mate," he said. He lit up immediately then gave them back. The plume of smoke he blew upwards drew a couple of random shots from the crew outside. They flew harmlessly over our heads and I heard a voice bark at the shooter to hold his fire.

They, like us, would have limited ammunition, twenty, maybe thirty rounds apiece, so ye needed to be a wee bit careful.

As well as the flying lead, our smoking antics also drew dirty looks from the big man.

"It will be dark in half an hour," he snarled. "Make that your last until this is over."

"Take it he's never indulged," said Mickey quietly.

"Never," I said. "Clean living boy is our Richard."

"I'll bet," said Mickey knowingly. "Can't be that clean though. Not if he worked for Joel Davies. I mean, I never had the pleasure myself, but the story goes that he was as ruthless as they come, then he just disappeared off the map, vanished into thin air."

I recalled the fearsome gun battle at Davies' mansion, and, although we'd always presumed that Goldsmith and crew had murdered him, why we'd never found his body.

"He's probably sunning himself on the Costa Del Crime, pal. People like him, and Jimmy in there, have a habit of riding their luck."

"Were you two close like? You and this McCreery bloke?"

"As kids, aye. We went to the same school, grew up two houses apart, but after I joined up, we lost touch."

"But he said you saved his life."

"That's not exactly true. I gave him first aid after he'd been shot. Chances are he'd have made it anyway. I'd been home on leave, and we met up for a beer and a curry, must have been late 1982. As he was getting the bill, some face shot him through the front window of the restaurant."

"So he was a player even then?"

"Aye, would seem so."

Mickey lapsed into silence for a minute or two. Then he tapped me on the shoulder.

"Des, can I ask you something?"

"Shoot," I said.

"If, well… if I don't make it like. Can you make sure my share of the cash gets to me Mam? I've no pen or paper, but if you can see your way to visiting her, tell her what happened, I'd be grateful."

"I've a good memory for names and addresses, Mickey, and I'd gladly do that fer ye pal."

He gave me the name and the place. I nodded, and there was no more to be said.

Rick Fuller's Story:

What had been a decent enough day had turned into a cloudy, chilly evening. With the light fading fast, I detected movement again out front. Peering into the gloom, I saw a group of men huddled behind what had been Jimmy McCreery's Range Rover. They sprinted out of cover, one at a time, keeping low one going left, the next to the right. They were attempting to skirt our building, trying to get in behind us.

It was all so predictable. After three men had gone, I waited for number four and slotted him the moment he broke cover.

This caused rumblings of discontent from some quarters of our enemy. Raised voices of protest were quickly followed by stern orders of calm. It wasn't that surprising really. After all, these guys had been making reluctant preparations for over two hours and all they had achieved so far was to lose another three men. This must have been extremely disheartening for those Big C crew, who had never experienced battle.

As for me, I was just getting started.

My only real concern was that I was yet to see Al-Mufti. I would never forget his face and never forgive him for what he did to Frankie Green. If this was to be my last stand, I needed to see Al-Mufti's corpse at my feet.

With dusk beckoning, the inside of our unit was close to pitch black. Another advantage.

I twisted my body and tapped the top of my head with my palm, a sign that all the team should join me. Once everyone was close, I lowered my voice to a whisper and gave my final orders.

Victoria and Lauren sprinted off left and right to the bunkers that Des and Mickey had forged from the pallets of fertiliser. The girls had the best cover, the best protection. They also had the widest arc of fire and could target our enemies as they approached from either flank.

Des, Mickey and I would be more central using each of the three C Class Mercs to best advantage. Unlike myself, they both still sported body armour. Kenny's crew had deemed it unnecessary to remove it. That said, if our enemies made good use of the two MP7's they had confiscated from us, lightweight Kevlar would be no more help than a tea bag.

As the girls had the best protection and position, they had taken two AK's and spare mags. We had been left with the rest.

This consisted of one further AK47 with a full extended mag, a Remington six shot pump with a shortened barrel, three Sig P226 SLP's and a very tired looking Smith and Wesson snub nose .38, with just four rounds in it.

We had a bag of cartridges for the shotgun and a quick inspection revealed that they were loaded with 00 buck. These very nasty cartridges, often used by the British cops, are real man stoppers. Nine lumps of lead, all the size of a 9mm slug fired simultaneously at your target. A direct hit would blow a man off his feet, or his head clean off.

I threw the pump and the bag to Mickey. He instantly checked the gun over and made it ready to fire.

The Sigs were all ten rounder's. Each weapon had already been fired, but we had another five full mags to reload with. All in all, I counted just over 25 rounds apiece, plus the AK, the pump and the .38. Hardly World War III starting material, but I reckoned we had enough.

As we settled into cover with our meagre arsenal. I saw headlights approaching and heard the sound of a big diesel engine. Moments later, the vehicle came into view. Things were about to get naughty.

From somewhere on the estate, our enemy had stolen a JCB. That in itself was bad enough but sitting inside the front bucket of the beast was a large metal drum, and strapped to that, was what looked ominously like explosives.

The earth mover was heading directly for us, dead centre, and whoever was behind the controls, had it flat out.

As the digger got to within twenty yards, the driver tipped the bucket and hit the brakes. The homemade bomb dropped to the concrete and was rolling straight for us.

"Incoming," I bawled. "Take cover."

It was a natural thing for me to shout, but really unnecessary. Des and Mickey were already on their toes heading for the girls' positions.

I sprinted to the back wall and tucked myself in behind the pallets at the fire doors, put my hands over my ears and waited.

The explosion wasn't as big as I'd anticipated, obviously Kenny was keen to keep his boss in one piece, and Al-Mufti didn't want to blow his money to bits, but it was enough to rupture the drum. Whatever was inside it, reacted to the shock of the explosion and it caused a huge plume of thick black smoke to fill the unit.

It was already close to full darkness, but now, we were totally blind.

The engine of the JCB revved hard once again and shouts came from outside. The boys were moving in behind the digger and using it as cover.

The smoke was dense and acrid. It burned my eyes and throat, but I waited until I saw the first muzzle flashes appear from the back of the earth mover before I opened up.

Now, the trick with fighting at close quarters, in reduced visibility, is to fire and move. The flash from your weapon is sometimes the only thing that identifies you as a target. It gives your enemy something to shoot back at.

I knew all my team would use this tactic if needed. It had been drilled into Des, Sellers and Mickey all their service, and I had personally tutored Lauren in CQ work. However, as they were all in great cover, I figured they would stay put and it would be down to me, to give the boys behind the digger a taste of their own medicine.

Kenny and Al-Mufti had obviously sent their least able men in first, and what was left of the Big C lads clearly figured they were safer behind the JCB. Each time they took a pot shot though, it was a simple task for me to double tap, move, and double tap.

As the smoke began to clear, the driver got an order and hit the lights on the JCB. Now the positions of all the players was no longer a guessing game. More to the point, as I alone had been using the shoot and move technique, I had just described to you, I found myself out in the open and immediately began to take fire. Sprinting back to my pallets for cover, I lifted the AK, instantly found my sight picture and dropped the digger driver as he sat in his cab.

I saw that I'd also taken out two men from behind the machine. Both lay bleeding and motionless on the floor. Another two, were on their hunkers behind the massive rear tyres of the yellow beast, seemingly very reluctant to come out and play.

That said, in all the uproar, our enemy had taken their chance and begun to move the big boys inside. They swarmed between the racks of products either side of our positions. To my right, I saw the remnants of Kenny's men. He was directing four masked, hooded figures. They'd got themselves tucked in behind whatever cover they could find and began to open up on us.

However, Kenny's crew were not alone. They were joined by other guys, ones I hadn't seen before. They appeared North African, skinny and dark skinned, Moroccan, Tunisian maybe. These were obviously Yunfakh, Al-Mufti's chosen crew. I once again scanned the unit for my man, but he was nowhere to be seen.

Des' idea to make two small bunkers with the loaded pallets had been a stroke of genius. From either position our shooters could target almost all the unit. Des and Mickey were giving the African boys a pasting. The Scot using his near miraculous talent with a handgun to great effect, whilst Mickey racked and fired the thunderous Remington, taking out his chosen targets and most of what they'd been hiding behind in the process.

Sellers and Lauren had the AK's of course. They had both selected single shot mode and were keeping Kenny's guys so busy, they couldn't get their heads up. When they did try, the sheer accuracy of the girls work was devastating, and Kenny was down to two within the first thirty seconds.

All our enemy had achieved, was to move twenty yards into even deeper shit.

As we were on the front foot and there was a brief lull in the rate of incoming fire. I risked a look out from behind my cover and what I saw raised my spirits. I thought all my birthdays and Christmases had come at once.

The man I'd sought for so long had arrived. He was only partially visible as he was masked by the JCB, but it was him, no doubt; maybe a few pounds heavier, but there was no mistaking my nemesis, Abdallah Al-Mufti.

He wore a pale suit, just as he had done all those years ago in Libya. And that hair, that ponytail, it was a little greyer at the temples, but his trademark was still there for all to see.

He grabbed at one of the Big C boys, hiding behind the digger and screamed in his face to move. The big lad was having none of it, he was terrified, and I watched him shake his head in defiance. Al-Mufti put a round in his skull in temper, then grabbed the second face, who instantly got the message and stood up, hands raised.

Using the last of the Big C crew as cover, Al-Mufti set off to join his beleaguered troops who were still taking fire from Des and Mickey. He got four paces, before I dropped his human shield with a single shot. However, those four paces took him halfway to his desired location and he managed to sprint the last yards to the relative safety of the racking.

Once again, he disappeared from my sight.

Kenny was a brave and clever soldier. He'd done a bit, no doubt, and using all his guile, had managed to get him and his remaining two men close to the portacabin where our prisoner was held.

Al-Mufti was also a smooth operator. He'd seen Kenny's progress and, determined to aid his comrades move to release McCreery, took a leaf from our book, and had his crew throwing the kitchen sink at us, keeping us in cover, unable to return fire.

I'd always had the feeling that this battle would be won and lost on how frugal either side could be with their ammunition and Al-Mufti obviously figured the same. After a minute or so, the constant pounding from his crew slowed and his boys adjusted their weapons from fully auto to single shot. Even so, his men were deadly accurate, willing to put themselves in harm's way, and made it tough for us to even see what was going on.

Just as I attempted to take a peek, one of Al-Mufti's boys let go with one of our suppressed MP7's. He got a roasting from his boss to conserve his ammunition, but it certainly gave me something to think about. As the specialist ammunition crashed into my position, wood splinters flew into my face, lacerating my cheeks and chin. I blinked furiously in an attempt to clear my vision. Mercifully, I had no splinters in my eyes, and moments later, I was able to see my arch enemy again.

Kenny had reached the door of the portacabin and within seconds, was inside. In any battle, you can go from a position of strength to being in total shit within minutes. And I felt that things were going suddenly against us. We weren't getting our rounds away, and the enemy had us pinned down.

"Come on," I bawled. "Make 'em fuckin' have it!"

Des didn't need any further encouragement and popped up with his Sig, arms extended, one hand cupping the other, the classic shooter's pose. The guy was nothing short of deadly. Anyone who has ever fired a handgun will testify that it is the most frustrating weapon to use. Most can hit a stationary target from twenty yards when under zero pressure. But a moving target that is equally determined and firing back? Well, that is an all new ball game. Desmond Cogan, however, as the old song goes, was simply the best.

The Scot ignored the incoming fire and slotted two of the Yunfakh boys within seconds. That seemed to give the whole of our team a lift and the girls opened up with the big stuff.

Mickey had turned his attention to Kenny's crew, who now had Mc-Creery untied and out of the cabin. He got off two rounds with his Remington and caught one boy in the gut. He went down screaming in agony, holding his entrails in with his arms, but Kenny stayed on point, kept his charge moving and his head down. The team leader was a cool, hard customer and was obviously more concerned with getting his boss home and dry than saving ammunition. He bawled to his last remaining fighter and the boy raked our positions with the second of our MP7's, forcing us all back into cover.

As the deadly armour piercing rounds clattered all around us, I once again risked a look.

Kenny, McCreery and the shooter were on their toes sprinting into the darkness and away from our position. It would appear that our big tough drug dealer was far more interested in staying alive than spending his five million quid.

As I cursed the loss of our prisoner, I felt a round fly past my head. It was close, very close and I saw that it had been fired by none other than Al-Mufti himself.

Now, it is always better to have a clear head in battle. The guys that suffer the red mist, often end up covered in the red stuff. But as I looked into the eyes of the man that had once again tried to kill me, I felt my rage overcome my common sense.

The Egyptian had watched Kenny and McCreery run for their lives. I could almost read his thoughts. He had just three men left. He was outnumbered and we had the superior cover. He gave the order to his remaining soldiers to open up on us, twisted his body, and as I ducked down behind my pallets, I saw him make his move and turn and flee.

"Let's finish this," I shouted.

My team had seen what was unfolding and were all over it. The girls popped up and lay down a blanket of fire on Al-Mufti's remaining crew, spewing white hot 7.62 into their positions. Des, and Mickey edged around our enemy's flanks, and ten seconds later, all was quiet.

Mickey was checking each body for signs of life as Sellers collected what weapons were still functional.

I looked around.

"Where's Des?" I asked, already knowing the answer.

Des Cogan's Story:

I'd seen Jimmy make a run fer it, but there was nothing I could do. Al-Mufti's lot were spraying so many rounds down on us, we couldn't even return fire.

That said, the moment, the very second, I knew we had the battle won. I was off. I knew Rick would want to go for Al-Mufti. It was personal to him, and he would have expected me to be alongside him, to take revenge for Frankie Green. But I had other ideas. I had unfinished business of my own, and that lay outside the unit, with Jimmy McCreery. Somewhere in the dark, in the grounds of the estate, Jimmy was running for his life, and as our orders were to eliminate the main players in this game, I intended to stop him in his tracks.

I sprinted across the tarmac, back the way we had been marched in, back towards our van. After all, if I were Kenny and I knew where a functioning vehicle was, that's the first place I'd be headed.

Once I was within fifty yards, I slowed to a walk and checked over my Sig. If I'd counted correctly, I had four rounds in the mag, so not much room for error.

I stopped and listened.

I could hear Lauren's voice from behind me. She was calling to Rick. There was fear in it, worry. I couldn't quite capture what she'd said, but I figured he'd gone after the Egyptian alone and she wasn't happy.

Then, there was silence, no traffic noise, just a light breeze and some rain in the air.

I wiped sweat from my face with my palm and got my head together. Edging ever closer to where I knew our van had been left, I heard the first murmurings. Scottish voices. Angry hushed tones.

I tucked myself against a low wall and held my breath.

The first voice I heard was Jimmy's.

"I dinnea fuckin' care one shite, Kenny. That's five mil of my hard earned back there, and I pay yees to look after these things."

"And ye willnea be spending it if ye go back there to try and collect it, Jimmy. I've six rounds left, and Billy here has two. Now work it the fuck out."

The camp was obviously not a happy one, and as far as ammunition went, it appeared we were all in the same boat. However, they were three and I was on my lonesome. I would only get one chance at this and I knew it.

I moved slowly, head down, until I reached the end of my wall and the last of my cover.

Jimmy was still whining about his cash. Kenny was doing his best to keep him calm.

With my knees bent and my back to the low wall, I took a deep breath. Four rounds, three targets, in the dark. A very tall order indeed.

Rick Fuller's Story:

I'd pulled an SLP from the dead hands of one of Al-Mufti's players and checked it over. Seven in the mag. Well, it would just have to be enough.

I caught Lauren's eye as I made to walk from the unit. She wore a concerned expression; she bit her bottom lip and shook her head.

"Ditch everything," I said. "All your weapons. Travel separately, and get to the lock up, keep your heads down and I'll be in touch… good job."

As I turned, Lauren called after me. "Rick," she said. "You don't have to do this."

I walked to her and took her in my arms, "I do. And you know I do," I said.

Al-Mufti had run towards the entrance of the site. I figured that the vehicle containing his drugs would still be out there, and that would be exactly where he was headed. Even in the jaws of defeat, he wouldn't want to lose another shipment. He would want to fight another day.

I jogged steadily, not knowing exactly where to look, or indeed how I would go about finding a man whom was undoubtedly an expert in urban combat. I figured that the vehicle would be a van or a large car. Worst case scenario was that Al-Mufti had left a couple of his Yunfakh goons watching over his precious consignment. If it was still guarded, I would be outnumbered, and that would put me right in the brown stuff.

As I reached the entrance to the estate, I noticed that the fake cop car was still there, lights flashing. However its occupants had long gone. Either they lay dead somewhere around the unit, or they had fled.

Seconds later, I heard an engine turn over and fire. It was off to my left and it was close.

I turned towards the noise and slipped off the safety on my weapon.

It was then I heard gunfire from the other side of the estate.

Gunfire and screams of agony.

Des Cogan's Story:

My first round caught Kenny square in the chest. The last of his guys was slow to react and I put two of my precious shots in somewhere around his diaphragm. He began to scream like a stuck pig. Under normal circumstances, I would have put one in his head and helped the boy out, but with just a single bullet left, the poor bastard would just have to scream.

Jimmy turned and sprinted away. In a split second he was out of sight, lost behind the van and I could hear him crashing through the undergrowth.

I had no choice but to follow.

With little ambient light to guide either of us, it was a guessing game. I couldn't see Jimmy, but I could hear him, tripping and cursing as he forced his way through the scrub. I caught a root with my right boot and went crashing to the floor, knocking the wind out of me. Evil brambles tore at my skin and my hands were lacerated in seconds.

However, I knew that Jimmy would be in the same boat. He would be struggling, and I had the advantage of experience. I knew all those horrible tabs through the jungle, would come in handy one day.

I heard a thump up ahead, and a cry of pain. Jimmy was down. I had to get to him, to finish this, once and for all. And I knew I was close.

It was so frustrating. I struggled to make any progress. Twine, creepers and whatever other local foliage wrapped itself around my ankles whilst the thorns continued to cut me to ribbons, I heard Jimmy begin to thrash about again. He was up and running and he still had a good few yards on me.

We were getting closer to the main road, and I began to see the odd shaft of yellow sodium light that illuminated my path. I forced my body forwards, head down, teeth gritted.

Seconds later, I looked up and could see the end of the scrub, the footpath and the silhouette of a very tired looking Jimmy McCreery.

He had his hands on his knees and was coughing his guts up. Even so, even in his state of exhaustion, dog tired, he had his wits, and he heard me approaching.

"Fuck you, Des," he shouted, then turned and began to run along the footpath, towards the main road and civilisation.

I powered forwards, no longer feeling the brambles, no longer worried about my footing. I had the bastard, and I knew it.

Moments later, my feet were on solid gravel and I was off. Now, I've never been the quickest, and, as you know, I do like a wee tab, but I've trained all my life, where Jimmy had not.

He was twenty yards ahead, blowing out of his arse.

He turned briefly, staggered, then stopped.

The temperature had fallen, and I could see his breath in the air.

He spat on the floor and held up a hand.

"Okay, fuck's sake, Des, okay."

Rick Fuller's Story:

The first thing I saw were headlights, then the plumes of smoke from the rear tyres of the 7 Series BMW. I couldn't see the driver, but as the car was flat out and heading straight for me, I had to presume that whoever was in control, was not on my Christmas card list.

The car would cut me off at the knees. I had nowhere to go, so I gambled everything, shit or bust and put all my seven rounds into the windscreen. Mercifully, I hit the driver, and the car lurched to the left, the accelerator flat to the floor, engine screaming. Whoever had the wheel had lost control and the car spun a full 180 before crashing, rear end first, into one of the small empty units that littered the estate.

The collision sent bits of plastic and glass flying into the air, raining back down on the shiny black paint of the Beamer.

The car burbled menacingly, ticking over, the interior in darkness, headlights blazing. No movement.

I kept my body bent and shuffled to my left. I needed to see if the driver was alive. Two more paces would do it, but I didn't get the chance.

Someone from inside the car started shooting, and I was suddenly taking fire in the open. Four, five, maybe six rounds flew around me and bounced off the tarmac. As I threw myself to the floor and rolled, I felt the unmistakable pain of being shot.

I was hit somewhere between chest and gut on my left side. It was as if someone had thrust a red hot poker into my flesh and was twisting it around for good measure.

I felt my blood seep into my shirt and my body begin to fall into shock.

That couldn't happen. Wouldn't happen. Not yet.

Lifting my knees, I dragged myself to my feet and staggered towards the car. The level of pain you suffer from a gunshot addles the brain. Confusion reigns. I still had my arm outstretched, empty gun in hand. Any fool can see when an SLP is empty, the action stays back, waiting to be fed. And my enemy could see that, too. The rear door of the BMW began to open, and I saw a pale suited leg drop to the tarmac.

Seconds later, Abdallah Al-Mufti stood in front of me.

He straightened his jacket, then produced his own gun from the back seat of the car. It too was obviously as empty as my own.

He threw the weapon to the floor and cocked his head. "Well, well, Mr Fuller. At last we come face to face, as men," he said.

I could feel the blood dripping into the waistband of my jeans, trickling down the inside of my thigh, I didn't have long to function, I knew it, and so did he.

I took a deep breath, balled my fists, and stepped in.

"Let's get this over with," I said.

Des Cogan's Story:

Somewhere back in the industrial estate, I heard the sound of small arms fire. So the fight wasn't quite over yet. However, I had other things on my mind.

Jimmy stood on the footpath, breathing hard. We were both bathed in the yellow streetlights. His face was lacerated from his attempts to negotiate the brambles, and I saw that his hands were in a similar condition.

I, too, had suffered from a similar fate, yet as I gripped my gun in my right hand, I felt no pain.

Jimmy looked up at the towering sodium light above him.

"Just reminds me of standing under my old lamp in Possilpark, eh, Des? Waiting for the next customer to pull up… good times those."

"I wouldnea know," I said, edging closer.

"No, of course you wouldnea. Ye was off fighting for Queen and country, eh? International man of mystery. That's you fer sure, Des."

"Ye make it sound glamorous, Jimmy. Stylish, sophisticated even. But ye always did have the talent fer that. Ye had the knack of making everything sound easy."

He lowered his voice. "It is, Des. It still can be."

I nodded and gave him a wry smile. "Ye going to pitch me now, are ye, Jimmy. Offer me money? Houses? Women? What?"

He shook his head.

"Naw, Des, I'm no."

He rummaged in his jacket for fags and came up empty. "Ye pinched mine, ye wee jobbie, eh?"

I pulled his pack and lighter from my pocket and threw them over. Jimmy leaned down and collected them. He didn't take his eyes from me, or the gun.

As he lit up, I felt my own craving, but pushed it to one side.

"Any other last requests?" I asked.

Jimmy blew out smoke and savoured the nicotine hit.

"So, this is it, then, pal, eh? Us two Bhoys, standing on an English pavement, and you, a proud Scot, about to do the Englishman's bidding."

"This has nothing to do with England, and you know it, Jimmy."

"No?"

"No."

"So yees no in bed with Her Majesty's Government then? They aren't paying your wages, telling you who to murder? Because, ye can dress this up anyways ye like pal. This is murder." He held up his arms. "I'm unarmed."

I snorted at that.

"I'm here to stop people like you lining the pockets of terrorists, Jimmy. The likes of Al-Mufti kill hundreds, maybe thousands, every year. Come to think of it, Jimmy, who's yer boy in Belfast? Ye do have three cities, I hear eh? Who's yer Belfast man. He wouldn't be connected now, would he? What do they call themselves these days? The New IRA, is it? Ye have blood on your hands, Jimmy. Ye might not be there when it's spilled, but it's there nonetheless."

"Blood ye say? And what about you? Y'see this is yer problem here, Desmond. You are playing judge, jury and executioner. Ye just like to give yersel good reason fer yer actions so ye can sleep at night, eh?"

He took another long deep drag.

"Remember that night at my flat? The night we went to the Barras? Ye walked out on me, cos of what I was sayin' about the army. Ye didn't like to hear the truth, did ye? Bloody Sunday, the Bogside Massacre, the 30th January 1972. Ye'd be what? Four? Five years old, same as me? But I'll bet my life, that it was the talk of your house and every house in the street, eh? Twenty eight shot, Des. Twenty eight unarmed civilians. Thirteen killed outright. They were fucking running away, Des. Square that circle why don't ye. Shot running away, some even while trying to tend the wounded. Every single victim a Catholic, Des. A Catholic just like me."

He pointed.

"And just like me now, Des, all of those poor fuckers were unarmed, posing no threat."

He finished his fag and curled his lip.

"So, there ye are. I've said my piece. I'm done. No cash offer, no holiday homes, no buxom blondes, just this…"

At that he turned his back and with his hands held out to his sides, began to walk away.

"Ye shoot me if ye must, Des. You decide what kind of man you are."

I stood, arms outstretched, the front sight of my gun dead centre in Jimmy McCreery's back. I had one bullet. One bullet left.

Clicking on the safety, I turned and jogged back towards the unit.

Was I right to spare Jimmy McCreery? Who knows? Like I've said to you before, sometimes you just have to be there to understand it.

Rick Fuller's Story:

I threw a mighty right hand into Al-Mufti's face. He parried it and turned his cheek just enough to allow the blow to glance off him. My momentum drew me onto him, and he grabbed at my wrist as it passed him. He was an expert fighter and twisted his body enough to apply pressure to my elbow joint with his other arm dragging me downwards. As he did so he lifted a knee and slammed it into my nose.

I knew immediately it was broken and felt more of my claret escape and run down my chin. I held onto his leg for dear life, hoping to clear my head, then dug in, knees bent and got my shoulder into his gut.

Swallowing bile, I staggered backwards, doing my best to keep my balance, the agony overshadowing my thought process.

My opponent spat on the floor at my feet.

"Now you die, Fuller," he hissed, and came again.

I couldn't move my left arm. It simply lay across my stomach, hoping to protect my wound from any further punishment. Blood had pooled into my boot and was dripping onto the concrete. I hadn't much left, and Al-Mufti knew it.

He went to kick my feet from under me, to get me on the floor. I staggered but didn't fall. As he came for me, I dropped my head again and led with my elbow into his throat. I got more of his chin than I'd bargained for, but he was hurt, struggling. He was flat footed, and I went in behind, kicked his knee joint and went for the choke.

I dragged him backwards until he lay on top of me. I had my back on the deck and my right forearm firmly on his throat. That should have been game over, but with only one good arm, I quickly realised that I was never going to choke him out. He just felt too strong and I felt so tired. I couldn't hold him.

He twisted his body one last time, and again he was free.

I rolled away, but I was too slow, I'd lost too much blood. Al-Mufti was back on his feet and he penalty kicked me in the guts.

I must have screamed, but I couldn't say for certain. My world was once again turning black, the way it once had on the moors in Manchester.

Al-Mufti sat on my chest and slapped my face to bring me back to consciousness. Slowly, I opened my eyes and locked onto his gaze.

"Get it over with," I said.

He sneered. "I've dreamed of this moment, Fuller."

"Dream on," said a Scottish voice off to my left.

Al-Mufti didn't get the chance to turn. Des fired a single round, penetrating the Egyptian's skull at the temple. It was a marksman's shot from any distance.

I pushed Al-Mufti's corpse off me and looked over to my only friend.

"I knew there was a reason I'd saved that round," he said. "Now, are you going to lie there all day, or can we fuck off?"

* * *

Des drove me back to the lock up in the beamer, and just after midnight, the whole crew were back together, safe, sound and happy. The round I'd taken had passed straight through me without any internal damage. Des and Lauren cleaned me up and got an IV into my arm. Once they were happy with me, they put on some music and cracked some cans. I desperately wanted to celebrate with them, but within minutes, I must have fallen asleep.

I awoke to find Lauren by my side. She was snuggled up against me. She looked and smelled wonderful. That lunchtime, Forrest went out for more supplies, the girls cooked up a storm and by that evening, I felt well enough to join in the fun.

By day two, Cartwright had given us the all clear to travel and we all made our separate ways home, to prepare for a lengthy break from terror and danger.

The final battle with Al-Mufti had been one of the hardest of my life and that evening, I stood in my shower inspecting my cuts and bruises. Luckily, other than my nose, nothing else appeared broken, but I knew from experience, and now, my age, that it would be a few weeks before I stopped wincing when I moved this way or that.

As the shower pounded my aching limbs, I considered that despite my injuries, I was the lucky one for a change. We had all emerged from the fight alive and our enemies were defeated. Des' decision to let Jimmy McCreery live was his own business. I hadn't really had the opportunity to ask his reason, but I knew the Scot well enough to know it must have been a good one.

The cops would be swarming all over the city for the next days and weeks. Due to the nature and location of the fighting, our vehicles and faces would eventually be picked up on cameras around the city and those images would be passed to forensics to identify.

Our only hope, was that Cartwright and any of his successors, were as effective as the old spy at keeping our identities a secret, and soon we would be able to walk the streets of Manchester again. It was a place with all the usual issues of any sprawling cosmopolitan city, and although I may have made out to you that it had more than its fair share of criminals and gangsters, it was the place that had become my home. With luck, Lauren and I hoped to make it so again, once the dust settled and we returned from our adventure to the Far East.

Sellers and Forrest were already en route to Dubai, yet I would wager that it wouldn't be long before they ended up in one of the war torn Middle Eastern regions, Iraq, or Syria maybe. Mercenaries get big money out there and they were both young enough to enjoy the ride. Sellers was a scrapper. She loved the fight, the danger, and the contest. And Forrest? Well, he had showed himself to be a more than capable soldier and as neither of them had anything to tie them to the UK, I didn't expect them to be back any time soon.

Des, of course was packing his gear and taking the train to Scotland. I knew he had great misgivings about beginning any form of relationship with Grace other than a platonic one. It was an unwritten rule that you didn't take up with a mate's missus, be he alive or dead, but what I'd learned this last few years, and certainly since losing Cathy, was that life is too short for rules like that. Des made JJ the promise that he would look after his boy and he'd already done over and above what most men would have. But to truly take care of a kid, a man has to be around. Now to me, that didn't mean every couple of days, or the odd weekend.

My old man went to war and never came back, killed in action. I was a little older than Kaya, but I remember this, once my old mum topped herself, I never once felt loved until I met Cathy. JJ's boy deserved love, as did Grace, and I couldn't think of another man on this planet who was more worthy of happiness than Desmond Cogan.

So, all in all, it was a good day… until my phone rang.

I pulled a towel around me, lifted the phone from my bedside cabinet and looked at the screen. 'Private Number,' it said. You know, at first, I almost nipped it. I mean, those numbers are usually a call centre, someone trying to sell you a kitchen, maybe life insurance or something. But then a more disturbing thought clicked in my head. In all the time I'd held this number, I'd never had a call like that. My phone, like my life, was restricted to the people that mattered.

"Hello?" I said.

"Fuller," said the caller. "I was hoping you'd answer."

My brain was putting a face to the voice, leafing through page after page of my chequered history. "Simpson," I replied, the penny dropping. "What the fuck do you want?"

"Now that isn't polite now, is it?" he hissed. "I always did think you had a foul mouth, Fuller. Common as coal, as my mother used to say."

"Look, Detective, I don't give a toss about what you or your mother used to say and I'm a very busy man right now, so unless you have something of importance to tell me, I suggest you hang up."

"Busy, you say?"

"Busy yes, so why..?"

"Packing I take it?"

I stayed silent.

Simpson did not.

"I can see you now, Fuller, just out of the shower, all those designer numbers laid out on your bed in a particular order, so as not to mess with your OCD. All nicely laundered and pressed. Do you still use the same lady? What's her name now? Lucy Meehan, isn't it? LM Laundry services? Too lazy to do your own washing, eh?"

Even though I knew it would be impossible for it to be the case, I took a quick look around my bedroom for a camera or two. Of course, he was playing with my head, the way he'd tried with Lauren.

"I think you need to be careful, Simpson," I said. "I mean, a man could get himself into all kinds of trouble for setting up surveillance routines on innocent people. Maybe even get themselves suspended again. Come to think of it, how did you get this number?"

"Never mind all that, Fuller," he croaked. "I suppose your tickets are all laid out, too, eh? PMT, that's what they say isn't it? Passport, money, tickets. Off to Amsterdam first, then Bangkok. What next then? Oh yes, Chiang Mai, Thailand. Nice place this time of year, I believe."

I dropped him onto speakerphone and hurriedly began dressing. I had a bad feeling, a really bad feeling.

"I'll ask you again, Simpson, how did you get this number, and how do you know..?"

"The darling Lauren, of course. Are you stupid, Fuller?" His voice was close to a whisper, leering. "She always did give me everything I wanted. Such a generous girl... in every way, if you know what I mean? So loving. A shame really."

"Where are you, Simpson?" I spat.

He let out a small laugh. A weird sounding giggle, the kind of noise a child would make to his peer when doing something naughty.

"I'm here, with Lauren, of course. She invited me over, ages ago. I even have my own key."

"Let me speak to her," I barked, an ever growing feeling of panic flooding my senses.

This time, Simpson's laugh was anything but childlike. It was guttural, it came from a dark place.

"She's busy," he said. "Too tired to talk right now. She's all worn out. We've been at it, see. At it for hours, all positions. She's a vixen, a pure animal between the sheets. That's what a man needs in a wife, Fuller, an angel in the daytime and a whore after dark."

"You're lying, Simpson. Where are you? Tell me the truth."

He lowered his voice again. Confident, cocky. "You can't have her, Fuller. No one can have her. No one but me. I told her so, and you know something? In the beginning, she wouldn't listen. She was a naughty girl at first, but all pretty girls can be temperamental, can't they? But now, we understand each other and …. She's all mine."

I'd heard enough, closed the call and dialled Lauren.

It was switched off.

I opened my wall safe, pulled my spare SLP from inside and pushed it in the waistband of my jeans. As I sprinted to my Aston, I called Des.

Des Cogan's Story:

Three holdalls. That was the sum total of my life since leaving Scotland. Not too much to show, eh? Well, apart from a bulging bank account. That said, money can't buy you happiness, or love. True words those, so they are.

Despite the elation of our victory, some parts of the job had left a sour taste, particularly the situation with Jimmy. That said, it was too late to change things and as I shoved my train tickets into my jacket pocket, I pushed all thoughts of drugs, gangsters and murder to the back of my mind.

I trod to the kitchen, opened the patio doors and stepped onto my wee balcony. The summer was showing signs of losing its grip on the year and dark storm clouds were gathering ominously over the city.

I pulled out my pipe, and just for a moment took stock of the things that mattered to me.

Ever since Ann had left, I'd always had a feeling of disappointment in folks. Ye know, just like when ye open the fridge after a few scoops, hoping to find some tasty morsel to eat, a pack of sausage or a slice or two of bacon, maybe some leftover curry even, but no, all that's there, winking at ye, is a tub of low fat cottage cheese.

That had been my life… until now.

I knew I had some really hard decisions to make. All my days I'd tried to do right by folk. It's my nature. I mean, I know I can be a wee bit tetchy if people piss me off, but I treat as I find, eh?

Now, Grace was a real problem, because doing the right thing by JJ must surely mean, that we could never take things any further than friendship. There are rules about that kind of thing. They might not be written down, or made to law, but they are there, nonetheless.

I tapped out my pipe and began to refill it. Before I could light my makings, my phone rang. It was the big fella and he sounded terrible, panicked, unstable even. I could hear the roar of the engine of his car and he screamed down the line.

"Lauren's gaff, now. I need you there."

"Okay, pal," I said. I'm on my way. What the fuck is up?"

"Just get there," he shouted, and ended the call.

The only car I could get my hands on, was the old Discovery that we'd used on the last job. If Rick hadn't sounded so desperate, I would have left it alone, as the cops would have had a field day with it, but it was needs must. I fired the engine, floored the accelerator and headed for Lauren's flat.

It was just after four in the afternoon and traffic was against me all the way. What would have been a thirty minute drive took me just shy of an hour and as I swung the Discovery in behind Rick's Aston on the driveway of Lauren's building, I was sweating and frustrated.

I ran along the gravel drive to the communal door. It had been wedged open by a stone from a nearby rockery. As I climbed the stairs, I pulled my Browning and felt the skin on my back begin to twitch. On reaching the landing, I looked at the carpet beneath my feet and saw it had been sprinkled with pink rose petals.

What the fuck?

Once again, the entrance door to the flat was ajar with no sign of a forced entry. Indeed, had I not known better; this had all the trappings of a romantic encounter where the beau had been lying in wait to surprise his lover.

Once inside the flat, however, it was a whole new picture. An overturned chair sat ominously in one corner; broken glass now mixed with the same rose petals on the floor. The contents of two suitcases were strewn across the lounge. This was a room where a violent struggle had taken place.

I set myself, Browning up in the aim, and trod slowly towards the bedrooms.

I knew Lauren slept in the second and larger room, but I cleared the first to be certain. It appeared untouched by whatever ill had caused the carnage in the lounge. The second bedroom door was open, and I edged myself ever closer to the jamb.

ROBERT WHITE

I took my first look inside, and instantly wished I had not.

Rick sat on the edge of the bed cradling Lauren in his arms. He was talking to her, whispering things I couldn't bear to hear. He turned and saw me. I went to step closer, but he held up a hand and shook his head.

There was nothing for me to do.

She was gone.

I said a few Hail Mary's to myself and sat on a nearby chair. Suddenly exhausted I became so overcome with grief I could hardly think. Tears welled in my eyes and with my elbows on my knees I let them drip onto the wooden floor. The room was so still and quiet, I could hear them fall. They matched the rhythm of my breaking heart.

Rick spoke, his voice quiet. "Her neck is broken," he said. "He broke her neck."

I lifted my head, wiped my eyes and looked at my best friend, his face as wet with tears as mine.

"Who did this?" I asked.

Rick took a deep breath in through his nose and held it for what seemed like an age, then he slowly exhaled and closed his eyes. Opening them, he shifted his body, and gently lay Lauren on the bed. He stroked her face and adjusted her hair, so it lay either side of her neck. I knew he'd never been a religious man, but he muttered something that again, I couldn't hear, but would have liked to believe was prayer.

Finally, he turned to me and his face darkened. He wiped his tears and bared his teeth.

"Simpson," he said with about as much venom as was possible from a human being.

"Larry, fucking Simpson."

I was wide eyed.

"Can ye be sure, pal? I mean, that's one hell of an accusation."

Rick pulled his gun from his waistband and checked it over. I knew exactly what was on his mind.

"The fucker called me. Goaded me, told me he was here with her. This is what he wanted, to punish me. To hurt me because I had her love. He wanted me to find her, find her... like this. He wanted me to see what he'd done to her."

I saw him fighting back more tears. He swallowed hard. "I... I had to fucking dress her mate. I think, well, I can't be sure but... I think... maybe."

He put his palm over his eyes, and I saw his shoulders heave. I stepped to him, took him in my arms and held him close.

"Come on mate, we need to call the cops."

He pushed me away, so hard I nearly fell on my backside.

"Fuck that," he said, "What? So the bastards can cover for him?"

"It won't be like that, pal, come on, this is murder we're talking. They'll put him away for good."

Rick's rage was building with every word. "Will they now? Oh, I can see it all. Can see the headlines, 'Top Cop has Breakdown.' Oh yeah, he'll be in a nice comfy side ward, tucked away from the mass population for his own protection, then before you know it, he'll be deemed fit to be released and be home free. And what about me, eh? Will I be free? Will I ever be able to close my eyes and not see this shit?"

Moving forwards again I grabbed him by the shoulders and looked into his eyes.

"Listen pal, if you do this. You do what you're thinking, you'll be hunted for the rest of your days. You'll be a cop killer and they won't care a toss about your reason. They will lock you away for the rest of your life and not bat an eye. So, I, for one, am no prepared to watch ye do that, ye understand me, pal? I cannea let ye do this. Ye wouldn't last the year out in the nick and I'd be attending yer funeral because ye topped yersel with yer bed sheets."

I stepped away and pulled my Browning. "If I have to, I'll put one in yer leg, pal. I mean it, ye know I do."

He glared at me, his mounting anger about to boil over into total rage. "Get out of my way, Des. You don't want to do this."

I clicked off the safety. "I dinnea, but I will."

It was the standoff to end all standoffs. Two men overcome with grief. Two lifelong friends full of hatred, anger and determination, but with one hoping to keep the other alive.

Thankfully, I didn't need to pull the trigger. There was a noise from downstairs, and the unmistakable chatter of a shortwave radio.

"Police," a female voice shouted. "Is everything okay? Can I come up?"

I held out my hand. "Give me the gun, Rick... Please."

He handed me his pistol and I shoved it into my jacket along with my own. Striding to the door of the bedroom, I shouted down. "Up here officer, quickly, and get some help, there's a woman been murdered."

Rick Fuller's Story:

Des did all the talking, and as the young officer inspected the scene, he quietly opened the landing window and threw both our pistols out into the grounds. I have no idea how he managed to keep thinking straight. I was broken beyond repair and so full of hate, I could hardly walk. My body twitched uncontrollably, and I had to run to the toilet to be sick.

There were dozens of questions that I hardly recall, I was put into the back of a police car and driven to the main holding station in the city. Des, taken to a separate location. Once I'd been booked in, my clothes were taken from me and I was asked if I wanted a solicitor present whilst I made my statement. Standard procedure of course, but I was made to feel like the villain of the piece which only fuelled my anger and hatred further.

I'd given a uniformed officer the rundown of what I knew, then I sat in an interview room wearing a paper suit, nursing an over-brewed sweet tea.

After what seemed like an eternity, a wizened old detective opened the door and sat opposite me.

"I'm Dave Cousins," he said quietly. "You must be feeling pretty bad right now, Mr Fuller."

"Rick," I said. "Call me Rick."

"Okay, are you sure you don't want a solicitor present, Rick?"

"Positive."

He nodded, turned on the recorder and began to ask me the same questions I'd been asked twice already.

"Why did you move Ms North's body, Rick?"

I could see my hands shaking as I clasped them together in front of me. I wanted them to stop, but they wouldn't.

That, and a tremor in my voice that I couldn't control. "First... well, first I went to see if she was alive."

"And how did you know she was dead?"

I looked into the detective's face.

"I was in the military. I've seen a lot of dead people, Detective. It was obvious her neck was broken, her eyes were open, she wasn't breathing, no pulse."

He nodded.

"Okay, so I'll ask again, Rick. Why did you move her?"

"You got a wife, Dave?"

"I have."

"Daughters?"

"Two, as a matter of fact."

I took the deepest breath.

"Well, if you went home tonight, Dave, and found your wife or one of your daughters with their clothes torn from them. Saw that they'd been assaulted in the worst possible way, and that you knew that people were going to come and take photographs of them, what would you do? I mean, I'm not stupid. I know that by dressing her, lying her on her bed, making her decent, I may have made things harder for your forensics guys, but I'll be honest with you, right here on this tape, I had no intention of calling you, because I knew who had done this terrible thing, and I was going to kill him myself. I was going to snap his neck and spit on him as he drew his last breath."

"Are you capable of such a thing, Rick? Could you kill a man with your bare hands?"

I looked into his eyes.

"More than capable, Dave."

He nodded again.

"And just who do you believe killed Ms North, Rick?"

"Larry Simpson," I said. "Detective Chief Inspector Larry Simpson."

Des Cogan's Story:

We were both released that same day and Larry Simpson was arrested for the murder of Lauren North. Two days later he was charged and remanded in custody. As Rick suspected, his legal team recommended that he undergo psychological testing and that the findings be reported to the court prior to his trial.

I'd moved into Rick's place and did my best to get some food in him between bottles of JD. It was history repeating itself. It was Cathy all over again, except this time, there was no need to search for the perpetrators. I think that actually made him worse.

When Cathy was murdered, the search for her killers gave him something to focus on between bouts of depression and near alcoholism. Now, he had nothing.

He spent half the day flicking through the news channels or scrolling the local online papers for any information on the upcoming trial, and the other half drinking himself into a stupor.

It was a full two weeks before Lauren's body was released for burial. The detective that had interviewed Rick on the day of the murder came to his flat to tell him where the funeral was to take place.

At first, I didnea think it was a good idea to go, but Rick couldn't be persuaded otherwise.

In all the time we'd known her, Lauren had hardly ever mentioned her family. I mean, from that day when she jumped in the back of that stolen campervan outside Leeds General Hospital, she had left everything and everyone behind. That must have been hard for her, and for her folks, although I got the impression that there had been bad blood between them after her divorce.

Families eh?

Even so, she had taken the plunge and become one of us. She had shown bravery, loyalty and love and I couldnea speak any higher of her. I did my best to keep things together for the big man's sake, but I was dying inside, too. So, despite my misgivings, I considered that maybe seeing the lassie put to rest would do us both good.

Just seventeen days after her murder, we went the see Lauren North buried.

The service took place in a small chapel in Headingly, just by the cricket ground. Rick and I sat at the back of the church, listened to the eulogies, the hymns, the prayers and then followed the priest and the mourners to the graveside to see our Lauren laid to rest.

As was the Lord's want, the heavens opened, and the wind blew. The small solemn crowd shed tears as the coffin was lowered into the grave. I looked into Rick's rain splattered face and he showed no emotion. He looked simply empty.

As the final words were spoken, the family began to shuffle away. Hands were shaken, tears wiped, condolences offered. The wind picked up further and blew the rain in sheets across the graveside. Standing opposite me was a stout woman. She didn't seem to notice that she was soaked to the skin. She stared at me; her eyes boring into mine.

Finally, she walked around the grave and stood in front of me, hands on hips, her face full of anger and I recognised her. It was Lauren's friend from the hospital, Jane.

"It's you, isn't it?" she said. "You, the guy… the fake, the fraud. The one who pretended to be a doctor that day, the day of the Manchester bomb."

I didn't answer.

She sneered and turned to Rick.

"And you're the man in the bandages, I'll bet." She bent down and lifted Rick's trouser leg to reveal the scars left by Stephan Goldsmith. "I thought as much," she said, her hair stuck to her grimacing face by the rain. "The mystery gangster. It is you, both of you. How dare you come here today."

She pointed in Rick's face.

"You are the reason she left us. You…" Jane began to break down. "You… took her away and filled her head with nonsense. Took her from me, her best friend, her family, her job, and for what? Just so she could end up with a broken neck. You are to blame, you and only you are the reason she is dead. This is all your fault. Shame on you… Shame on you both."

And with that she strode away.

Rick didn't speak. He walked to the grave, peered down into it, picked up a handful of soil and dropped it onto the top of the coffin. Then he turned and strode off.

"Rick," I called. "Come on, you cannea blame yourself. The woman was just upset."

He didn't stop, didn't turn around, just held up a hand that told me not to follow him.

As I watched him disappear through the cemetery gates, I wondered if I'd ever see him again.

END

Printed in Great Britain
by Amazon